the edge of glory

m.j. parisian

Published by Dream Life Publications
ISBN: 978-0-578-87985-7

Other books by M.J. Parisian

What We Know Now

This is How a Heart Breaks

To Live in This World

To Mary Karen,
who taught me the technique for the sport,
and the lessons for life.

Hello, Friends. I am grateful you have picked up this book, and my wish is that you fall in love with these new characters. I have chosen to create a world in the year 2020 without the pandemic and all that we have gone through. I know there will be many stories and books that include all that has happened in our world, but I wanted to stay in my fictional world without the anxiety, sadness, and loss. Believe me when I say, I didn't take this decision lightly—I only wanted to create an escape for you. And that's what books are... an escape. Something to take us away from our reality and bring some joy into our lives.

That is my wish for you.

Continue to stay safe and take care of one another...

XO, Mo

Things You Need to Know

Popping: When a skater stops rotation mid-jump. An example would be a triple jump opening up to a single or double.

Short program: *The short program features required elements which include jump elements, spin elements and a step sequence. With fewer elements to perform, the short program leaves less room for error, and skaters rely on clean performances and high component scores to earn points heading into the free skate.

Free skate program (aka long program): *The free skate, the second and longer segment of competition, features a broader set of requirements and a maximum number of elements a skater may perform. If a skater performs more than the number of well-balanced program elements permitted, there are no deductions, but the skater will not receive credit for these additional elements. After a skater completes his or her free skate and receives a free skate score, that score is added to the short program score to determine overall standings.

Regionals: First step in the qualifying competitions. The top four skaters qualify to compete in the sectional competition, in this case, Midwestern Championships.

Sectional Championships (Mids): The second step in the qualifying competitions. The top four skaters in each group qualify to compete in the National Championships, held in a different arena every year.

U.S. Figure Skating National Championships: aka Nationals. Highest level of competition in the U.S. Figure Skating qualifying series. Usually, the top four skaters qualify to compete in either the World Championships or Olympics if it falls on an Olympic year.

*Taken directly from the U.S. Figure Skating Website.

INTERVIEW - PART 1

Air date: March 16th, during World Championships.

Interviewer: Trish LaMonde, NBC Sports Analyst and former figure skating Olympic medalist. The NBC commentators, Trish and Thomas, could make or break a skater with a single comment.

Interviewee: Adeline Gray, U.S. Figure Skating's newest rising talent.

[Pre-story video showing Addie in an empty ice rink. The lights are dim, but we can see her trying the same jump over and over again, falling each time. The last clip is of the same jump with a clean landing and a small nod to herself as we fade to black.]

TL: Thank you for taking the time to sit down and talk with us. I know your world feels like a fishbowl and you don't do many interviews.

AG: *(shy smile and small nod)* Thank you for having me. Doing interviews is probably scarier than stepping on the ice before my short program.

TL: *(chuckles)* I remember that feeling, and I promise

this will be easier than any program you'd skate. This year has been quite the rollercoaster for you, hasn't it? I'd actually like to go back to Nationals in 2020... that is where this story ultimately begins, right?

AG: It probably started long before that, but for this interview, and where I'm at today, Nationals last year was definitely the moment everything changed for me...

LESSON 1

You can't go back and change the beginning,
but you can start where you're at and change the
ending.

~C.S. Lewis

The Law of Threes

The train was getting closer—its horn blowing three times—and yet my feet were glued to the tracks. Paralyzed with fear, the light from the front of the engine blinded me immobile. The roar of the tracks vibrated through my entire body, and I braced myself for impact.

I woke up with a jolt and blinked a few times, my hands grasping for the sides of my bed. A cold sweat coated my skin, and the bed creaked as I slumped back down to my pillow.

For the last few months, nightmares had become my thing.

Being chased down by a swarm of killer bees. A near miss with a semi-truck, only to swerve into an oak tree planted *unusually* close to the road. Sitting the front pew at my mom's funeral when all of the power goes out at the church.

Full disclosure: that last one actually wasn't a dream. It was a moment in time I chose to keep reliving.

My friend Marcy thinks I need to see a therapist— she even has a friend who can help me.

I've reminded her that she *is* my friend *and* a

therapist. In reality, she's a high school guidance counselor, studying to become a life coach, but that's the same thing, right?

I haven't always been this way. But in the last year, my thoughts have swayed toward the worst-case scenario as opposed to the Hallmark movies Marcy likes to watch.

The end of the year was near, and I'd never been more excited for a fresh start as I was now.

The last twelve months had been the worst on record, and I wanted to get out before anything else could go wrong. Marcy thinks I'm crazy, but I'd always believed that bad things come in threes. One could argue that good things do too, but stick with me here.

In June, my mom found out she had stage four ovarian cancer. It got to stage four because, apparently, this type of cancer likes to sneak up on women. "The silent cancer," they call it. By the time anyone really notices something wonky is going on in their body— BOOM—it's stage four.

Good luck with that, the cancer whispered.

In July, we buried my mom. Yes, it really happened that fast. She never even made it to her first chemo treatment, scheduled for July twenty-third. They called to remind me of the appointment, and I let them know she wouldn't need it any longer.

In August, Kevin—my husband of two years— came home and told me he had fallen in love with his secretary. The next day, he moved into her townhouse. Divorce papers arrived in September. Divorce hearing scheduled for January.

It was as if a reality show had taken over rights to my life.

He said he had planned on doing it earlier, but we found out about my mom, and he thought it would be cruel to hurt me like that. Like that extra month of him sticking around really grounded me in support. I felt warm and fuzzy just thinking about it now.

Truth is, I didn't even notice him much while we were trying to get my mom's health back on track. My sister, Sheila, would come home on the weekends to help as much as she could, but the brunt of the work and care fell on me. My dad sent his love—and money—from Boca, but that was the limit of his affection. Love from a distance was the best he could manage. Truthfully, I would've been okay with neither. After all these years, we've learned to live without him and have been just fine, thank you very much.

In the universal law of threes, I was due one more tragedy before I could move on with my life. Every day, I woke up wondering if this would be the day that I was thrown out a window of a tall building or somehow bit by a rattlesnake—difficult for December in Detroit—but I'm not excluding anything at this point. The threat of another blow had me on edge, and I knew this was the cause of my nightmares, but you don't mess with universal laws.

I looked around the rink where I coached figure skating every day and envisioned myself being crushed by the Zamboni.

Stranger things have definitely happened in the skating world, and I wasn't ruling anything out at this point.

～〜

The most important thing you have to understand about figure skating is that appearances are everything.

Everything.

What you see isn't necessarily what is real… it's just an illusion. Under all the glitter and glory, they are regular teenagers with normal everyday problems. But the audience will see only what the skaters *want* you to see. The ones who make it have not only nerves of steel but also a laser focus that helps them put their body through hell day in and day out, just for the chance to make it big.

And the really lucky ones have the vision—a crystal clear picture in their head—of exactly where they're going, and more importantly, why.

The ones without that vision, or God forbid, following someone else's dream, will suffer the consequences.

What are you doing with your life?

The nagging voice in my head started almost immediately after Kevin moved out. Marcy calls it the old hag in the attic—my newly acquired voice—and encouraged me to shut it down. I don't think I have ever shut anything down in my life, let alone a bully in my own head.

In case you hadn't guessed it already, I fall into the latter group: the ones without any kind of vision. Gliding through life, untethered by goals or dreams. Just surviving to get through another day so I can crawl back into bed for another episode of Natalie's Greatest Fears. This year had kicked my ass, and I was so over it.

I wasn't always like this—I used to have a life. I'm not sure it was what I dreamed of or even worked for, but it existed. I have the pictures on my phone to prove it. It all sort of just happened.

And now it was all gone.

Except for skating. That has been the one and only constant in my life, and the only thing I felt I had any control over. My safety net.

It was the only reason I ever got out of bed. Literally. Being on the ice at six every morning wasn't for everyone. Certainly not in the middle of winter, but it did give me a reason to wake up. It became my life preserver in the last two months.

When my mom was still alive, she begged me to find another job and try something else in life. Anything else. I never listened, because ever since I was ten years old, I knew this was what I'd be doing.

Well, either this or backup singer for the Backstreet Boys. Being the first female singer in a boy band would've proved I was talented beyond the social norms. Looking back, it was probably good the skating thing has worked out so far.

"The shortest sentence in the English language is 'go.'"

I blinked, looking down at sweet Ingrid, an eight-year-old phenomenon who showed more talent in her pinky than I did in my entire body.

"Why are you telling me this?" I asked. She led with a serious disposition, and I always tried to match it.

"You say 'go' approximately thirty-two times during every Breakfast Club skate." She emphasized this fact by pushing her glasses higher up her nose.

My stomach growled at her statement. She looked at the center of my body, and the right side of her mouth twitched up.

The music blasted, and the other skaters were already on the big circle. I bent forward to meet her eye to eye.

"Ingrid?"

"Yes, Miss Natalie?"

"Go."

She graced me with a wink before she took off after the pace skater. "Thirty-three times!"

She was eight, going on eighteen, only without the teenage attitude. She wasn't my student, but I loved working with her in the Breakfast Club power class I ran every day. Part strength, part endurance, all mental. The class was for any skater who wanted to improve their stamina. The fact that it ran at six-forty a.m. weeded out those who skated for fun.

This class was the opposite of fun.

I supposed I could participate in this class and die from cardiac arrest. That could be my third calamity, but I really don't want to freak out the skaters with that image.

Plus, I don't want to die doing the one thing I love. That would be such a shame.

The Beautiful Yes

"So, let me get this straight," Marcy said, sitting down on the couch. *Seinfeld* was on TBS, and an almost empty bottle of wine sat on the coffee table. "It's your birthday, and you wanted to stay in tonight instead of going out to celebrate?"

"It's Winesday," I said. "Our rule is to celebrate at our houses. Why you made me come to *your* house on *my* birthday is beyond me."

"You live in the sticks."

She had me there. It was true, my home was off the beaten path, but it was the only thing I asked for in the divorce, and Kevin was complying. He was already living in her townhome anyway, and there was no way she would want our small home. The best part was the tiny lake in my backyard. Since he moved out, I had repainted the whole downstairs a creamy ivory and found nautical accessories to work with. It was slowly becoming my own place, but every now and again I still came across a piece of our history.

"I do live in the sticks and prefer it that way," I said. I loved that no one would just be 'in the neighborhood' and stop by on a moment's notice. It pleased me that you had to go through six roundabouts to get to my street. There wasn't a direct way. Granted it sucked in the middle of winter, but it didn't matter. It was my home now.

Marcy shushed me and grabbed the remote. "This is the best part."

George, Elaine, and Jerry sat at a table going over George's life and how every instinct he's ever had was wrong. Jerry's response was, "If every instinct you have is wrong, then the opposite would have to be right."

Marcy smiled at the classic line. "God, that was so brilliant," she said, pausing to take a sip of wine. "You know… this same wisdom could be applied to your life, as well."

I sat up. "Are you seriously implying all my instincts are wrong? Way to kick me when I'm down." I reached for the bottle of wine and emptied the contents into my glass.

She set her wine on the coffee table and turned to face me. "No, of course not *every* instinct is wrong, but I do think that you have areas in your life where you keep choosing the wrong thing."

"These *areas*… what do you mean?" Finger quotes are less effective when you're holding a glass of wine, and she held back a smirk.

"What I mean is that you are beautiful, smart, talented in ways most people dream about. And you are internally cringing right now because I just brought the best parts of you into the light. And for whatever reason, you continue to wait for something to go wrong in your life instead of focusing on living again."

I walked to the kitchen and emptied my glass in the sink.

"Okay, that went south super fast," she said, as I walked back into the living room.

"Do you really think I'm... beautiful?" I batted my eyes, and she threw a pillow at me.

"Yes, I do, and you know it too."

I sat back down and grabbed an Oreo. Double Stuf just for my birthday. Marcy reached beside the sofa, then set down two presents, both wrapped in tan paper and tied with black twine. I eyed her suspiciously.

"Open the big one first."

I pulled the twine off the corner and tore the paper carefully. A luxurious pale pink, cashmere scarf tumbled out of the box as I lifted the corner. It was exquisite—something I'd never buy for myself.

"Oh Marce, it's *gorgeous*," I said, wrapping it around my neck. "I absolutely love it."

"I knew it would be perfect with your skin tone," she said, pleased with herself. "The next one comes with a challenge."

"Oh, God, do I have the choice to not open it?"

"Nope."

"And I have to accept the challenge without even knowing what it is?"

"You're gonna have to trust me on this one."

"I'm not really in the mental place for a challenge

right now," I said.

"Tough cookies. This present is going to be the gift that keeps on giving. You'll see."

I already knew what it was—well, sort of. Every year, Marcy would give me two gifts for my birthday. One that was pretty (no exceptions), and one self-help book. Every year without fail. Usually the books were interesting, but they really aren't my style. I'm more of a grin and bear it kinda girl.

I sighed. "Okay, I guess I'll accept your challenge, but if it has horrible outcomes, I'm blaming you."

"Bring it," she goaded.

I pulled the twine and paper off to reveal a white cover with hot pink lettering—*The Beautiful Yes*. The cover dared me to say the obvious.

"Noooo—no, no, no, no, no."

She threw her head back and laughed like a hysterical person. "I believe the actual word you're looking for is yes. Y. E. S. Yes!"

I shook my head and read the inside flap. Another actor-turned-writer, dropping her wisdom of how she transformed her entire life by saying yes to whatever life threw her way.

"You do understand that this actor doesn't live in the real world, right? She is saying yes to things that include yachts and Teslas."

"I've read the book and I'm asking you to give it a chance. I think you will see how closed off in life you have become. The book isn't a comparison of lives—

it's the message of allowing good things to come into your life."

My eyes rolled so hard that my head tipped backward. "Come on, you're killin' me. It's as if you don't even know me."

"No, it's more like I know you better than you know yourself," she countered.

"Then you know I don't want to say yes to anything. I barely say yes to showering, most days."

"What if I said I was going to say yes with you," she said, eyes twinkling. "Yes to something I've only talked about for so long."

"You're finally going to write a book?"

She squeezed her eyes shut and nodded. "I'm giving myself a year to figure it out and write a first draft."

"Well, that's already better than anything I could do this year."

"No way," she shook her head. "A—this isn't a contest, and B—I'm really only saying yes to this one thing. You're gonna say yes to everything. Dates, exercise, and who knows what else comes along."

This was going to be horrible. "Everything?" I squeaked out.

"Yes."

"But I—"

"This isn't up for debate. You have to at least try," she said, balling up the wrapping paper on the floor. "You saved me a few years ago, and I'm going to do the same. Not that you need saving, but you definitely need something right now. New year, new you, and all that jazz."

"I have a very bad feeling about this," I said, pulling my scarf a little tighter around my neck. It felt comforting to be wrapped up so snug. "But I really do love this scarf."

She stood and kissed the top of my head. "My bet is you're going to be a little uncomfortable this year, but I'm certain it'll be a year to remember."

"I don't know why I'm so worried," I said, following her into the kitchen. I set the wine bottle in the recycling bin and threw away the Oreo package. "It's not like I ever have anything to say yes to. I think you might be disappointed with the opportunities."

She gave me a low laugh. "Famous last words. I can't wait to see how it all unfolds."

I shook my head. "I gotta go, it's late, and Breakfast Club is full tomorrow."

"Are you good to drive?"

"Uhhh, I only had one glass. You drank the rest. Good luck with that in the morning."

She leaned on the cupboards and covered her face. "Why did you let me drink so much on *your* birthday?"

"I was letting you say yes to wine," I said with a smirk. I pulled on my coat and slid my book into my tote. I pulled her into a hug. "I don't know what I'd do without you. Thank you."

She patted my back. "I got you," she said into my shoulder. "Drive safe out there."

I heard the lock bolt behind me as soon as I walked down her steps to the sidewalk. A thin layer of snow covered my car, and I pushed the auto starter, wishing I had thought to do it sooner. Out of all the extras my car came with, this was by far the best one. I slid in, the leather seat freezing beneath me. I found my skating music playlist on Spotify, always on the hunt for new program music, and headed home. I let the music and the choreography in my head keep me company on the way home.

I was almost getting used to living alone again.

Almost.

There were even times I could forget about everything I lost last year, but something would always trigger a memory from the depths and tighten around my heart.

Focus.

Music.

Choreography.

Yes...

How it Started

It was the kind of day that made you want to go back to bed. A day that started off bad and would only get worse as it progressed. A "Netflix day," Marcy called it.

My only thought during Breakfast Club was crawling back into bed. I'll say yes to naps... that'll show her. I felt my phone vibrate in my pocket.

Jonathan: Can you meet me at Starbucks when you're done?

I had to read it twice to make sure I wasn't reading it wrong.

Me: Yes!

I giggled to myself, certain this wasn't what Marcy meant.

Jonathan Leoni was our skating director and my favorite person at the rink. Okay, full disclosure, I had a slight crush on him, but it didn't matter because he was married and certainly wasn't the cheating type. It was just a deep admiration. Plus, he was the most brilliant coach, and I've learned everything I knew from him. He took me under his wing when I became serious about coaching five years ago.

He mentored me and introduced me to all the higher coaches at competitions and conferences. He encouraged me to seek continuing education and get rated to bulk up my credentials.

Best of all, he always gave me the best learn-to-skate classes.

Me: I'll be there by seven forty-five.

He gave me a thumbs-up emoji.

The rest of class dragged on at a snail's pace. It was freezing this morning—well, every morning, really—and I lost feeling in my fingers and toes thirty minutes ago. It was a strength day, so I made the skaters do crazy things like push-ups and planks on the ice. If looks could kill, I would've dropped dead a long time ago.

But they kept coming back for more.

On my way to the car, I dialed Marcy and filled her in on the morning text. I don't know why, but it felt serious.

"So, explain to me... why do you have to meet Jonathan? And outside the rink? That's just weird, isn't it?"

My stomach flip-flopped. "Honestly, I don't know." I sighed. "He just texted this morning and asked if I could meet him."

"Hmmm, sounds fishy," she said. "Do you think he knows you love him?"

"Absolutely, and he's going to tell me that he's leaving his wife," I shot back. "Seriously, you watch too much *Grey's Anatomy*. No one ever gets what they want in real life."

"That's what you think," she said. "But one of these days, you'll start listening to me."

"Is that why you're still at Orchard Lake? You and I both know that's not what you want."

It was a truth she couldn't deny. Marcy was a high school counselor at the same school she went to as a teenager. All she wanted since she started two years ago was to quit.

"Excellent point, but I have a plan to get out of here," she said. She had started to get her certifications to be a life coach at the end of last year. She consistently ignored my opinion of staying where she was until she made a dent in her student loans. Her degree was in accounting, but being a CPA lasted about three months, and she hated that even more. Working in a high school was at least tolerable, and she loved the students. "But let's go back to your meeting... he didn't give you any hints?"

"Nada," I said. "Just that he wanted to meet when I left the rink."

"I don't know, Nat," she sighed. "This doesn't sit well with me."

I turned into Starbucks. It was a staple in our lives.

"Look, I'm here," I said. "I'll text you when I'm done and give you all the details."

"You better," she said. "And we're still on tonight?"

"It's Thursday, isn't it?"

"Oh, crap! Gotta go," she said. I heard the school bell ringing as she disconnected.

I smiled and shook my head at her hasty hang-up. Classic Marcy.

Jonathan's SUV wasn't anywhere in the parking lot, and I looked at my phone to make sure I didn't miss another text. I grabbed my bag and pulled my mittens back on. Every winter, I wondered why I still lived here. It was gray, freezing, and we had roughly three hours of solid daylight each day. It's no wonder so many people had seasonal affective disorder during winter. One of the coaches actually bought something on Amazon called a SAD light. We all made fun of her, but I had to admit her moods seemed to be a little better than most lately.

The walk from my car to the door was short, but enough to force every warm cell left in my body to escape. Luckily, the heat from inside was as cozy as the glow of the lighting.

Come, it beckoned me. *Sit and warm up.*

Yes, my Starbucks called to me like the Giving Tree. I didn't care.

～

I was next in line and felt the presence of someone behind me.

"My treat," he whispered in my ear, making the hair on the back of my neck stand on end.

"You scared me," I said, pulling away from him

slightly.

He smiled and shrugged. "You're just jumpy—as usual."

In my defense, I wasn't always jumpy. I just found it impossible to relax around him outside of the rink.

"Why don't you get us a table, and I'll get the coffee?" He flashed his app that supported his caffeine addiction.

I felt a smile spread across my face as I walked towards the row of tables by the front. This time of day was unusually empty, and I picked the one closest to the wall for more privacy. I sat facing the counter where he waited for our order and watched him. An uneasiness swept over me, suddenly, and I worried this was something serious.

He sauntered over, carrying two coffees and a pastry bag. "I knew you probably didn't eat breakfast, so I got you the blueberry scone you love so much."

"Yessss," I whispered, taking the bag from him. "How did you know?"

"Because you live alone and don't have any food at home?"

"Fair point," I said, pulling out the scone and breaking off a piece. "So, what's this about? Why are we meeting outside the rink?"

He paused and took the lid off his coffee and took a sip. "I'm not quite sure how to say this, so I'm just going to blurt it out."

He blinked at me, and I waited, holding my breath.

"Beth has taken a job—a promotion, really—and is being relocated to their Cleveland office," he said. He stared at his coffee, waiting for me to respond, but what was I supposed to say?

"Um, congratulations to Beth?" I said. "How are you going to manage living apart?"

He grimaced. They didn't have kids, so it wouldn't be too difficult to have two homes.

"We won't be having separate homes," he said, locking eyes with me. "I'm going with her."

"But—" I stopped, my brain trying to understand what he was saying. "You can't leave. What will your students do?"

He smiled gently, as if he expected this question. "I haven't told them yet—you're the first to know, but they will be fine. I'm going to recommend that you take on Addie and Will, and the rest will go to whoever has time. Those two are the ones who I want to make sure are set before I break the news."

"Wait—*what*? You want *me* to coach Addie and Will? I don't have any students even close to their caliber. I wouldn't even know where to begin with them."

"But that doesn't mean you can't take them on as your own," he said. "I don't trust anyone else with them, especially Lydia."

I blew out a breath I'd been holding. "I still don't understand—how can you just leave? Your students are going to be devastated."

"Natalie, this is my life. My wife has worked so hard for this, and I can't tell her to stay here because of my students."

His wife, Beth, worked for Global Systems—a VP in one of their tech divisions. Their marriage seemed to be one of convenience rather than love. They didn't have kids, and I wondered if they ever would. For him to go so willingly felt off to me.

"But you have worked hard for your students too," I said. "What about everything else? You run the damn rink!" He shrank from the rising octave in my voice.

I had left my coat on when I first sat down, and suddenly realized I was sweating. I tore it off in retaliation for his calmness. My heart felt like it was breaking, and yet it had no right to feel that way. His only response was to tip his head, and a sad, sympathetic smile played on his lips as if he knew my reaction wasn't about the rink at all.

"Natalie," he said my name slowly. "The skaters and the skating program will get figured out, and Skateland will run as usual. I'm planning on announcing this after Nationals and just wanted to give you the courtesy of knowing before then." He reached for my hand and squeezed my fingers. "Everything is going to be fine."

His last words echoed in my head, *everything is going to be fine*, even though my heart felt the opposite. The pit in my stomach felt hollow and empty, and I scanned my surroundings to see if anyone else could feel my despair. That's how big it felt.

Would everything be fine? Somehow, I couldn't quite wrap my brain around "fine" right now. I had this same feeling when Kevin left me. Abandoned. Again.

"Say something," he urged.

"I can't believe you're leaving," I said quietly. "It's like you're the one person who holds that rink together, and you're just going to up and leave us. Everything is not going to be fine, and you know it. No one can do what you do."

He sighed and leaned back in his chair. "I don't know what else to say, but I do believe I'm doing the right thing."

"Look, I have to get going," I said, looking at my watch. "I appreciate the heads-up, but how am I supposed to act normal for the next two weeks?" I grabbed my coffee and coat then walked away from him without waiting for a response. A cold blast of January air hit me in the face as I walked out. My heart raced all the way to my car as I fumbled with the keys to open the door fast enough.

It wasn't until I pulled out of the parking lot that my eyes started to water. I wiped them roughly, not wanting to let this weakness add to my misery.

My mind couldn't understand what he was doing and why. I get that his wife got a promotion, but in the skating world, you never just up and leave your students. Especially ones of this level and talent. It just isn't done.

I briefly wondered if it were possible to go back to bed and erase everything that had just happened. To go back one hour and change the direction of that conversation. I was so sure it was going to be something completely different, and now I just felt pathetic for thinking something could actually work out for me. I would have to tell Marcy I was right: no one ever gets what they want in life.

And Jonathan was wrong. Everything would *not* be okay, no matter how much he said it to me.

National Championships

I had everything I needed. A glass of wine. My laptop. A cozy blanket. And my phone.

The rink was all abuzz today with Addie skating her short program tonight. The programs wouldn't be on TV, but most of us had a subscription to watch the event online. Those of us who didn't just used Jonathan's credentials since he didn't need them. There are several coaches—all of whom will remain unnamed—who use his account more frequently than even he knew.

The site had a special cam just for the practice rink, so we could stalk every portion of Addie's Nationals experience. She was easily a contender in the top five, and if enough skaters made horrific mistakes, she could even medal.

Not that we were wishing harm on anyone. Just a few well-timed mistakes.

Stephanie: Anyone watching?!

Dana: I'm not home yet!

Ronnie: Present.

Me: Watching practice-ice. She looks tight.

Dana: Ugh.

Something looked off with Addie. Her posture was stiff and withdrawn, and she wasn't going anywhere near Jonathan, who was standing at the far end of the rink with the other coaches.

Stephanie: Nat—text J and see what's wrong with her. He'll answer you.

It wasn't any secret that Jonathan played favorites with me, especially at competitions. He would often text to vent or seek wisdom for dealing with teenage girls. But something about this situation didn't look right to me. Knowing what I know about Jonathan leaving made me even more cautious about pressing him for information. I had to trust that if he needed something, he'd text.

Me: That's a hard pass. She looks too tense for me.

Ronnie: Don't blame you. My spidey-sense says to steer clear.

Dana: Don't mess with the spidey-sense.

The event started in twenty minutes, but Addie was lucky to draw in the last group. Like groupies, we would sit on our laptops and watch Will and Addie, cheering from far away, no matter what time it was. One year they were competing in France, and I set my alarm for two a.m. to get up and watch. We all did, texting like teenagers in the middle of the night. Every one of us had a dream to get to Nationals or an international event, but most of our skaters were still too young.

Of course, I could only think tonight about the next event and how I would be the one taking Addie and Will. It didn't seem real yet, and I worried about how they would react when they found out. And what would the other coaches think? They already called me his favorite, so what would this do to our relationships?

I took a sip of wine and tried not to think about it yet. I had a week to deal with it.

Dana: WHAT AM I MISSING????

Me: Relax. She's in the last group and the first group is just starting.

Ronnie: Why is Janelle wearing a catsuit???

The camera scanned the group of skaters standing by the door, waiting to be called onto the ice. Hair slicked back into tight buns, sequins for days, sparkling in all their glamour for the camera. The tight expressions etched on the skaters' faces with heavily made-up eyes darting around. They opened the door, and one by one the skaters took the ice like tiny but fierce ballerina dolls. The training, dedication, and sheer mental will it took to get here made them the top twenty skaters in the nation. That alone is an accomplishment. But each one of these skaters had that dream of standing on the podium by the time Saturday was done. The only way to even have a shot at that was to skate clean tonight. Not just clean, but lights-out perfect so the judges would have to reward them with the highest scores. Addie had been doing flawless programs for the last two weeks. Even during Hell Week.

Ronnie: Did you really not text him? I thought you would anyway.

Me: Nope. Can't do it... too much tension for me. She will figure it out.

Stephanie: I'm doing a class in ten minutes. I'll catch you guys in a bit.

Ronnie: Step away from the Peloton. Walk towards the light. We're waiting for you... come.

Me: lolol

Dana: hahaha

Ronnie constantly criticized Stephanie's addiction to her Peloton. There wasn't a day he didn't get on her about it for some reason. Some days, he would just text our group chat for no reason other than to trash talk. It only encouraged her to post about it and tag him.

The groups crept by slowly, with very few clean programs. No one even came close to Addie's program, in my opinion. One after another only proved what we already knew: she had a gift. She had that "it factor" that all of the skaters wanted but only a few ever had. Jumps, spins, and the ability to skate a program that entertained and inspired. On top of all that, she was genuinely likable. Other coaches loved her, and she seemed to be everyone's little darling. There was a reason U.S. Figure Skating was making her their next big thing.

I couldn't take the not knowing any longer and finally texted Jonathan.

Me: Tough warm-up ice. How is she mentally?

Jonathan: Today is not going as planned.

That was a vague answer.

Me: What is going on? Is everything okay?

Jonathan: Nothing is okay. I don't know what she is going to do tonight.

Me: It's just nerves. She will be fine—you both have worked so hard for this. It'll be fine.

I didn't know if I was trying to convince him or myself. She wasn't my student yet, but I felt so much emotion in this moment and only wanted her to skate clean.

The texting bubble appeared and then disappeared. That was the last I heard from him.

～～

Ronnie: I'm gonna puke.

Stephanie: Stop! You're making us more nervous.

Me: I'm with Ronnie. This is impossible to watch.

Dana: Why does she keep popping her jumps?

Ronnie: why are they keeping the camera on her???

It was true, the camera didn't leave her. In a sport fueled by drama, this one was unfolding for everyone to see, and the producers knew a goldmine when they saw it. Watching her was making my stomach turn.

Stephanie: Why does Sophia always have to wear feathers?

Dana: It's hideous. And could someone get her a cheeseburger?

Ronnie: She's practically see-through. How does she have the strength to do triples?

Stephanie: And what's with Gina? She looks like she's been crying.

Ronnie: Nope. That's just her face.

On and on it went. One comment after another, which on any other given day, I'd be laughing. But now, I just felt nauseous. I turned the text group to mute and strictly concentrated on Addie. Jonathan still hadn't replied from before, and I sent him a heart emoji so he knew I was thinking of them.

No response.

I watched skater after skater, judging them mentally against Addie's program. Technically, she had one of the harder short programs, but only if she skated clean. A clean short program would set her up perfectly for the free skate and put her in the final group of skaters. That's what all of them wanted in the free skate: to be in the final group.

Finally, the skater before her sat in the kiss and cry. It was Gina Garlin, or GG as everyone called her, and her program was flawless. She collapsed into her coach's arms at the door, happy tears flowing down her face. We caught a glimpse of Addie before she stepped on the ice, pale and stone-faced.

GG's score was met with an eruption from the crowd. The highest score of the night. The camera panned down to Addie standing in front of Jonathan at the boards, his eyes searching hers and his head nodding. I imagined he was telling her that she had this... make it happen. He said this to everyone around the rink—"make it happen"—and it became the go-to cheer for everyone.

She gave him a curt nod, so unlike her. The two of them were usually so close, and he always found a way to build her up right before she skated.

Her name was called.

She circled the ice and presented to the crowd, then took her spot in the center.

The camera zeroed in on her as she waited for her music to begin, her eyes focused above the judge's heads.

I could tell from the first few steps this was going to be the longest two minutes of her life. A tiny misstep— no one else would even notice—but I did, and then it happened. A fall on her connecting steps leading into her triple flip. She picked up the program after the landing—didn't even attempt to do the jump, and while she fought for the rest of her jumps, it was too little too late. You don't just skip a required element in a short program. Plus, the other elements were sketchy at best.

A bobble here.

Downgraded levels on spins.

It was disastrous.

The most interesting part of the whole night was when she got off the ice. She was calm—stoic, even— and had very few words to say to Jonathan. The usual lightness was missing, and I wondered if he had told her already that he was leaving. Something was off. Anyone who knew them could read it in their body language, and Addie didn't seem concerned or upset by any of this. With two skaters left, her score put her in thirteenth place.

She had zero chance of placing, let alone even getting in the top ten.

What the hell was going on?

INTERVIEW - PART 2

TL: Can you give me your frame of mind the week going into Nationals last year? Were you mentally ready?

[Addie looks past Trish and shakes a memory from her head.]

AG: I think I was prepared physically... my run-throughs were mostly clean, and I was consistently landing my triple-triples every time. I was excited for Nationals.

TL: And mentally? Were you prepared there?

[Addie shakes her head, eyes downcast.]

AG: Umm, no. Not even close. We had just found out that week that our coach was moving to Cleveland shortly after Nationals. I couldn't stop thinking about it, and Nationals didn't even matter at that point.

[Camera zeros in on her downcast eyes. Trish leans in and waits for more.]

AG: I remember not understanding how he could just walk away so easily from something he worked so hard for, and I guess a part of me wanted to punish him—I guess a part of me thought that if I skated badly, he'd see how much we needed him to stay.

TL: So, finding out about your coach made it impossible to stay focused on your skating at that time. Is that correct?

AG: I don't think I had ever been so confused or scared to compete as I was that week. My emotions were all over the place. I trained so hard for that moment, and I tried to keep it together, but as we all know, that didn't exactly work out that way... I had lost sight of the one thing I wanted most.

Go.

Ingrid was right. The shortest sentence in the English language is 'Go.'

And right now, I was screaming it in my head—to myself. Go! Get out of this office.

"Natalie, all I'm saying is you've been here the longest, and it's your responsibility to take over now until we can find someone to fill Jonathan's shoes." Roger paused. "Er, uh, I mean skates."

Roger Clayton was the GM of Skateland, and his office was getting smaller by the second.

"But I have no interest in being the skating director. I have enough on my plate just by taking on his students," I vented. There was no way I could do this job.

"Oh, so who's going to take over? There isn't anyone here who has your dedication to this club or the sport. You practically grew up in this rink!"

"So now you're going to punish me for where I grew up?"

"This isn't a punishment! Some would take this as a compliment—a promotion."

He was trying to handle me. Persuade me to take

this job because he knew no one else would take it. The skating director position was legendary for causing migraines, depression, and hopelessness, in that order.

"Roger—" I stopped. How was I going to get out of this? "Seriously, you're not listening to me. I don't have the time to manage the skating program as well as maintain my coaching duties. Jonathan couldn't do it and bailed the second something else came along." By something else, I meant his wife took a better job in Cleveland.

"Jonathan only bailed because of his wife, and you know it," he reminded me. "And he has maintained all of his skaters along with this position for years. And he has a wife! It's just you, right?"

"My marital status is none of your business and shouldn't have any influence on this," I snapped.

He held his hands up defensively. "You're right, I know. That was uncalled for on my part."

"And it won't convince me any faster."

"I guess if you don't take it, we'll have to go to the skating board and see if anyone there is interested…"

"You wouldn't." No way could we allow a parent to take this over.

"If I ran out of options, I guess I'd have to," he said, shrugging. "But if you just took it over tunil we have someone solid in place, we wouldn't have to go in that direction."

My body felt as if it weighed a thousand pounds. Maybe hopelessness was first in the order.

"What does this entail?" I don't even know half of what Jonathan did, or how he managed to coach and do all this administrative stuff.

Roger raised his eyebrows as if to say, *I own you now*. "Well…" He shifted in his seat. "It's overseeing the coaches and figure skaters. The contracts, the schedules, the communications. And then there's the learn-to-skate program, but that runs itself now. You would just have to maintain what he had in place."

"You mean maintain the hundreds of extra skaters that walk through those doors every week? Is that all?"

"That's a bit dramatic, but yes, his numbers have grown over the years. Best learn-to-skate program in the area—and that's saying something since there are so many rinks around us now."

I narrowed my eyes. "You're not helping to convince me," I said.

"C'mon, Natalie." He stood and shut the door to his office. "What if I could convince corporate to start you at the same salary that Jonathan left with? He worked years to get to this level, but I can recommend you start you at this hourly salary." He slid a piece of paper across the desk.

My eyes bugged out. "Jonathan made *that*? On top of his coaching fees?"

"The only rule is that you have to clock in and out, according to your coaching schedule. No double-dipping."

I nodded. That seemed fair. I had to admit the extra

money would be helpful, but did I want all the headaches that came with this job?

"Can I think about it?"

"As long as you can give me an answer by tomorrow. I don't have to remind you it's friggin' January, and the learn-to-skate numbers are insane. We need someone who can hit the ground running."

I blew out a breath and looked at the calendar hanging on the wall behind him. The new session would start in four days—not a lot of time to acclimate myself to the program. "Okay, I will let you know tomorrow before I get on the ice," I said, standing.

He reached to shake my hand. "I can't tell you enough how I hope you make the right decision."

"No pressure, though, right?"

He chuckled. "Honestly, there isn't anyone I'd rather have running these programs. I know you'll be able to handle it just fine."

I knew I could handle the bump in pay, but that was about all I could handle right now.

"Oh. My. God. That woman makes me crazy," Dana groaned in the coaches room. We were getting our skates on before the first session, and this was the only safe place in the rink. No parents allowed. The coaches room was located just behind the main office, tucked in the corner of the lobby. If you didn't see the door, you wouldn't even know we were here.

"Let me guess, Kari's mom?"

In Webster's dictionary, under the term "skating mom," was a picture of Jeanette Wilson.

"What'd she do this time?"

"Quote-unquote 'No matter what diet we try, she just can't lose weight.'"

I spit out the water I had just sipped. "She did not say that."

"I swear on my mother's grave," she said, looking upward.

Her mom wasn't dead, but she had an odd habit of saying this.

Kari Wilson was twelve, with the body fat of an Olympic marathon runner. It was never good enough for Jeanette, and she put her on diets all the time. Kari was the youngest member of Weight Watchers two years ago, and Jeanette bragged about it to the other parents in the lobby. If you watched closely, you'd see the glazed look in the other parents' eyes as they slowly backed away.

"I'm happy to meet with the mom if you ever want," I offered. I knew they wouldn't listen to anything I had to say, but I always offered just the same.

She rolled her eyes. "Never in a million years would I subject you to that woman. Besides, unless you recommend flat-out starvation, they wouldn't go for it."

"That poor girl is skin and bones as it is," Stephanie said. "Has she even started her period yet?"

"No, but she is only twelve," Dana said. "Could be

anytime now."

"Not with that little body fat," I said.

"Honestly, I think Jeanette is just fine with that too. 'No boobs means faster rotation, right?'" Her imitation of the crazy mom was spot on. If I closed my eyes, I'd swear she was in here with us.

Stephanie snorted. "I'd have knocked that mom's block off by now—you're a saint."

"If Kari wasn't the sweetest kid, I'd have dropped her a long time ago," Dana said. "Some parents just aren't worth the stress."

"Amen," I agreed. I wanted to bring up my conversation with Roger, but I didn't know how they would react. "So, I have some news…"

Both Dana and Stephanie stopped what they were doing and eyed me.

"You're finally online dating?"

"You met someone!"

I stared at both of them. "No—wait—why would you think that?"

"Because you've been a nun since Kevin walked out," Stephanie said. "It's time to get back on the horse."

"A, it's only been a few months, and B, my divorce was just final last week! So, no, that's not what I was going to tell you, but now you're seriously going to be let down."

"Spill it. I saw you leave Roger's office a while ago," Dana said. "Is that it?"

I took a deep breath, unsure how they were going to react. "Roger asked if I could oversee the program until they find a permanent skating director." I paused to see if I could gauge their reaction. "I have to give him an answer tomorrow morning."

"I was more excited with the idea of online dating," Stephanie said, disappointed. "Are you going to take it?"

"It's kind of a sucky job, Nat," Dana said. "Jonathan was always here."

"I don't know," I said honestly. "I really haven't had any time to think about it yet, and I'm not sure it's something I can even handle."

Steph rolled her eyes. "Oh, please," she said. "You're the *only* one who can handle it, and besides, no one else wants it."

Lydia walked in, huffing and puffing about the Zamboni being late again. "If Roger thinks I'm going to put up with late ice every day, he's got another thing coming."

Dana looked at her wrist. "Jeez, look at the time," she said. "I need to get out there." Lydia never noticed she wasn't wearing a watch.

"Take your time," she yelled at Dana as she left. "Didn't she even hear me?"

I could only shrug as I threw on my coat as fast as I could. No way was I getting stuck in here with her.

Just as Ronnie came in, Steph and I headed out the door. His look said *thanks a lot*, and we snickered through the lobby into rink one. No one ever wanted to be in the coaches room alone with Lydia.

"So what are you going to do?" Steph asked on our way.

The skaters were already on the ice, and now was just not the time to talk about it.

I shook my head. "I don't have a clue yet."

Lizzo's inspired edge work couldn't ease my mind right now, even though it was brilliant to watch. I couldn't wait for Lydia to come out and complain about the loud music. Every day brought the same complaints...

It's too cold.

Music's too loud.

The damn Zamboni is late.

Is that something I really wanted to deal with?

No-no-no-no-no.

Shopping Therapy

If Wednesday was for wine, then Thursday was for stocking up. For the last two years, Marcy and I have had a standing date at the grocery store by our neighborhood. Fresh Finds is a mom-and-pop store that specializes in organic produce and farm fresh meats and cheeses. They also have a killer wine selection and coffee bar that kept us coming back. The prices were probably more than we'd pay at a big box store, but the owners were like family at this point. We would never shop anywhere else.

We started the Thursday night shopping excursion a few years back when Marcy decided she wanted to lose weight—her freshman fifteen had turned into thirty—and she asked if I'd help her figure out what to eat. Since I've been an athlete for most of my life and majored in nutrition in college, she came to me instead of joining a weight loss scam. The shopping turned into more of a therapy session for both of us. We were able to catch up on the week and see what was causing us to eat a pint of ice cream in one evening. The upside was that she lost the thirty she was going for—and then some. Marcy was a hottie, and it was clear that she knew it by the way she carried herself. In my opinion, it was the weight loss that led her on the life coach path. She exuded confidence. I'd give anything to look like that, just once.

"You seem extra angsty tonight," she said while looking for the perfect cantaloupe. "What's happened today?"

I took my time bagging a couple lemons. "I was offered the skating director position today," I finally said. "Roger said I have to let him know by tomorrow if I want it."

"*If* you want it? You didn't accept on the spot? You didn't say *yes*?" Her eyes bugged out of her head. "Nat, this is what you always dreamed about—running your own program."

I puffed out a sigh. I hated that she knew everything about me. "That was always easy to dream about when I didn't actually think it would happen. I'm not in the habit of dreams coming true for me," I said. "This is real and it's scary. I don't think I can manage everything Jonathan did."

"So do it your own way," she said. "Who said the way Jonathan ran it was the only way? This is so exciting!" Her entire face lit up, her blue eyes sparkling. "Look at these oranges... have you ever seen more beautiful oranges?"

"Well, it is orange season," I said. "How about you—what is going on in your world?"

"Oh no," she said, shaking her head. "We're not

done with you yet. What are you going to tell him tomorrow?"

I shrugged a shoulder. "I figured I'd sleep on it and see how I felt in the morning."

She stopped pushing her cart and squared off to face me. "Tell me you're kidding." She did that one eyebrow thing that meant she was serious.

"Umm…" I paused, searching for the perfect pineapple. "I don't think it's a bad thing to take a night to think over a giant career move like this."

"A giant career move you've always wanted," she said, turning back to her cart.

I sighed, knowing she was right, but I couldn't help but feel like this was all too much too soon. "What if I take it and realize that I can't do what he did?"

"He started out just like you did, not knowing anything. In fact, I would bet you know more than he does right now. And the whole point is to make the skating program your own. You don't have to follow what he did."

The weight of this decision was burning a pit in my stomach. Everything she said was true, but did I have the guts to actually think I could run the skating program? Who did I think I was to take over like this?

"See? I know what you're doing there." She circled a finger around my head. "You're thinking you're not good enough, right?"

I closed my eyes and shook my head slowly. "Here is what I need," I said.

She blinked, her eyes waiting for me to finish.

"I need for you to let me make this decision and not care about what that choice is. I need you to support me, no matter what I choose. Even if it isn't yes."

Her shoulders slumped a little. "I suck," she said after a moment. "I'm sorry, and I suck. From here on out, I'm on Team Nat and support whatever you want."

We pushed on towards the vegetable section. "First of all, you couldn't suck as a friend if you tried. You're just trying to help me. And I would worry you had a head injury if you didn't try to tell me what was best for me. It's what you do," I said. "But I need you to know that I have to make this decision for me. Not for anyone else."

"Got it." She saluted me. "The best thing you can do is trust your gut and not to overthink it."

I rolled my eyes at her. "You can't help yourself, can you?"

She held up a cucumber and wiggled her eyebrows.

"Just once, could you not defile the vegetables?" I said, laughing. She did this to me every week since Kevin moved out. Every single week, and every week we would giggle like teenagers.

"I'll make you a deal. When you get off the abstinence train, I'll stop wagging the cucumbers at you."

"It's not a train! I'm just not interested in anyone right now," I said.

She bagged a gourd and tossed it in her cart. "You

know I'm just giving you crap. Plus, it's good for a laugh every week," she said. "At this point, you'd fall over if I didn't do something obscene at the veggie stand."

"Probably true, but still..." She was right. I'd know something was seriously wrong if she stopped. Finally, we headed to my favorite, the gourmet cheese section. My mouth started to water just looking around.

"Honestly, you need to get a grip on this obsession with dairy," she said. "Your eyes are darting around like a junkie."

"Ohhhh, they have the garlic cheddar back in," I drooled.

"You're killin' me." It was a sad fact that Marcy was lactose intolerant and couldn't enjoy the wonders of the cheese stand. I only felt bad for a minute but quickly got over it. "I'll meet you at the deli," she said over her shoulder as she walked away.

Her loss was my gain, and if a block of cheese helped me make a decision, then so be it. Could I really create a program of my own? I mean, logically yes, I could, but I don't even know where to begin to make changes like that. I thought of Carey Vernon in Utah and wondered how she started her empire of a figure skating club. Her students always seemed happy and well-adjusted instead of stressed out and anxious.

That was what I wanted. A club that focused on training a skater in a positive atmosphere and not just a competitive one. It has only been the last couple years that the mood around the rink changed, and only because of the rankings that a few of our skaters held. Suddenly, almost overnight, the rink vibe became more serious and driven. I don't blame Jonathan completely for the change, but I don't think he did anything to change it either. He had parents to please and upper management who expected big numbers on every session. It was a no-win situation.

And I wanted no part of that version. In that second, I made my mind up, and I looked around to see if Marcy was nearby. She was pushing her cart towards me and she stopped when she saw my expression. A smile grew on her face, and she nodded.

I knew what I had to do tomorrow, and I wasn't sure I'd be able to sleep tonight. I would call Roger first thing in the morning and go over the details of what I would expect to take the position. It would have to be my way.

It was the only way.

Yes.

LESSON 2

When you lose, don't lose the lesson.

~Dalai Lama

First Night

My heart had been racing since this morning when I woke up from my thirty-eight minutes of sleep. That was a solid eight minutes more than the night before. The first night of learn-to-skate began a half hour ago, and another wave of people for the second hour started filing in. I longed to be on the ice with my clipboard and list of skaters to oversee. Instead of a clipboard, I had a spreadsheet with all of the skaters listed, the classes they signed up for, and any late additions.

The name tags were spread out on the gray table like a color-coded junior military camp. Every class in the first hour was filled, and the second hour would be full by the end of the night. We'd had at least six walk-ins who never thought they needed to sign up for a skating class in January.

I felt like I was walking up a mountain. Without water or shoes. That girl from the movie *Wild* passed through my mind, and "unprepared" wasn't a big enough word for how I felt.

Our hockey director, Mack, came behind the table and sat on the bench next to me.

"Roger told me to come help out," he said so quietly

it was almost whispered.

I'd noticed him around the rink—mostly because he looked like he walked out of a magazine—but I'd never talked to him. His eyes were the bluest eyes I'd ever seen. Caribbean Sea blue. Photoshopped blue.

He raised his eyebrows, waiting for an answer.

"Oh!" I said. "He did? Is that normal?"

"Do you want some assistance?" He said each word slowly, as if I were hearing-challenged.

I went from 'a cute boy is talking to me' to 'oh-my-God he hates me' in a matter of seconds. And as much as I'd love some help right now, there was no way I was asking him for anything.

"I think I'm good," I said with a sharp nod. "Tell Roger not to worry."

He looked at me wearily, like not taking his help was the wrong answer. "Whatever you say," he sighed. He stood and walked towards the office, no doubt to tell Roger I was failing miserably and didn't want help.

A woman looking for her son's name tag raised her eyebrows at me. "I don't think I'd ever turn down help from him," she whispered and winked. Her eyes lit up when she found the yellow name tag. "I forgot he moved up to basic three." She waved the tag at me and turned to find her son in a sea of people in the lobby.

I quickly chugged a long drink from my water bottle before the next skater came up. I knew her from the last few sessions on the ice.

"Miss Talula," I said, smiling at her familiar face. "Did your parents let you drive here all by yourself again?"

Peals of giggles escaped from her. "Nooo, Natalie. You know I'm only seven," she said.

"And you've been driving for years now! Shame on those parents!"

More giggles. Her mom across the lobby waved and smiled at us.

"Don't forget that you practice first tonight. You moved up a whole level, and the time is a little different," I reminded her.

"I won't forget," she said, walking towards her mom.

It was that precise moment I realized that I wouldn't be on the ice to teach her anymore—at least for learn-to-skate. I loved teaching the littles and wondered if I'd be able to still be a part of their lives this way. My heart sank a little more as a dad known for his high expectations walked up, red-faced.

"I stopped by to pay for my daughter's class, and they said she wasn't signed up and to come see you because the class is filled," he huffed.

"Did you sign up?" I didn't mean for it to sound condescending, but his reaction proved it was.

"We have been taking classes for a year now. At the end of last session, I stopped by the front desk and told them to put her down."

This was the third person tonight who said the same

thing. "I'm sorry, but if you didn't pay for the session at that time, they wouldn't have been able to take the registration," I tried to explain. "Winter session is too busy to hold any registrations."

His face started to turn purple. "Are you kidding me? Where's Jonathan? He will take care of this."

I took a deep breath. "Unfortunately, Jonathan isn't working here any longer. My name is Natalie, and I'll be running the learn-to-skate program from now on," I said, holding out my hand to shake.

He looked at my hand as if I spit on it first. "You're joking, right? You really think you're going to be able to take Jonathan's place?"

"Sir, what class is your daughter supposed to be taking?"

A line started forming behind him, and I didn't need to have an argument in front of all of them.

"Basic five," he said.

The pit in my stomach grew. Sheila was teaching that class, and she already had eight in there, which was the limit. She'd kill me later, but I didn't see how I had a choice.

"Get her skates on her—she will practice first—then you can go back down to the office to pay and get her name tag. I'll let them know I cleared it."

He rolled his eyes and turned away from me. On and on it went, until the last of the parents came through. By then, the lobby filled back up with the first group of skaters leaving. There was a trail of sweat down my back and pooled at the base of my spine. I was grateful I was wearing black today, so no one would see.

I remembered thinking this morning that I was as prepared as I could be, but an hour ago I started a list of things I needed to accomplish before the Saturday morning classes began. The list was daunting, and I could only imagine how many hours I'd have to put in this week.

And that didn't include the Club's board meeting I had to still attend tonight when I was done with this. How did Jonathan do all of this and stay sane? As I saw it, my entire life would change with these new responsibilities. And I knew I chose this, but I didn't have a clue as to how much I had gotten myself into.

~~

The meeting room was just off rink one, separated only by floor-to-ceiling windows across the entire length of the room, and all the heat in the entire rink was located in this one room. From here, you could see everything that was going on in rink one.

In this case, a high school hockey practice. From where I sat, half of the team were solid players, and the other half looked as if they had never skated before. "Ankle benders," we'd call them. It was a good distraction to the mind-numbingly inane meeting going on inside this room.

"But you can't just ask them to give their money back. It was a gift for qualifying for Nationals,"

Margaret said. She was everyone's favorite mom.

"And look where that got us! One was injured, and the other barely made it into the top ten," said Clarissa. She had taken over the treasurer position after Jonathan left.

I had always avoided the board meetings after hearing Jonathan talk about them, but I had no idea they were this bad. This conversation was bananas.

I cleared my throat. "Um, maybe I'm stepping out of turn here, but the gift was based on expenses and an accomplishment from Mids, if I'm not mistaken. What happened at Nationals shouldn't be your concern."

Ten pairs of eyes zeroed in on me. Clarissa turned her head so sharply I heard her neck crack. "I think, given this is your first meeting ever, you should just observe instead of giving your opinions."

I slumped down in my chair, my entire body overheated from embarrassment. I unwrapped my scarf and pulled off my fleece.

"She's right, though," Margaret snapped at Clarissa. "And I'm sorry, but she is the new skating director. Show some respect."

"Okay, let's just take a step back," said Lance, the Club's president. "We're not asking for anything back. Natalie's correct—it was given after Mids—and regardless of what happened at Nationals, we are lucky to have skaters make it that far. Let's not forget that. We have gone through massive changes, and now is not the time to alienate anyone, especially the skaters or the new skating director."

Clarissa shot me a look that was anything but kind. Jonathan had coached her daughter, but she was with Dana now. I silently thanked Jonathan for sparing me this mom. No amount of talent was worth the stress of an aggressive mom.

The conversation went in circles about budgets, ice show decorations, and a national conference coming up in May. Clarissa talked endlessly about missing funds and still hadn't located receipts from last year. At some point, they began discussing the date for the holiday show in December, and I had to keep my head down, taking notes in my planner. My face burned from the heat and the monotony of the conversation. I rested my chin on my hand and worked to keep my eyes open for just one more topic on the agenda.

My mind wandered to Jonathan and where he might be right now. Would he keep coaching down in Cleveland? Would he quit for good? How did he ever sit through these meetings for all these years?

I felt a hand on my shoulder. That's odd, why was someone nudging me?

"Nat-a-leee," Clarissa was saying my name very slowly. "WAKE UP."

My eyes snapped open to see those same ten pairs of eyes zeroed in on me, again. I wiped my chin and noticed a blob of drool on the table.

No, no, no, this isn't happening. I did not just fall asleep and drool on the table in front of the entire Club board.

"Seems like someone is up past her bedtime," Lance said with a chuckle.

"I know this isn't the most exciting conversation, but still," Clarissa said. "Somehow, all of us manage to stay awake every month."

Margaret and several others shot me sympathetic looks, and I wondered if they'd notice if I slithered under the table.

"As much as I'd like to say you're the first to fall asleep at a board meeting, you're not," Lance said. "Just last year, sweet, little Mabel fell asleep for the whole damn meeting."

They all had a good laugh at sweet little Mabel, who was the oldest board member up until last April, when her term was up. At ninety-two, she still volunteered at every competition and ice show, and being compared to her wasn't doing sweet little Mabel any favors.

"Remember, next month is when we start planning the annual banquet. We will need to have a committee take that over," Juanita said from the corner. She was the head of the social committee and usually ended up planning everything by herself.

Well, with the help of Mabel.

Committee was her middle name.

Lance stood and walked to where I was seated as everyone else packed up their notepads and binders. "So, congratulations on the skating director position," he said.

I dipped my head, shaking off his compliment. "I'm

really sorry about the whole sleeping thing," I said. "I guess my week has caught up to me."

"All good." He waved me off. "Listen, I'm wondering if we could meet for coffee sometime in the next few weeks. I want to run some ideas past you for the show this year."

Lance was a legend when it came to the ice show. He made props, painted scenery, cut out decorations, and when dress rehearsal came, he helped put it all together. The room emptied out quickly, and it was just us left in the room.

"I'm counting on it," I said truthfully. We couldn't run a show without his help. "I'll email you tomorrow, and we can figure out a time to meet. I'll need your help more than ever this year, given all the change going on."

He slumped a sigh of relief. "Oh, thank goodness. I was hoping you'd say so."

I had known Lance forever, but this was our first conversation together. He seemed a little desperate for the show, if you asked me, but who was I to say no to free help?

I couldn't think about the show right now. The first order of business was bed. The rest would fall into place, I hoped.

Office Antics

I had no idea how much paperwork was involved in any of what Jonathan did. Between the learn-to-skate registrations and the figure skater's ice time contracts, I began to understand why Jonathan was so picky with his coaching time. There wasn't enough time to do it all, so he zeroed in on his favorite skaters, and spent the rest of the time running both programs. It was mind-boggling for me because I now had a full schedule with the skaters plus the added time here in my tiny cubicle.

The office had an open layout with three offices along the outside wall and four cubicles in the center area. The receptionist sat in the front, closest to the entrance and lobby. I shared the cubicle space with Mack, the hockey director, Amanda, the office manager, and Todd, who was Roger's assistant and head of maintenance. Our GM, Roger, and program manager, Janie, had two of the outside offices. The third office was more of a storage room for the learn-to-skate and hockey programs. We kept the clipboards, toys, markers, and coats stored in there and locked up when not being used. Roger and Janie rarely closed their doors, so the office had an open feel—which meant there were no secrets.

If you were having a bad day, everyone knew it.

If you had onions at lunch, everyone knew it.

And the constant joking was relentless. Hockey players, I'd learned, have a tendency to treat the world as one big locker room.

I'd spent the entire first week feeling exposed and annoyed.

"Nat, you're scowling again!" Roger yelled from his office. "Please tell me you'll lighten up at some point."

I stuck my tongue out at him and turned to face my computer. "Maybe if there wasn't constant chatter in here, I could get something done."

At that moment, Mack walked through the office door, eyebrows raised. Roger gave him the *shhhhhh* signal, and Mack gave him a thumbs-up.

I still had six emails to answer from parents in learn-to-skate before I could leave. Roger had made a point to tell me to leave my work email off my phone, and to never take work home with me. Solid advice, but it also forced me to finish my work at the end of each day.

I checked my watch. It was six thirty-five, and I was supposed to meet Marcy in twenty-five minutes at my place. I shot her a text telling her we were off tonight.

Marcy: WTH???

Me: Too much work tonight. Stuck at the rink.

Marcy: Okay... see you tomorrow. No bailing!

Me: Wouldn't consider it.

I started with the first email and worked my way down, answering the most mundane questions possible. Class changes, day conflicts, make-up passes, and even misspelled names on the name tags. It appeared that people had even more questions once they got home than when they were here.

My to-do list before Saturday classes had also grown, but that would have to wait until tomorrow before lessons. I needed to get out of these four walls.

"Hey, Bishop," Mack said, peeking over the cubicle wall. "You're going to make us all look bad."

"Do you call everyone by their last name?" I asked, not looking up from my list. Something about this guy rubbed me the wrong way. He had the cocky confidence only a former hockey player could acquire. Entitled. Arrogant. Overly good-looking, and his hair had this annoyingly perfectly messy look. One would have to spend a great deal of time looking in the mirror to master that look. I imagined his girlfriend was the perfect, Barbie look-alike type, who slept in his old jerseys.

"Actually," he said. "Now that you say it, I guess I do use last names all the time. Huh."

Roger chuckled at my eye roll. "Nat, he's just giving you a hard time. Wanted to glue all your things to your desk this morning, but I wouldn't let him."

"You know, sort of an initiation," he said, smiling. I had to look away before I smiled back at him.

Jonathan reminded us constantly of an unwritten rule that the hockey and figure skating programs competed over ice time. One group always wanted more of what the other had. Given this was considered a hockey city, the figure skaters had to earn their right to more ice time. That meant we'd have to prove we could profit more per hour than a hockey team could. It led to overcrowded sessions and learn-to-skate classes with multiple teachers. It also meant Mack was the enemy.

"Can I ask you a question?" I said, turning to face Mack.

"Of course," he said. "I'm an open book."

"Why were you so rude to me the other night during learn-to-skate?" His eyes darted to Roger, and the charm visibly melted away. "You just seemed so stressed, and I didn't know what I could do to help."

"In his defense, that's my fault," Roger said from his office. "We were watching you on the lobby cam and could tell the parents were being difficult. Mack thought you were handling it, but I asked him to come down."

"You used the lobby cam to spy on me?"

Roger got up and leaned against his door jamb. "It's mostly used for security, but every now and again, we check to see how the parents are behaving," he explained. "I don't have to tell you how quickly their stories change when they know they are being recorded."

I remember when we installed the cameras two years ago: several families complained of missing or damaged equipment. All complaints have stopped since then, and the cameras were invaluable during skating competitions or hockey tournaments.

"So, basically you hired me, but then didn't trust me to be able to do the job?"

"It was your first night," Mack said. "No one can handle the demands of that job on the first night. Roger was just trying to help. To me, you seemed like a jump-in-the-deep-end kind of girl, so I wanted to let you be."

"For your information, I hate the deep end and would've gladly taken some genuine help." I turned back to my computer, and the office fell into an awkward silence. I didn't care that I was ruining their office antics. I was hired to do a job and wanted to make sure I didn't fail anyone, especially the coaches and skaters who depended on my ability to keep the programs up and running.

More than anything else, I had to make sure our programs didn't lose any of our ice time. That was my only goal right now.

After adding my tasks into Outlook and categorizing them, I powered down my computer. My stomach growled, and my head pounded. All I wanted was a giant bowl of popcorn, a glass of wine, and *Dateline*.

I hollered a lame goodbye as I walked out, zipping my coat up to my chin. Michigan winters were brutal and unforgiving. Given that it was dark by five-thirty every night, it felt like midnight whenever I left the rink. Every night, as I got into my car, I said a silent prayer of thanks to my dad for encouraging me to get the luxury edition when I bought my car. I didn't give him credit for much in my life, but this was definitely advice I was happy I took.

❧

Thankfully, the highway was empty tonight because a small dusting of snow passed through an hour ago. Not enough for snowplows yet, but the roads had that unstable, slippery feel to them.

"Did you call me so I could listen to you curse at the roads?" Marcy said.

"Sorry—icy patch," I said. "I didn't think the roads would be this bad."

"You're really putting in the hours this week. Will this be the normal schedule?"

"God, I hope not, but I really don't know yet." I sighed. "There is so much more to this than I ever thought. It's overwhelming."

"It'll get better," she said. "I promise. New jobs are so hard to break into."

"I know it will. I just wish I didn't have to deal with the office politics on top of everything else."

"There's politics already? That's fast."

"Nothing new, just the same battle for ice time with the hockey players. And the hockey director is a total tool—thinks he's God's gift to everyone."

"Oh, do tell... he sounds interesting already," she said. I could hear the smile in her voice.

"Don't even think about it," I warned her. "He is my sworn enemy and appears to be best friends with the GM. I will have to work twice as hard to make sure our numbers are up every session."

"Huh, you have strong feelings already. I might have to meet this guy. What's his name?"

"You're gonna love this... it's Marcus Mackinnon, but everyone calls him Mack. He's Canadian and a former hockey player. Hurt his knee or something in juniors, so he had to quit, and now he's here."

"Ohhh, Canadians are nice," she said. "But you're right, he sounds horrible, with that cute nickname and all. How are his eyes? I love a cute boy with nice eyes."

"Who said he was cute?"

"It was implied with the God's gift reference."

"Well, I guess some people might think he was cute. To me, he's the competition."

"Uh huh, sure. Nothing wrong with a little competition to keep us on our toes."

"And he's only half of my problems," I huffed. "I have these two new students and don't have a clue how to make them like me. It's like this surface-level politeness, and we're getting nothing done."

"How about we pump the breaks a bit," she said.

"How long has it been... two weeks? Things like this take time, especially with teenagers. They don't trust anyone."

"That's probably true, but Will has been a little better than Addie." I exited the highway, my car slipping in a slushy patch. The heated seat began to melt my coat, so I turned it down to the lowest level. "Addie is just taking all of this so hard. And after Nationals, she is just so down on herself. I don't know what to do for her."

"Have you reached out to Jonathan about it? He might be able to shed some light," she said.

"I've texted and called but haven't heard anything back from him. He's totally ghosted all of us."

"That is so weird, considering this was his life for so long," she mused. "Why would he just up and leave everything he worked toward for so long?"

"I don't know—he's not even updating any social media, which he never ignored. The whole thing is bizarre, and I'm beginning to wonder if it's more than just his wife getting a new job."

"Sounds like it, but who knows? Maybe he's just busy getting his new life settled. Major life events affect everyone differently. Best to give him the benefit of the doubt for now, but I want to go back to Addie... is she showing any weird behaviors other than normal teenage angsty stuff?"

I was grateful for the change of topic from Jonathan. "Honestly, I'm not sure. I know Jonathan had some issues with her at the beginning with her mom. She's pretty demanding and thinks her daughter should be in the Olympics. Jonathan had to put his foot down with her from the beginning, but he's never said a negative word about Addie, ever. Just that she's super hard on herself."

"Often, when someone is hard on themselves, it's because they're trying to please someone… like Mommy Dearest. Maybe you should have a meeting with the parents and skater to go over goals and expectations."

"On it. The meeting is tomorrow after lessons. The dad is a surgeon and has been pretty hands-off with her skating. Not sure I've ever seen him," I explained. "So, Addie, her mom, and I are meeting in the lobby and going over the year. It's weird to go over goals and expectations with a skater of this caliber. It's like Jerry's Bizarro world."

She laughed. "Yes! This is like the opposite of what you usually do, so this is working. You'll be brilliant."

I snorted. "I'm not sure brilliant is the word I'd use, but it's definitely the opposite of my norm. I've always had such a laid-back approach with my own skaters, so this is just another thing in my life that is completely different."

"Hey—just remember, all of this is a major life change for you as well. Make sure you're taking care of yourself through all of this."

"I'm not sure I did that before, other than meeting

with you, I mean." I sighed. "Back to Addie... how should I approach it?"

"I see what you did there, but I'm going to let it slide this time. For Addie—why don't you list out what you'd like to see her accomplish this year. Break it down into quarters, so she has goals to meet every few months. Have that list ready, but I would have them speak first and see what the mom expects."

"That sounds doable," I said, my mind already hitting goal markers for her. "I could list out the competitions too, just to give us more checkpoints."

"Good, best to be proactive with an aggressive mom. Nip it in the bud, if you can—or better yet, get her on your side. Then it'll feel a little safer for Addie."

"Okay, I like it. Mind if I shoot you the list later to see what you think?"

"Fine with me," she agreed. "If you want to FaceTime to go over it, we can do that too. Kind of a virtual wine night since I didn't come over."

"Yes! Great idea," I said. "I'm almost home, so let me get settled. I'll call you in a bit."

"Aye, aye, Cap'n. Catch you in a bit," she said before disconnecting.

I unzipped my coat, suddenly so hot I could spit fire. My mind raced for both Will and Addie and what to accomplish this year. This was exactly what I needed to do to feel more in control of the situation. "Always have a plan," Jonathan used to say. I don't know how I forgot that.

A plan was exactly what I needed.

I pressed the hands-free button on my steering wheel and asked Siri to call Jonathan. Figuring everything out on my own was not part of the agreement.

A high pitch beep came on immediately, followed by, "We're sorry... the number you are dialing has been disconnected."

A million questions popped into my head as I hung up, but the loudest one of all was, *what in the hell are you hiding from, Jonathan?* My mind raced to the last month he was here. Our last conversation. Every moment together to see if he left any hints of why he really left. On top of everything else I was going through, now this... more questions instead of answers, and I knew that I'd have to figure everything out on my own from here on out. I didn't even know if I'd ever see or talk to Jonathan again, but it didn't matter: I had to save everything he passed onto me without his help.

The skating program, his skaters, and my reputation... These things were all mine to lose.

Morning Lessons

"One. Two. Three. Four. Five. Six. Seven. Eight." It was a known fact around the rink that I was a yeller. Loud. Borderline obnoxious. I'm not sure what happened, but when I put skates on, a higher force took over my body and made me do and say things I normally wouldn't. I was still searching for that force when I taught Will and Addie, but it was alive and well on this morning session with Bri.

She was younger, only ten, but showed so much talent from the beginning. We were working on her moves in the field—required elements that focused mainly on edge quality, power, and quickness. Moves were one of my favorite things to teach, but the students generally hated them. They'd rather work on jumps and spins, but this is where the skaters became great—in my humble opinion.

We were preparing for testing next week, and Bri would have to perform these in front of judges to see if she was ready for the next level of skills. She wouldn't be moving on to anything if she couldn't get this rhythm down.

"Sweetie—can you hear me?" I asked when she

finished.

"*Everyone* can hear you."

"And you understand your steps have to match my counting, yes?"

Her shoulders drooped. "I hear you, but I can't make my feet do those steps that fast."

"Of course you can," I said, taking her hand. "Let's walk through them together." She stepped through the eight-step sequence easily and with the rhythm needed.

"I don't understand," I said. "You know what to do—why can't you do it out on the pattern?"

She bit her lip. "Can I try without you yelling?"

I zipped my lip shut and motioned for her to try again. This time, she skated through the steps without any problem. Beautifully, even. Skated like that, she would gain a few tenths on points, ones we could use on her back power threes.

She skated back with a smirk.

"I know what to do, but sometimes, all I can hear is you yelling the count, and it messes me up."

"Point taken," I said. "That was definitely passing. Skating like that in the test will help boost your total score. Let's see the next move."

She nodded and skated towards the end. I made certain the skaters had a testing mentality and knew what would pass and what wouldn't. Not only that, but each skill was judged individually, so if they made a mistake on one, those points could be made up somewhere else. Perfection wasn't required, but knowledge was. In a sport where a test could pass or fail by a tenth of a point, you have to learn to play the game early.

It was six thirty in the morning—many skaters came in before school—and I noticed Mack watching from the lobby. He gave me a small wave. Creepy, if you asked me. Why was he even in at this time? Usually it was just the maintenance workers that opened up around here. The rest of the management rolled in around nine every morning.

I gave him a lame wave and continued on with my lesson, trying to ignore the fact he was watching me.

Bri and I spent the rest of our lesson making the power threes look easy, which was shockingly difficult to do. By the time she got off the ice, Mack was nowhere to be found, and I took off my skates and sneaked out of the rink in record time. No need for him to see my bedhead under my winter hat. Fashion wasn't the main focus for morning sessions, and the skaters adjusted quickly to the just-rolled-out-of-bed look.

⌣

I stopped at Starbucks on the way back home and scanned Spotify for new music this year. I was a little behind with Will and Addie, but not horribly so. My meeting with Addie and her mom the other day ended up being more about getting to know each other than a planning session. Her mom—Nicole—looked like she came straight from one of the Housewives shows but was down to earth and friendly. Not at all what I expected. She had nothing but great things to say about Jonathan, but I had the distinct feeling she was relieved he was gone. We agreed to keep the same blocking system that Jonathan started a few years back to train, peak, and recover for each competition this year. We agreed she would be lucky to get an international spot for the Grand Prix, but it wasn't completely out of the question. A good skate in July would help but wasn't mandatory to qualify for Nationals again.

Today, Addie and I agreed to each bring in music for the upcoming year. We wanted to do two new programs, and let the past remain where it was— behind us. Our choreographer, Fredrick, would be in next week and requested to have the music at least by Saturday so he could start 'processing' it in his head. I had several pieces that I loved and could see her skating to, but also wanted to have her be a part of the choice. She needed to own it.

On the drive home, lulled by Agnes Obel, my mind drifted to Mack and why he was at the rink this morning. A normal person would've stopped by to inquire, but there was something about him that set me on edge. His eyes, for starters, were something only seen in movie stars. Bright blue, with the longest lashes I've ever seen without mascara. Lashes like those made me jealous.

He was quiet—soft-spoken—but his face lit up like Christmas when someone said something funny. I watched him interact with his youngest hockey players, the mini-mites, and swore he was a little kid himself. I remember during the holidays, he dressed up like Santa for the learn-to-skate and hockey programs. "Hot Santa," Stephanie called him. "He could come down my chimney any time," she whispered in between classes. We had a staff meeting today at noon, so maybe he needed to get some other stuff done before that.

Either way, I had to get home and figure out the music situation for Addie. For Will, we would just be a new short program, and had quickly agreed on a song already. Everything about Will was easier, and he seemed to balance Addie out as well. I knew they were keeping something from me, but I didn't know what yet. I needed to build up their trust first.

What I'd rather be doing is taking a nap. The lack of sleep I'd had since all this started was mind-boggling, and Starbucks wouldn't cut it for much longer.

Reality Check

"So glad you could make it, Natalie," Roger said, looking over his readers at me. We met in the small conference room located in a long dark hallway between both rinks.

Four pairs of eyes stared at me from the table in the middle of the room. I looked at my watch, which said exactly twelve noon.

"I'm sorry, I thought noon meant *noon*," I said, peeling off my coat and setting my planner down at the only empty spot next to Janie. Mack sat across from me, biting his lip.

"We usually get here at eleven forty-five to make sure we're ready to go by noon," Roger clarified. "It's your first time... you'll get used to it." He handed me a meeting agenda. "The skating programs always go first, but given that you just sat down, I'll let Mack go first today."

I looked at the agenda and a pit grew in my stomach. I didn't have anything prepared about either of my programs. Granted I had the numbers memorized— seared into my brain, more like it—but no printed reports. I slid down in my chair and looked for a pen in my bag.

I only half-listened to Mack as he droned on about how high his numbers were this year compared to last. "At this rate, I don't know where we're going to put all the players for next session," he said. I looked up, and he raised his eyebrows at me. "You ready yet, Natalie?"

I had scribbled down the numbers from each program and contract totals for winter, but I haven't yet compared them to last year. If I was being honest, I hadn't even thought to do that. I took a deep breath and looked up at Roger, who nodded for me to go.

"Well..." I started. "I know this is my first official meeting, but I really didn't know what to expect, so I feel a little unprepared."

"Someone probably should've given you an idea of what to prepare," Janie said. "Why don't you just give us what you have for the current sessions. I think they're up from last year, but not sure how much."

Janie was the eyes and ears of the entire rink. That much I knew. Program Director wasn't a big enough title for everything she did.

"So, for learn-to-skate, the number—last I checked—was at two hundred and twenty-three skaters. The Beginning Tot classes are overfull, as are the basic one classes. I have multiple teachers and helpers for each of those, and no complaints yet. The higher levels seem to be normal, although the freestyle class is at three skaters total. Three of those skaters from last session moved into private lessons, so that's a gain in my opinion."

I looked up and Roger was scribbling notes on his notepad, so I continued. "For the contracts, we're a little lower than fall, but I'm still missing some of them. I noticed a couple skaters on sessions yesterday that haven't turned anything in yet."

Roger's eyes snapped up. "Aren't they supposed to be signing in for every session?"

I swallowed hard. "They are, but it's Lydia's skaters, and they always think they don't have to follow the rules. I will speak with her today and make sure they are turned in before they get on the ice next."

He nodded but didn't look convinced. "Janie— you're up."

The rest of the meeting dragged on as only one would where you feel publicly shamed in front of your peers. I couldn't believe Roger was being so tough on me already. It wasn't like I knew any of this coming into the job, and thanks to Jonathan, I had an uphill battle to climb.

"It looks like we're on track for another record quarter, with the exception of the figure skaters. We need to get those numbers up, Natalie," Roger said, closing the meeting. "That is prime ice time they're using, and we can always shift some of the times to increase the number of skaters on the sessions."

"But the majority of sessions are at capacity already," I said. "Some of those sessions are downright dangerous."

He nodded and shrugged. *Not my problem*, he seemed to say.

Everyone packed up their stuff, and I remained seated. I needed a moment alone to process the mental beating I just took. The door behind me opened again.

"You okay?" It was Janie.

I sighed, not wanting to cry in front of anyone.

"I just don't understand how I'm supposed to know everything from day one," I said. "I've never done anything but coach, and I'm doing the best I know how, but that doesn't seem to be good enough."

She shook her head, smiling. "You're doing fine," she reassured me. "I promise. Jonathan took forever to learn some of this stuff, and to be able to pull those numbers off the top of your head like that was quick thinking. How would you know we compare everything to the year before? Hell, sometimes the five years before for the average. It's insane how number-driven this company is."

Her rant made me smile.

"I mean, I know why they're so important, but it's like we're not even talking about people anymore when we make them a number. I like to keep the focus on *why* we're doing all this work."

"Whew, okay," I said. "Thanks... I needed to know I'm not the only one who cares about the people on the ice. And thank you for helping me through this. I promise to be more prepared next time."

"And don't get me started on the monthly meetings," she said. "Corporate sends someone down the first week of each month, by the way. Wouldn't want you to be blindsided."

Janie couldn't have been more than late twenties but had been here since she graduated from college. She was African American with a petite frame. You'd never have known she played college hockey for Brown, but her competitive nature was unmistakable. I had no idea why she was helping me so much. She had barely said a word to me since I'd started.

I opened my planner and wrote down eleven forty-five for the February meetings and starred the one on the first Friday of the month. I'd be so prepared for the next one, Roger won't know what hit him.

Looking at the clock, I realized I had a couple hours before my first lesson. There was still so much to do before learn-to-skate tomorrow.

Agree to Disagree

The learn-to-skate program lived by a color-coded system to differentiate the class levels. The Beginning Tots—five and under—were light pink and blue. I was busy cutting out name tags for these groups when I heard a yawn on the other side of the cubicle.

"You sound tired over there," I hollered.

"How do you guys do it, coaching so early every day?" Mack's head suddenly peered over the wall.

"Honestly, I think we just get used to it after a while," I said. "And naps on the weekends are epic."

The corner of his eyes crinkled when he smiled, and I wondered how old he was.

"Why were you here so early today?"

"Todd couldn't make it this morning, so he asked me to open for him," he said. "I don't know why anyone would willingly take the morning shift every day."

To me, Todd seemed like someone who didn't want to be around a bunch of people. The mornings here were quiet, and the skaters and coaches kept to themselves. It made perfect sense to me.

"Well, I'm here most mornings, so I could always open if needed," I offered. Why was I being nice to him?

He started to say something but hesitated.

"What?" I asked.

"I just wondered what you were teaching this morning when you noticed me," he said. "It was just a bunch of steps, but they looked tricky. I mean, nothing a hockey player couldn't do, though."

I stopped what I was doing altogether and turned to face him. He was winking at Roger, like I wouldn't see it. "Nothing a hockey player couldn't do?" I repeated. "You're joking, right? My ten-year-old, Bri, could skate circles around most of your hockey players. And here I thought you were serious." I turned back to my name tags, moving on to the red Basic One class.

He walked around to the entrance of my cubicle. "It's a known fact that hockey players are better than figure skaters. We're faster and have more power."

"Oh boy," Janie said from her office. "Here we go."

"I don't know where you're getting your information, but you are clearly misinformed. Figure skaters can out-skate a hockey player any day. And you can't even compete with our edge work."

Mack looked in Roger's direction, and they both busted out laughing. I felt heat creep up my neck into my face.

"Aren't we all supposed to be on the same team?" Janie yelled from her office. "Let's just agree to disagree."

Mack held his hands and backed up in mock retreat.

"I can agree to disagree if she can," he said, back over on his side now. "As long as we can agree it's a hockey world, and we're just letting them skate here."

My head snapped up, and I looked at Roger. "Is that really what you all think?"

He chuckled and shrugged. "He's just getting you all riled up, Nat. Don't pay him any attention. He just misses the trash talk with Jonathan."

"Tell me again why he left in such a hurry?" Mack asked.

"His wife was transferred to Cleveland," I answered. "More money, I'm assuming. Seemed like a promotion the way he explained it, but he's been completely off the grid ever since."

The chatter and trash talk quieted down, and I finished up the beginning levels for Saturday classes with a half hour to spare. I grabbed my earbuds and headed to the coaches room to lace up my skates. If I could get on the ice before any of the skaters, I'd be able to see if any of my music would work or not.

Unable to know what Addie would like, I had a few choices from classical to show tunes, as well as a couple contemporary songs. Most skaters had at least one program with current songs—and Addie was no different. I found several this year, with and without lyrics, and I added them all to a playlist. Choosing music was somewhat competitive, and I didn't want anyone to steal the choices I had found for her, so I made sure to not use the overhead speakers. The first was my favorite—a tango-themed piece, featured in an old Jennifer Lopez movie. It had everything I wanted from her—emotion, tension—and felt current enough for today's competitive scene. The others were all good as well, but I could see this, and I knew Fredrik would kill to choreograph this program. I turned it up and let my own body move to the music, feeling every beat.

There is something so utterly peaceful about a quiet and darkened rink with the overhead lights off. Some people dreamed of beaches, but this... this was my heaven. I felt this song in my bones and played it over again from the beginning. I could see it. I could see the image of her on TV at Nationals, the camera zeroing in on her face right before the music started. That glint in her brown eyes as she narrowed them towards the judges.

This music was the perfect choice. It had to be. Now if only I could convince her.

The lights suddenly snapped on, jarring me from my musical bliss. Janie waved to me from the lobby as the first few skaters stepped on the ice. Playtime was officially over.

～〜〜

The best part of any session was the first five minutes or so. Will was legendary with his taste in music and became the self-appointed DJ for any session he was on. Every session he would play a song—a different one every single day—for the skaters' warm-up. The intricate edge sequences they practiced had to be completed to the beat of whatever song he put on. Like human metronomes, the skaters would weave back and forth, turning on a dime front to back, then repeat down each side of the ice. It was like a chorus of dancers, and all of them marched to the beat of Will's drum. Today's choice was a Taylor Swift song I'd never heard of before. The beat was a little slower, so the skaters had to create bigger edges to stay on time.

It was magic to watch. Mesmerizing.

Addie broke from the group first to stretch at the boards. Both rinks were frigid during the winter months, so even though they warmed up off the ice, they still had to get their body moving again out here, then stretch.

"I think I found some really good music choices," I said to her.

For the first time since I started working with her, her eyes lit up. "Really? Can I hear them?"

"I'd prefer to send you the playlist and have you listen tonight... I don't really want to play them overhead before you decide."

She nodded knowingly.

"And if you don't like them, it's okay," I reassured her. I desperately wanted her to start warming up to me—to anyone—again. Since Jonathan left, she looked like the spark left her eyes. She was almost indifferent in lessons with me, and while she still worked hard, something was missing.

Will came up beside her to stretch. "Nice song choice today," I said to him. "Haven't heard that one before."

"It's from her CD a couple years ago. Not a popular track, but the perfect beat for edges," Will said. He was much more outgoing with me so far.

I leaned on the board and watched them stretch in unison. I always knew they were close, but until now, I hadn't realized how much.

"You know," Will started. "Today is Friday Funday." His dark eyes twinkled. His dad was Caucasian, and his mom was Asian, and his features favored both of them. He had his mom's eyes, but his dad's smile and charm. Will was one of the nicest skaters I had ever worked with.

"Okay, I give up," I said, playing along. "What happens on Friday Funday?"

My previous schedule had me off on Fridays, so I didn't have a clue what Jonathan used to do with them. This could be a complete lie on their part, and I wouldn't know it.

Addie looked at Will with wide eyes and a wrinkled brow. If I had my guesses, she didn't know what Friday Funday was either.

"Welllll," he said, looking back at Addie. "Jonathan always let us do our lessons together, and we'd work on jumping exercises for balance and agility."

I called BS in my head but refrained from saying it out loud. "These jumping exercises you speak of... care to elaborate?"

His eyes twinkled when he smiled. "I'll even show you once we're warmed up. The whole point of Friday was to stay loose and learn something new, outside of our programs. We would do different spin combinations... step sequences too. Anything out of our ordinary. Sometimes we skate each other's programs to see something different."

Addie smiled but wouldn't meet my eyes. "Yesss, Friday *Funday*," she said. "It's the best day of the week."

I raised my eyebrows and looked them in the eye. "I supposed I can't break a Friday tradition, but we are still working today. No goofing around."

"We would never," she said, skating towards the middle to warm up her spins.

"She seems to be a little better today," I said, nodding towards Addie.

He nodded, but his eyes narrowed. "There is something still going on with her, but she won't tell me what it is."

I held up my hand. "I don't want to break any confidence you have with her. Just let me know if you ever think I should bring her mom into the picture."

He looked at Addie, then at me. "I don't think you should *ever* bring her mom into any conversation. If you ask me, her mom has always been her biggest problem, and Addie will tell you that herself. It's no secret."

He skated away, leaving me with my mouth hanging

open. What the hell was that? I didn't get that impression at all when we met. Her mom seemed pretty open to whatever Addie wanted and on board with the plan for the year. If anything, Addie seemed in control of all the decisions.

I didn't want to rock the boat today, but I would definitely have to address this later if it became a problem. We continued on with our Friday Funday, and I think I had more fun than the skaters. And given what they accomplished today, I didn't see why we wouldn't keep this "tradition" going. It forced them to skate outside their box and pushed them to learn intricate skills—and make them look easy. It was brilliant, and I couldn't wait for next Friday. I even recommended Will create a playlist just for Fridays to see if we could do the sequences to a beat.

As I was leaving the rink, I thought more about what Will said about Addie's mom. I knew she and Jonathan had become friends after that unfortunate first year with him. I wondered if emailing Jonathan about her would help. I just wanted to make sure that I was able to give Addie everything she needed, and that meant I needed to know everything about her. I decided to give it a little more time and see where things went with Addie. A bubble of hope bloomed inside my chest, and for the first time, I felt like I didn't completely suck up the day.

It wasn't exactly the positive self-talk Marcy wanted me to do, but it was a start.

INTERVIEW - PART 3

TL: Take me through the short program. That was your first indication you were in trouble, right?

AG: *(laughing softly)* Yeah... you could say that's when the wheels fell off the bus.

TL: I remember watching you and feeling shocked for you. The look on your face at the end of your program broke all of our hearts.

AG: I knew it was over, and all I wanted to do was hide. Hard to do with a camera in your face.

TL: What was going through your head as you sat in the kiss and cry with your coach at that time?

AG: My only thought was to not break down in front of the cameras. I just wanted to hold it together until I got back in the locker room. *(she pauses and looks down at her hands...)* It was actually at that point when all hell broke loose.

Show Fever

We had a problem in the rink for the past couple of weeks that had made everyone edgy, exhausted, and partial to sudden tears. It was a little thing Jonathan always called "Show Fever," and I've caught it before, but never to this extent.

My introduction into show production had been filtered with fear, angst, and overwhelm. I had no idea how much went into the planning and execution of an ice show, and I felt like it was me against the world most days. The coaches were pissed about extra coaching time for rehearsals. The rink staff hated having show props around the office and glitter covering every surface possible. The skaters, God bless them, were the only ones ecstatic about the additional ice time, crazy costumes, and perfecting new programs in less than two weeks.

It was two weeks of insanity, and it was almost the end.

Thursday—dress rehearsal day—was the day we finalized the decorations and dressed the rink up as if it were prom. While I had covered the boards with black paper, Roger and Mack were in the middle of the ice on a lift, hanging colored spotlights to shine down on the skaters. Next, they would hang the curtain that blocked off a quarter of the rink at one end, creating a backstage for the skaters.

Lance had been here till midnight last night, finalizing the props that would hang on the boards and curtain. He also made a giant balloon archway for the lobby, which took up most of the entryway. When Roger saw it this morning, he gave a look that said *what the hell?*

I was well aware of the fact that Jonathan had been able to do more of the heavy lifting with decorating, so I'd gone out of my way to be extra nice to anyone who was willing to help out today. Stephanie and Dana were covering the glass of the lobby with fabric to block out any light. In all honesty, Stephanie would do anything that allowed her to use a staple gun. Ronnie was in the lobby, untangling more Christmas lights and organizing Lance's props to bring onto the ice when the big stuff was done. Janie was helping in the office, making signs and sizing the show T-shirts.

My task lists have had tasks lists, and at any point I could fall over and sleep until next Monday. My only goal was to make it through the next two days without any injuries, threats, or panic attacks.

By three o'clock every muscle in my body was screaming for relief. I had three more hours before the rehearsals even started, and then it was another four hours at least. Just as I was about to rest my head on my desk for a quiet moment, a Starbucks cup was set in front of me.

"Thought you could use a pick-me-up," Mack said. He smiled with a hint of sympathy. "I hope you like mocha."

I had to physically will myself not to tear up in front of this guy. It was a simple gesture, but my exhaustion had left me a little emotionally unstable. I swallowed the emotion down hard.

"This might be the nicest thing anyone has ever done for me," I said. I met his eyes, and something inside me melted. "Thank you."

"If that's the nicest thing, then you seriously need better friends in your life," he replied, moving back to his cubby.

"Maybe it'll just give you an indication of my mental instability," I joked. "I don't think I've ever been this exhausted. And sore."

"This show is no joke. I came on board right after last year's, so I didn't realize how much went into it. No wonder the maintenance guys hate this."

The first sip of mocha hit my tongue, and I instantly knew it would be all okay. It felt like I was in a Starbucks commercial.

"Pretty sure the skaters are the only ones who love it."

"Not true," he said. "Yes, your workload has tripled in the last few weeks, but you've also been happier, singing all those damn show songs."

That can't be right. I don't sing.

Ever.

I looked at Roger, who was pretending to work, but listening to us. "Do I sing around here?"

He grinned wide. "Only when you're in the office," he said. "Of course, we don't follow you around, so I can't be sure about outside the office."

"You guys are just pulling my leg. I would never sing in front of people."

"Natalie!" Janie yelled from her office. "Normally, I'm on your side, but the guys are telling the truth. You've done nothing but torture us by singing the last few weeks. Half the time you have your earbuds in and can't hear yourself."

I wheeled away from my desk to see her face. She was nodding.

"Oh my God," I said. "I really sing? I'm so sorry!"

They were all laughing now.

"My personal favorite has been 'Fly Me to the Moon,'" Mack said.

I could feel my face heat up and knew it was beet red.

"I don't know," Janie chimed in. "Her rendition of 'Hallelujah' is pret-ty moving."

"Okay, I get it, I sing," I said. "Trust me when I say I'll never do it again!"

"Can I get that in writing?" Roger was holding a pen out to me.

I grabbed my coffee and my list and walked out of

the office. No one was sitting in the concession area, so I grabbed a chair and made myself comfortable, wishing I had remembered my phone.

After sitting out here for ten minutes, checking and double-checking my timeline and list, I saw Mack head towards me. I tried to focus on my list and not the smirk planted on his face.

He pulled out a chair and sat down. "Thought you might need this," he said, setting my phone on the table. "It's pinging like a crack dealer's phone."

I took a sip of my coffee and eyed him.

"We're sorry," he said. "It doesn't bother me when you sing. It's kinda funny... keeps things light in there."

"I guess we could all use that," I said.

It was no secret that our numbers had dipped this spring with all the programs. Roger had started making the staff meetings a weekly guilt trip. I knew he was only relaying the information from corporate, but it still felt like he didn't have our back right now.

He peered over my sheet. "What else do you have to do before rehearsal?"

I pointed to a stack of giant cardboard music notes that Lance had been painted and glittered. "Those need to go on the curtain and boards," I said. "I'm just trying to gear myself up for that right now."

"Drink up," he said. "I'll help you."

The other coaches were down in the other rink with regular practices. I could say no, but hanging these by myself would take hours—which I didn't have.

"It's not like you can run the lift by yourself," he said, noticing my hesitation. "And I think you need someone to make sure you don't fall asleep."

I gulped down the rest of my coffee and stood up. "I'll let you help me, but don't think for a second you get to pick the music this time."

"Shoot," he said, following me. "Skip the music, and you can just sing."

"Ha ha." I slugged him on the arm before picking up the notes. "Can you get the rest of those?"

He followed me through the backstage area, both of us leaving a trail of glitter behind us. I had been wearing a fanny pack all day loaded with scissors, duct tape, and fishing line.

I was the MacGuyver of show producers.

"So, we have twenty notes total," I said. "We'll use ten on the curtain—five on either side of the entrance—and use ten on the boards."

The overhead lights were off, and just the spotlights were shining down on us. In my head, Dana and Stephanie were snickering at me.

"Let's do the curtain first so you can get back to the office. I'll finish up the boards easily."

He nodded as he stepped into the bucket of the lift. "C'mon, if you're nice, I'll let you drive."

The bucket on that thing was about three feet by four with the control panel closest to the arm. Not a ton of space for two people. Plus, there was the whole heights thing. Suddenly, I saw myself like Wile E. Coyote, falling from the top.

He stared at me while I debated my options. I noticed a scar on his bottom lip, just on the underside of it. I wondered how he had gotten that.

"Or... you can stay down there and tell me where you want them," he said, breaking my thoughts.

"I don't love heights," I blurted out.

He shrugged. "Okay, I can hang them where you want, if you get them ready."

"Perfect," I said, scanning the curtain. "Now, we'll want to have some of them higher and some lower... staggered. Let's start up here with one." I motioned to the top left part of the curtain.

We worked for the next hour, me cutting the fishing line and tying to the top of the notes, and Mack tying them at various heights from the top of the curtain. After we finished with the last one, he wheeled the lift to the backstage area, out of the way of the skaters, and I started to tape the remaining notes to the boards.

"How are you not freezing?"

"Who said I wasn't? I can't even feel my fingers anymore."

"I still don't get how you go this overboard for two days—what five hours combined?"

His cheeks and nose were red, and he blew hot air into his hands.

"You can go back to the office," I said, trying to avoid his eyes. Unfortunately, in avoiding his eyes, I was drawn to that damn little scar. "These will take less than a half hour."

He grabbed my hand and inspected my spot where the skin had been torn off.

"What happened to your thumb?"

"Duct tape isn't so forgiving on skin," I said, stealing my hand back.

"Okay, hand it over." He held out his hand expectantly. "I'll tear the tape and you hang these damn things."

"But—"

"No buts. This will take ten minutes, tops, if we work together."

I stopped and looked at him. "Why are you being so nice to me?" I asked. "Usually it's 'this is a hockey world, and you're just livin' in it.'" It came out more like Barney's voice than his, but this nice act had me defensive suddenly.

"Do I really sound like that?"

I smiled. "No, but that's what I hear when you say stupid things like that."

"I did say that once, didn't I?" He cringed.

"More than once, Mr. Hockey," I said, taking the tape back. "Go on, I got this. Wouldn't want your little fingers to get too cold."

His eyes met mine, friendly, but sad too. "I'm sorry if I ever made you feel uncomfortable. Jonathan was better at dishing it out and didn't give a rip if we trash-talked him."

His eyes were sucking me into his apology. I shook my head to clear my head again. "I'll be back in the office shortly to get ready for tonight. If you see Dana or Steph, let them know to come find me."

He saluted, winked, and turned to walk backstage towards the exit.

For the first time in an hour, I took a deep breath in and let it out slowly. No way was I going to let him distract me from getting everything done.

I finally started to feel like I could get through today.

The Edge of Glory

Ever since I was a little girl, the ice show was always a highlight in my year. First as a skater, and then a coach. Never did I once think I could run—or "direct," as Dana liked to keep saying—the overall production. It was too massive for one person, and the smallest detail missed could ruin it completely.

Okay, maybe that was a bit dramatic.

But my mind had been racing for the last month. Music, costumes, props, rehearsals, the music list, parent information, tickets, programs, and ads. At best, it was overwhelming.

At the worst, it was miserable.

Your favorite aspects when you're a skater are far different than when you cross to the other side and become the coach. You're excited to skate under spotlights and see the rink all decorated. You love getting a costume, especially if it's one of the cool ones with a fringe skirt. And the biggest love of all is getting to perform, and not just for the judges.

As a coach, you love the creativity of choreography, especially with group numbers. The inside jokes. Competing to see who has the worst show number, aka "show death." The energy working on the Elite number. There is nothing like being in the trenches with the other coaches—laughing, and sometimes crying—over this beautiful thing we call the ice show.

Every year we also take bets on who will have the best show program. Two years ago, Stephanie coined it "the edge of glory number," when there is a perfect storm of music, choreography, and ultimately, performance. A former skater, Gia, skated to Andrea Bocelli's "Time to Say Goodbye" for her final show number.

"That, right there, is an edge of glory moment," she had said with tears streaming down her face.

Ever since, we'd vote on which coach will get the title and bragging rights for the year. To maintain balance, "show death" is also awarded to the coach of the worst number.

It was the last performance on Saturday, and I'd been counting down the hours till I could go home and go to bed. The second half of the show had just started, and I'd taken over the music to let Dana have a break. Stephanie volunteered to announce this year so we could keep Lydia backstage, but I made her promise not to use any curse words while she was on the mic. Poor Ronnie had the hardest job of all in gathering the skaters and making sure they were backstage at their appointed time. Last night, some of the older skaters had taken to playing a friendly game of hide-and-seek on him, just to see him panic. A near meltdown during last night's performance earned them a brief talk before today's show.

Most days, I was a glorified babysitter.

The order of the show always stacked the better skaters in the latter half of the second act. "Give them something good to remember," Jonathan used to say. Dana walked into the box with coffees for Steph and me.

"Is that the Baileys-flavored creamer again?" I choked out. To say she served a heavy pour was an understatement.

She winked in response. "Ohh, goodie. This is my favorite number this year," she whispered as Steph introduced Ingrid, who was skating to Beyoncé's "Single Ladies." Ronnie choreographed it, and Ingrid had moves Beyoncé didn't even have. Her fearlessness in performing in front of a crowd made it even more entertaining.

"Is this the edge of glory for the year?" I asked.

"Hmmm, I think Will might have it this year, in my opinion." Steph said. "I smile the entire time watching his program. We'll vote after the show."

I couldn't help but smile inwardly at the Will comment. It was the first time I choreographed a program for a male skater, especially one of his level, and skating to "Fly Me to the Moon" carried some weight. The prospect of failing terrified me, so I made sure to get his input every step of the way. And I wanted to agree with her, but Addie's show program made me prouder than anything else I've ever done. The way she felt the song "Hallelujah" took my breath away—skating with so much heart, feeling every note in that program. It brought tears to my eyes last night.

As the skater before Addie curtseyed to the audience, my stomach began to clench and twist. I felt more nerves for her performance than if I were skating it myself. So far, her year had been a series of disappointments, and I knew she teetered on the verge of quitting. A bad skate would only solidify her reasons for wanting to throw it all away.

Will came into the hockey box with us to watch her performance. He caught my eye, and I knew he felt it too—the need for another good skate. I nodded to give us both confidence, but my heart rate began to take off.

"Here we go," Steph said before turning on the mic. Addie skated out as Stephanie announced her. Will cheered and yelled louder than any other skater, and she looked towards the box and smiled before taking her beginning pose at center ice.

Dana squeezed my shoulder from behind me. I glanced over to catch her eye and noticed Mack watching from just outside the box. Dana gave me googly eyes when she noticed him too, causing a breath of laughter to escape me.

The first note of "Hallelujah" isn't even a note—it's an audible breath. Addie visibly relaxed.

Then a quiet strum of a guitar.

My favorite songs happened to be the simplest, most

scaled-back versions, with a voice and one instrument. Acoustic.

Her steps were as quiet as the music, still and steady, opening with a gorgeous double axel. The voice echoed through the rink with its odd lyrics and hypnotic, waltzing rhythm. The cut of her edges sliced through the ice with a satisfying ripping sound. Something you can only appreciate in person.

Every step, spin, and jump glided over the ice as though she was floating. Her landings—gentle and strong, simultaneously—lead her through the element flawlessly. Addie matched the intensity of the artist as she used her body to mimic the building energy. She finished with her classic layback, pulling up into a Biellmann.

The audience stood on their feet, and I blinked back tears. Will stood up and cheered with his hands clapping over his head. It was a moment for her that she needed more than anything else. I looked over to Mack, and he nodded in appreciation.

"I take it back," Stephanie said before introducing the next skater. "That's your edge of glory. Freaking *brilliant*."

Will ran out of the box to meet Addie as she came off the ice backstage, and she fell into his arms. He wasn't much taller than her, but he managed to lift her off her feet. My heart soared watching them, and it was the first time this year I felt like I had done something right.

If that performance didn't convince Addie that she

still had some fire in her, I didn't know what would.

We would get back into our competitive programs this week, but I knew the roar of that crowd would be something she'd relive before she went to sleep every night.

At least I hoped she would. There were no guarantees with Addie, and I knew that better than anyone. What I needed was for her to say yes, too. I hadn't realized how much I wanted that until now. I needed her to stay on this journey with me, no matter where it took us.

Getting to Know You

"Who can tell me, what kind of food is round?"

"Pizza!"

"Cookies!"

"Apples!"

We asked the same question every week, and every week we would get the same answers. Kids loved round food.

Mack stood beside me, his initial anxiety in working with three-year-olds starting to dissipate. He's lucky this was week five and not the first week, when all these adorable faces would be crying out of fear and frustration.

"Should we ask Mr. Mack what we want to make first?"

"Yesssssssss!" they all shouted.

Six pairs of eyes looked up at him.

"Ummmm, it's my birthday tomorrow," he said. "We could make a cake?"

"YEAAAAAAH!" Even more excitement than before.

"Mr. Mack," I said, brightly. "You didn't tell me it was your birthday!"

"Well, Ms. Natalie," he replied, matching my forced enthusiasm. "I believe I just did." He looked at the kids. "What kind of cake should we make?"

"Chocolate!"

"With sprinkles!"

"And ice cream!"

Mack looked at me wide-eyed. "Are they always like this?"

"When cake is involved, yes."

We proceeded to show Mack how to make the cake bigger by wiggling backward, and then made him a pizza, and finished with a cold glass of chocolate milk. What could be better than that for a birthday dinner?

Mack and I had made a bet based on spring numbers—who would have the most new registrations—and I won by three. Not a lot, but the loser had to help with the winner's class of choice. This is how he found himself helping me with the beginning tot group, our youngest skaters. Coaches either loved or hated working with beginners under five, and Mack seemed to be a natural. The boys in our group gravitated towards him like he was Spongebob and Superman rolled into one.

It made me wonder why Jonathan never thought to use hockey players as coaches for the beginning levels, since half of my skaters would end up in hockey anyway.

"You're pretty good at this," I said in between classes. "Did Jonathan ever try to get you out here?"

He tossed me a *yeah, right* look. "Jonathan didn't want anything to do with hockey players. He hated it when they would join my program from his."

For the second half of the hour, Mack and I supervised the practice area, and by the end, we were both sweaty and exhausted from playing with all of the skaters.

"I'd say this calls for a drink at Pauley's," he said as we walked towards the office.

Pauley's Pizza was less than a block away and had the best pizza in town. The owners had kids in hockey, so we always got the best service there, too.

You have to say yes, I heard Marcy say in my head.

"I guess we could," I said. "I have a couple things to wrap up first." My hope was that he wouldn't want to wait for me, and I'd be off the hook.

"That's cool... I do too," he said.

Ugh. "Okay," I said brightly—borderline manic. "Say twenty minutes?"

He gave me a weird look but agreed. I stopped at the learn-to-skate table to collect name tags from the skaters as they left the building. My stomach was still churning when the last skater walked out and I had to pack everything up. I knew Dana and Stephanie were still in the coaches room, since I hadn't seen them leave yet. They were going to give me so much grief over Mack, and I wished I had my shoes at my desk instead.

Both of them stopped their conversation when I

walked in.

"That new coach tonight was a hottie," Stephanie said.

"Mmm-hmmm," Dana agreed.

"Sure wish I could get a class helper like that. Instead, I got Ingrid, who the other skaters confuse as a classmate because she's so small."

Dana giggled. "She is your mini-me. Sarcastic as all get out."

"Actually, she is a hoot to have as a sidekick. She whispered 'slacker' to a kid who refused to get up last week," she said. "Don't worry, no one heard her, and she had a smile on her face the whole time."

Somehow, that didn't make me feel any better.

"Mack lost a bet—that's why he was out there with me tonight," I explained. "And somehow, it's turned into getting drinks at Pauley's."

Their eyes grew wide.

"This is great news," Dana exclaimed, clapping her hands.

"Pauley's is the perfect place too. Super casual." Steph nodded. "Well done."

"It wasn't my idea! I just couldn't say no," I said. "This is the last thing I want to do."

"Having a drink with Hot Santa? Yeah, I can see how that would be such a bummer."

"Will you stop calling him Hot Santa? It's May, in case you haven't noticed."

"And I will never unsee him in that little red hat,"

Steph chimed in.

"You two are the worst," I said. "I shouldn't have said anything."

I pulled my coat on and raced out, wanting to hide from the glaring spotlight I felt was on me. I knew they meant well and were just teasing, but fear continued to gnaw at my stomach from the inside out. Why was he being so nice to me? I know Marcy would ask why I was so resistant to his interest.

I pushed through the office door and swallowed my fear for the moment. My cheeks blazed from the change of cold to warm—on top of all the thoughts going on inside my head.

"Ready?" he asked from his side of the cubicle.

"One second," I said, sitting down. "I just need to shut down my computer and get my stuff."

Amanda was at the front desk for another hour and she eyed us suspiciously. I was grateful no one else was still in the office tonight. May was the month things started to slow down a bit for youth hockey, and adult leagues took over. Staffing was much lighter during the late spring and summer months. It was a welcome reprieve from the grueling fall and winter seasons.

Mack was still typing something out on his computer, so I messaged Marcy to fill her in.

Marcy: OMGOMGOMGOMFG

Me: Ok, let's not get carried away.

Marcy: You said yes! It's working.

Me: And you owe me pages from the latest chapter.

Marcy: I'm working on it now. This chapter sucks.

Me: Nothing you have written sucks. It's brilliant.

Marcy: *eye roll emoji*

Me: I'll check in later

Marcy: I'll be waiting :)

I had no doubt that if I didn't text her later tonight, she would call me.

⌣⌣

Pauley's Pizza had been voted the best pizza in Farmington Hills for five years in a row. The first year I started teaching, Dana, Steph, and I would come here once a week after learn-to-skate. The staff grew to know us and saved our favorite table for us in the bar area. It all ended when I got married and wanted to spend every waking moment I wasn't teaching with Kevin in our new home.

Everything was perfect for about a year.

I shook the thought from my head as we sat down in one of the side booths in the bar. The restaurant side was large, made for big parties and group events, but I have always gravitated to the cozy bar side.

I ordered a glass of white wine, and Mack ordered a Bud Light. Our waitress, Paige, was the owner's daughter, and has worked here since she was fifteen. She could run the place blindfolded. She winked at me before she turned to place our order.

"So, I'm guessing this isn't your first time here," Mack said, observing our unspoken language.

"I may have been here once or twice," I said, shrugging.

"I've gotten their pizza a hundred times, but have only eaten here once, with Roger on my first interview."

"He brought you here on your first interview?"

He chuckled. "He did. Ordered us beers and everything. It wasn't like any interview I had ever been on."

Paige dropped off our drinks and a basket of breadsticks, then dashed away.

"So Skateland really is a boys club, isn't it?" I asked.

"Yes and no," he said, hesitating. "The company is sort of like that, but Roger is pretty fair, I think."

"He's fair as long as the numbers are up," I complained. "If those go down, then so does my ice time."

"But that has nothing to do with you. Every week, the company is on him about our budget, and if numbers are down, he has to explain why. I wouldn't take his job for anything—we have it easy in comparison."

"I guess," I said, not really wanting to agree.

"No more shop talk," Mack said suddenly. "We spend half our lives there, and we both need a break."

He picked up a breadstick and broke it in half, dunking it in the marinara sauce before taking a giant bite.

"How did you end up here in Farmington Hills? You grew up in Canada, correct?"

He nodded. "I did, in Sarnia—not too far from the border." He took another bite of breadstick and chewed. "I was playing juniors in the Soo when I blew out my knee."

"Oh, that's horrible," I said. I took a sip of wine. "I do love Sault Ste. Marie, though. It's so pretty up there."

His whole face lit up. "Can't disagree with you there."

"You didn't want to go back home?"

He shrugged. "I did, but I also knew my mom wanted me to get out and experience life too. I stayed at Lake State and took classes in business. Hockey was my life, and I didn't know what else to do. I took a job at the rink on campus and got a taste of the other side. I felt like working in a rink was a way to still make an impact."

He took a long drink of his beer, and Paige stopped by to see if we needed anything else. Mack looked to me to see if I wanted anything other than breadsticks. I didn't think I could even eat those, so I shook my head.

"What about you?" he asked. "You grew up skating here, right?"

I nodded, taking another sip. "As long as I can remember, I've wanted to be a coach," I said. "Being on the ice is about the only place I'm ever comfortable anymore."

"It shows," he agreed. "You're like a different person on the ice."

"How so?"

"I don't know," he stalled. "It's like this confidence exudes from you—you're less guarded."

Less guarded. Huh. "Are you stalking me? Should I be worried?"

I was joking, but he blushed immediately.

"No! I just catch you when I'm walking by or something," he said. "I do like your group class in the morning, though. You might enjoy torturing skaters a little too much."

"Breakfast Club is my favorite time on the ice," I said, smiling. "It's not for everyone, though."

"You couldn't pay me to take that class. You're demented. But the idea of it is something I've tossed around for hockey players. Kind of an endurance class to build strength."

Something sparked in my brain. "Yes, and you could incorporate edge work too," I said. "It would make them better players."

"Have you worked with hockey players before?"

I shook my head. "I haven't, but I know Jonathan

did. He always said the average hockey player would benefit from the most basic of edge work that we teach at our beginning levels."

Mack smirked. "I don't know if I'd go that far, but I do think it would help."

"Summer is the perfect time to start it, too. They're needing off-season training," I said, ignoring his jab.

"If I can get Roger to agree, would you help me with it?"

I blinked. "Let me get this straight—you're asking a lowly figure skater for help with a hockey class? Are you sure I'm up to the task?"

He tipped his head. "Okay, I deserved that," he conceded. "And yes, I am asking you for help. Your class runs like a well-oiled machine. I want to create something like that. Plus, you have all the cool edge drills."

I smiled on the inside at his compliments. "Honestly, I'd love to, on one condition..."

"Oh boy, here it comes."

"Nothing horrible," I said. "But if I'm going to help with a hockey program, then I'd love it if I could get you or another hockey instructor to help during learn-to-skate. Kind of a cross-coaching to boost both our programs."

He blinked, twice. "That's actually kind of brilliant. Working together to boost both programs? We'd have to sell it to Roger though," he cautioned. "If he doesn't go for it, then it's dead in the water."

"What do we have to lose? We can figure out the details this weekend and present at the staff meeting next week."

"Done and done."

I sat back and folded my arms over my chest. That was almost too easy. "Why are you being so nice to me?" I tried to ask with some lightness in my voice, but his face grew serious.

He took a swig of beer, keeping his eyes focused on the table.

"You just always seem so sad to me. Other than the ice show, if you're not on the ice, it appears that you're needing something. And I'm not just being nice because of that... I just want to stop working against you in the office. I think we could get further if we work together, and I feel bad for how difficult I made it for you when you started out. You didn't deserve that."

For some ungodly reason, my eyes started to water. I could not show him my weakness—now that I know he feels pity for me.

"I can handle anything you dish out," I said, pulling myself back together.

He held his hands up. "Oh, I'm well aware of that. But I'd much rather have you on my side than against me."

"Fair enough. Besides, my friend and I have a bet going, and I can't say no to anything this year."

"This *year*? You have a year-long bet?" He asked

wide-eyed. "That's a bit extreme, isn't it?"

"My friend doesn't mess around."

"Wait—you have to say yes to *everything*?"

"Yep."

"So if I asked you to go for a ride on a motorcycle, you'd say—"

"Yes."

"Go-kart racing."

"Yes."

"Alligator hunting."

I laughed. "I guess if we were in Florida, I'd have to agree."

"Why on earth did you agree to the terms of this bet? What does she have to do?"

"She has to write a book she's been talking about for years," I explained. "And to answer your question, she thinks I've gotten a little closed off in life. This is her way of making me say yes to life, whatever that means." I had no idea why I was telling him all of this.

"How's it working out for you, if I might ask?"

"The day after I agreed, I was asked to take over Jonathan's skaters... and then the skating program."

"Holy shit, no joke? That's when you started?" He barked out a laugh. "That's why you had the deer in the headlights look about you for the first month." He paused to think about this. "Would you have taken it if it weren't for the bet?"

"Hmmm, excellent question..." I said. "I truly don't know. I was happy before, or at least I thought I was, but doing this has shown me a different side I didn't even know I had. Had I known the workload ahead of time, I don't think I'd do it. It's overwhelming."

"That's just because you're learning everything for the first time. A year from now, you'll do this all in your sleep."

His confidence in me felt reassuring. I drained my glass of wine, wishing I had just a little bit more.

"You surprise me," I said. It slipped out, and his eyes met mine.

"I could say the same about you," he said. "And now that I know you can't say no, life could get more interesting around the rink."

I dropped my head to my arms on the table. "Why did I tell you? You have to promise you won't tell anyone else."

He gave me a joker's smile and shrugged. "We'll just have to see, won't we?"

Ugh... "Yes."

Hell Week

Our training for the last couple weeks had ramped up, and the skaters were beginning to push themselves harder than they had since before Nationals in January. We were in the summer sessions, and on the ice more than during the school year, and exhaustion was setting in every day. Even the lower-level skaters were showing resistance to the extra training efforts.

Will and Addie had done everything I'd asked—and they were well aware of what stage we were at in the training block—but the week before we would taper was always called "Hell Week." Jonathan came up with the name a few years ago after a particularly brutal run of training before Regionals. The only reprieve they had was knowing that the following week was a welcome relief from all the stress and a time to relax and enjoy the benefits of working so hard.

We were officially halfway through our first Hell Week, and I had never pushed skaters to this extent. My skaters have always been younger and definitely lower levels, so this kind of intensity was making me question myself. Addie wasn't helping me either.

Every double run-through, every off-ice class, and

every Breakfast Club made her more distant and irritable. Will did his best to encourage her, but Addie's stubborn streak was epic. The thing that bothered me most was the fact that I had never seen her act this way with Jonathan. She used to thrive during this week and outwork everyone else. Jonathan even joked she was our very own *Survivor* because Addie would outlast everyone else. She led the pack and lifted everyone up, but this year she needed some help. Technically, her skating was on target. Her programs were mostly clean—level four spins and step sequences—but there was still something missing.

Her heart.

I was pushing for that feeling I had when she skated her show program, but instead she was void of any emotion.

We were on the last session of the day, and I gave Will the choice of skating the second half of his program at full intensity, or the whole program with singles only.

"I choose C," he said while I waited in the music box.

"There is no C," I said. "What's your choice?"

"Second half, full intensity," he groaned.

"Excellent choice." I sped his music up to the middle section. "Make it count!" I yelled.

And he did. He nailed everything except his last triple lutz. When he finished, he took a slow lap around the rink to bring his heart rate back down.

I queued up the next skater's music and met Will on the ice.

"That was zero fun," he said, taking a drink of water.

"It isn't called Hell Week for nothing," I reminded him.

"Tell me again why we do this?" He peeled off his sweatshirt.

I chuckled. "To prepare you mentally and physically for competition. It makes performing under pressure seem less intense."

"I'm pretty sure Jonathan only started it to torture us," Will said with a smirk.

"So you don't believe it helps you, then? Do you propose another plan to prepare for competition?"

"Actually," he said, raising his eyebrows. "Addie and I have been talking about it."

"Oh no... this isn't going to be another Friday Funday sneak attack, is it?"

He waved Addie over, who had been skating through her step sequence over and over again. It was no secret to anyone that it tripped her up when she was exhausted. Being at the end of her program made it even more challenging to complete well.

Her hair was in a flurry, a thin hair elastic clinging for dear life at the back of her head. Her cheeks were flushed, and her dark eyes looked weary.

"What's up," she said, looking from Will to me.

"Are you having fun?" Will asked her.

She eyed him, eyebrows scrunched together.

"Ummm, it's Hell Week," she said. "It's not supposed to be fun."

"But what if it could be." He paused. "What if we could do it differently?"

We both stared at him, waiting for more.

"I mean, Jonathan created Hell Week because that's what worked for us *then*," he continued. "And I feel like we need something different now that we have a different coach. No offense, Natalie. You run a mean power class, but Hell Week doesn't feel right. If I have to look at Addie mope around here anymore, I'm going to take a couple days off."

She shook her head in offense. "Mope? Did you just say I was *moping*?"

His eyes grew wide as if to say *duh*. "You're bringing the energy down in the whole rink, and Skate Cleveland is too important to the rest of the competitive year. We only have two competitions before Regionals and both of us have to get through that to get to Mids."

I closed my mouth that had been gaping open. "Will, I think this might be a little harsh at a time when we all need to just be focusing on the programs."

"Exactly, but you have to admit the energy is down."

I sighed. The last thing I wanted to do was throw Addie under the bus, but she was bringing negativity to most of the sessions. Her body language said it all.

Shoulders slumped. Head down. Eyes focused in the near distance on nothing in particular.

Will met my eyes, and I motioned for him to beat it. I'd deal with him later, but right now, I needed to figure out where Addie's head was. Will was right about one thing.... well, most of it, but Skate Cleveland was too important to throw away. We'd have to figure this out. In my head, I was trying to figure out what Marcy would say right now.

I grabbed my planner, which was sitting on the hockey bench behind us. I mostly used it to keep track of lessons and noted anything unusual just in case a parent ever questioned something we'd done.

"On a scale of one to five, tell me how much you want to be here this week," I said to her.

She pulled her warm-up coat on and zipped it up. "Can I say zero?"

"Yep, you just did," I said, writing her name down and a big zero next to it. "What is something we could do to bring that up even just one number?"

She looked annoyed, but then really seemed to be thinking about it. "I hate double run-throughs."

"Okay," I said. "What else?"

"I hate that every moment this week is planned on trying to break us. I don't feel like it's making me stronger this year. I really feel like it might break me."

Warning bells went off in my head. Addie never talked about how she felt.

"Okaaaay, keep going. We need to figure out what

isn't working before we can change it to what will."

She met my eyes and scanned the ice till she found Will. Her body seemed to visibly relax watching him.

"All I can see in my head is my short program from Nationals this year. I replay it over and over again, and I don't know how to stop it from taking over everything."

She was still watching Will, transfixed, but she knew I was listening. This was so far over my head of anything I've ever dealt with, and I only wanted her to see how good she was. To *remember* how good she was. I closed my planner.

"Do me a favor," I said. "Let's face the boards, and I want you to close your eyes." She looked at me with that weariness again, but in the end did as I asked. "Okay, now I want you to take a section of your program—I don't care what part—and I want you to see yourself skating it exactly as you want to skate it. Jumps, spins, connecting moves... all of it as if it was the best you've ever skated it. I want you to feel it in your whole body by seeing it in your head."

I stood beside her and waited. Her body swayed and moved with her thoughts, and after a minute, she blinked her eyes open. A small smile on her mouth.

"Close your eyes and do it again, but this time, make it even better. Feel it."

She gave me less resistance this time and closed her eyes. When she was done, she faced me.

"Now, go out there and show me the section you just

skated in your head, exactly how you saw it. I want the emotion you just felt watching yourself to come through."

She bit her lip. "Can I do it without music first?"

"Of course, however you want," I said. All I wanted was to find a glimmer of hope for her.

She skated towards the end and began her step sequence she was fussing with before Will called her over. Her whole body seemed to relax into every edge and turn, and her body moved exactly how Fredrik had designed the program. I could hear the tango music just watching her, and she oozed easy confidence. Halfway through, Will stopped and noticed the change—in fact, several skaters did. By the time she was done with that section, she was smiling, and many of the skaters whooped and clapped for her.

"That was pretty incredible," I said. "I could even hear the music just watching you move."

She was breathless from that. "I haven't felt that good in a long time," she said. "That's how I want my Hell Week to be."

"That's how it should be," I confirmed. "Do you want to try that section with music?"

She nodded eagerly. "I want to see it again in my head first," she said.

"You do that, and I'll cue it up." I skated across the ice to the music box, where Will was standing.

"I don't know what you did, but keep it up," he said.

"Not sure I agree how you got us into that

conversation, but I'm glad you did. Thank you," I replied.

Addie skated down to the end again and waited for the precise moment of the music. Her whole body transformed into the music this time. It was as good as last time, but *more*. More emotion and extension. All of it. Her whole body seemed to be one with the music. This was her magic when she was on, and it had been hiding for way too long. Most of the skaters stopped to watch again, sensing the change.

She covered her mouth with her hands when she was done. She knew how good that was, and I'm sure she was thrilled with how it felt. I met her back over on the other side again.

"So what have we learned?" I asked.

She looked thoughtful and was breathing hard. "That I've been wasting a lot of energy focusing on bad stuff. Only seeing the mistakes and freaking out about that."

"We know you hate the double run-throughs, but we still need to train this week. What could we do instead? I can't send you into competition unprepared."

"I promise I'm not trying to get out of work," she said. "I just have a hard time feeling good about something when I hate it so much."

"We'd have to find something to prepare you both mentally and physically, too. Your head has been working against you for some time now—probably since January, if we're being honest."

Her eyes clouded over. "I don't want to think about that," she said and stopped. "What if we did a mental double run-through?"

A smile spread across my face. "You mean, go through the program in your head first, then skate through the whole thing?"

"It's worth a try," she said. "This felt so good today, and if I could even get a portion of that, it would help."

I couldn't argue with that. "Let's try it tomorrow. Bring your headphones out so you can immerse yourself mentally, and then we skate through it at one hundred percent effort."

"Deal," she nodded.

"That was pretty incredible, Adds." Will came up beside her. "I want to see more."

"Tomorrow," she said. "I want to try another section right now, if that's okay?"

I held my hands up. "Go for it. I'll let go for today, and we'll get back at it tomorrow."

She nodded. "Thank you," she said quietly. "Sorry to be such a pain this week."

"Ha! *This* week?" Will said. "You're always a pain. This week was just apparent to everyone."

She laughed but punched him on the arm.

"On that note, I'm leaving you two to figure it out. I'll see you both bright and early. We still have two days left in this week, and we're using them."

Addie smiled and rolled her eyes. Will saluted. "We'll be ready," he said.

I skated off, thinking this was the first time this year that I felt like I didn't screw something up more. Maybe all those self-help books were finally sinking in.

Maybe I could say yes and have it turn out okay...

Skate Cleveland

The work had been done to the best of our ability. It was the first competition of the season, and even though it had no relevance on the remainder of the season, you always wanted to open well. Show off the new programs. Work out the kinks. Get some good feedback from the judges.

I was leaving for Cleveland first thing in the morning, so Marcy came over tonight for "good luck pizza," as she likes to call it. I passed on the wine, knowing I needed to be up at six.

"I still don't understand how Jonathan just fell off the face of the Earth," she said. "He didn't respond to any of your messages?"

My mouth was full of pizza—sausage and mushroom—but I shook my head no. For what it was worth, I didn't understand either. "I really don't know. Maybe he didn't even go with his wife and he's hiding somewhere."

"But why? He had everything going for him here, and he walked away and never looked back. It's just so weird."

I had left him several Facebook messages last week,

hoping he could meet me for coffee or at least come see the skaters. The radio silence was maddening, especially after everything I'd done for him, and I was just glad I hadn't said anything to Will or Addie. Both of them seemed to be moving along okay without him, despite my rocky start with Addie. The last thing any of us needed was a setback of any kind.

"It is weird, but there is nothing I can do about it. My only priority is to keep the skaters mentally prepared so they can put something decent out there. I don't want to be known as the coach who took over these skaters and drove them into the ground."

"Seriously, you need to chill," she said. "You have done your best, yes?"

I nodded.

"Then, the rest is up to them. This is actually a great learning curve for you too... you can't control everything. Only yourself. Addie has to take care of herself, and Will does too. You can't skate the programs for them, and you can't want it more than them."

"I hear you. I know all of this, but it's so hard, and it's so daunting to be going to this competition with high-level skaters. This is not my comfort zone."

"We could say this year has been out of your comfort zone so far," she countered.

I glanced her way. "And it's all your fault."

She giggled. "I'm okay with that. You are doing an amazing job."

"It doesn't ever feel amazing *in the moment*, but I am happy with most of the stuff I've done. And I want to have this weekend be a positive step forward for all of us. I need to know I can handle this level of competition—not just the lower-level skaters."

"You're going to be great," she said. "I promise."

"I'd be better if you agreed to come with me."

"If I weren't going to this conference, you know I'd be there."

"You're always going to some conference or another," I pouted. Her life was so much more exciting than mine.

"This is my last one, and then I get certified."

"And the book? How is that coming along?"

"After this weekend, I'll get back at it. I just needed some space from it to cram for this weekend."

She turned the TV up. "Ugh, this bachelor is the worst. Why is he making out with everyone on week two?" *The Bachelor* shows were our hidden secret. I'd record them so we could watch together on Wednesdays. Rarely did the contestants prove to be looking for true love... more like their fifteen minutes of fame. It made for interesting TV and never disappointed.

Marcy left shortly after the final rose was given out, and I stepped out onto my deck that overlooked White Lake. It was small but always busy with kayaks and paddleboarders. It was my favorite place in the world, and I wished I had gotten out today.

With a heavy sigh, I went back inside and shut out the lights. This weekend would be long enough, and being tired wouldn't help anyone.

⌣

Thursday was a travel and practice-ice day. Events didn't start until Friday with my lower levels in the morning, then Addie and Will in the evening with short programs. Will had been skating clean programs all week and seemed to be quite relaxed. He loved his programs and was helping to keep Addie focused and engaged.

I was heading into my third hour of practice-ice—exhausted from the drive and stress—and wandered into the coaches room for some hot tea. The room was divided into two areas, one with snacks and some drinks, and a seating area on the other side. A group of coaches sat on the other side, commiserating in between sessions. Competitions were grueling at worst, and boring at best.

I had my back to them, pouring hot water into a Styrofoam cup, when a voice caught my attention. I stepped around the corner and peered at the group of coaches, not wanting to look like a stalker.

There he was. His back was to me, but I'd know that voice anywhere. My heart started racing, and I felt the blood drain from my face. One of the female coaches I knew that had worked here looked up at me.

"Are you okay?" she asked, and they all turned to

look at me.

The moment Jonathan's eyes met mine, he looked bewildered, then covered it with a forced smile.

"There you are," he said, getting up to hug me. "I was wondering when I'd get to see you."

I continued to look at him like he had a third eye in the middle of his forehead.

"I can't wait to see Addie and Will," he continued on. He proceeded to introduce me to the rest of the table of coaches—all from Cleveland—and reminded them I took over his position at his "old rink." I felt like the biggest idiot, not being able to process a thought to save my life.

Wait—how would Addie and Will react? What was going on?

"It's nice to meet all of you," I stammered. "But I have to get back to another practice-ice."

"I'll walk you out there," Jonathan said, following me out.

My tea sat on the table. There was no way I could hold it, let alone try to drink anything now.

As soon as we entered the hallway, I turned to face him eye to eye.

"What the hell—what are you doing here?"

"Keep your voice down," he shushed me. "This is not a good time for me to talk right now."

"Oh really," I said. "Just like the last *seven months*? Have you been coaching here the whole time?"

His downcast eyes said everything.

"Wait, did you move down here just to switch rinks? Was it all a lie?"

"I had my reasons for leaving, and no, it wasn't the only reason. My wife really did get transferred, and I needed to have a fresh start."

"A fresh start? Do you want to tell Addie and Will that? They're here this weekend, by the way."

His head dropped. "I know. I saw the list of skaters earlier this week."

"And you didn't think it would be nice to let us know you'd be here?" I rubbed my forehead and looked at my watch. "I need to get going," I said, distracted.

"Can we meet for coffee in the morning before your first event? There's a Starbucks down the street... could be like old times."

The nerve of this guy. I met his eyes and shook my head slightly. "No, I can't." My brain wasn't functioning fast enough for the words to come out quicker. And my heart was beating out of my chest.

He was coaching here.

What was that about needing a fresh start?

"Okay, well, let me know if you need anything while you're in town," he said.

"You mean you would respond to a text if I sent one now?" His eyebrows raised a hair, and his smile dropped. "I mean, I've only tried to message you every possible way, and you've ignored me for seven months. Why would you respond *now*?"

"I guess I deserved that," he said. His head drooped. "I really am sorry about how I handled everything."

"Do you have any idea how Addie is going to feel knowing you dumped her for a fresh start? Did you ever think about anyone but yourself?"

"It's not going to be easy seeing her—or her mother—but I'll take whatever they dish out. I know it hasn't been easy on anyone, especially you."

I gave him a curt nod, but honestly couldn't bring myself to say anything else. What else could I say without making a scene? I turned and walked back down the rink for practice-ice. Shaking off the last ten minutes, I pasted a relaxed look on my face, and hoped no one would ask about how weird I looked.

A cool blast of air hit me when I walked through the doors. This session was specifically for higher-level skaters, so Addie and Will were both on the ice. Do I tell them now? Do I wait? My gut said to get it over with or he could come out here and surprise them. I needed them to be prepared.

Not many coaches were here tonight, and I found an empty spot on the side with the hockey benches. Only one other coach was in this box, thankfully. I had no idea how this would go.

Both Addie and Will skated over when they spotted me.

"You look weird," Addie said.

"Yeah, what's wrong?" Will asked.

I took a deep breath, unsure how to start.

"Umm, I just came from the coaches room," I started. Will's eyes narrowed. "And you'll never guess who I ran into."

They looked at each other, eyebrows scrunched in that way only a teenager can master. That look that said what the hell is she getting at? Both looked back to me, straight-faced.

"Jonathan," I blurted out. "Jonathan is here." They continued to stare at me like I wasn't speaking English. "Jonathan was in the coaches room, because he is working here now."

"But…" Addie started. Her mouth opened then shut.

Will didn't say anything, but his eyes immediately scanned around the rink, looking for Jonathan.

"Why is he here?" Addie asked. "Is he coaching?"

She said "coaching" like it was equivalent to eating bugs.

I took another breath and blew it out slowly. "Yes, he is coaching here in Cleveland," I confirmed. "I don't know any details—I didn't talk with him for long—but you will most likely see him around this weekend. I would bet money he'll be watching for both of you."

Will puffed his cheeks out as he blew out a breath. "Okay, we'll deal with it when we see him. I need to get moving though."

He skated away and started his edge work over again at the far end. Addie watched him skate away, then looked back at me.

"What am I supposed to do?"

She was taking this even harder than I thought she would. "The only thing you can do, Addie," I said. "You skate your ass off. Show him you're still standing."

She gave her head a little shake with an eye roll. "It's not that simple," she said.

"You have come too far to just throw it away because Jonathan is here," I pleaded with her. I tried to lock on her eyes, but they were bouncing around the rink. I knew she wasn't really listening to anything I was saying. I felt like I was losing her.

"Okay," she said finally.

"Okay?" I asked.

"I'll skate my but off," she said, the right side of her mouth lifting.

My heart melted for her. She had somehow warmed up to me finally, and I wanted to protect everything about her.

"Let's get a move on then," I said. "Start your warm-up again, and we'll go through your short on this session."

She nodded and headed towards the middle for spins. I exhaled, not realizing I had even been holding my breath. I knew we weren't out of the woods, but we would be prepared now for whatever Jonathan threw our way. I pulled out my phone and tapped out a quick text to Dana and Steph, warning them. I slid my phone back into my pocket, giving the skaters my full attention.

They would need that more than ever now, and I'd have to step up and stand up for them if needed. What did Jonathan have up his sleeve, and why was this all a big secret?

Secrets and Lies

I tossed and turned all night, my mind racing to all the worst things that could happen this weekend. Despite Marcy's positive woo-woo texts, my default mood was still set to drama.

I hated drama.

It wasn't enough that I dealt with skaters in a high-pressure sport that demanded perfection, I now had to deal with feelings of abandonment and betrayal where Jonathan was concerned. Dana and Stephanie were dumbfounded by the news that he was coaching here, and questioned whether I had the information correct. They'd see for themselves when they got here later today.

My first event was at eleven thirty, but early morning practice-ice forced me to get up way earlier than I wanted. Walking into the rink—Starbucks in hand—I felt more prepared than last night. I'd greet Jonathan this morning as if nothing had changed, and then carry on with my day. My thoughts got too carried away from me last night, and I knew I'd have to face him and deal with the situation like an adult.

The facts were on my side:

—The skaters were in good shape, despite their coach dumping them with no warning.

—The learn-to-skate numbers were holding steady from the last two years. No major dips.

—The coaches were happy and had no complaints.

—I survived the ice show without needing to check into Betty Ford.

Every challenge that presented itself to me this year had been greeted with a yes, and regardless of how I felt last night, I knew I was stronger than I was six months ago. The fact that Jonathan was the first person I saw when I walked in was proof that God had a sense of humor where I was concerned.

"So, you do still drink Starbucks," he said, a twinkle in his eye.

He clearly slept better than I did.

"Of course I do," I said tightly. I scanned the lobby for someone else to talk to—a parent or another coach—to avoid getting drawn into his eyes.

"Busy day?" he asked. "I see Will and Addie have good placement in the skating order."

"Oh?" Why was he even looking? "Listen, I'd appreciate it if you could keep a low profile where they are concerned. It hasn't been the easiest road for them since you left."

He nodded. "I do know that, and I'm sorry for putting all of you in such a difficult position. Unfortunately, I do have a couple skaters in Addie's group. Avoiding her completely won't be possible."

A pit burned in my stomach, and my heart began to race. I closed my eyes and shook my head slowly. "Why are you doing this? Why did you leave just to start over down here?"

He blinked, mouth tightening. "I don't expect you to understand why I had to do this. From the outside, no one would understand."

"Then tell me," I pleaded. I was whispering, but our body language would not be mistaken if anyone were watching us. "Tell me why all the secrecy."

"It's out of my hands," he said. "I'll stay out of your way if you just stop pressing me for answers."

Now I was intrigued. It felt like he was forced to leave. What did he do? My gut rolled over at the thought of the horrible possibilities, and I thought of Addie.

"I don't know what you did, but I don't want you to talk to Addie or Will if I'm not present," I said.

His face dropped. "Do you really think I'd say something to hurt them?"

"You're not giving me any choice," I said. "By not being up-front with me, I have to make sure they are protected."

"Oh, for God's sake, Natalie. Being a little dramatic, are we?" He turned away, and then back to me. "Fine, I'll stay away from them, but don't you dare start anything with me where they are concerned. You don't know *anything*, so stay out of it."

With that, he turned and walked away. I felt the heat

rush to my face, and the coffee shook in my hand. I glanced around to see if anyone had noticed, but thankfully, everyone was drawn into their own conversations. I stood there alone, fuming, and the fear trickled into my belly. There was a reason he had to leave, of that I'm certain.

But what? What could he possibly be running from? Or maybe it's a who. Either way, I knew he was hiding something, and I would bet money it had something to do with Addie. The way she reacted had always been off to me.

I knew that now wasn't the time to investigate—I'd wait until we got home. But maybe if I got to the bottom of that, I could get Addie on track once and for all.

⌣

Practice-ice was uneventful. Jonathan did have a few skaters on one of the sessions, but we stayed on separate sides of the rink. That would be impossible tonight for the ladies' short program, but I would keep my focus on the skaters and nothing else. It was imperative that Addie not get wrapped up in anything other than her own programs.

I sat in the bleachers of rink one, waiting for Dana and Steph to find me. They both had a two thirty practice-ice in between events. My next skater wasn't until six tonight, and I pondered going back to the hotel for a catnap. The majority of time at a competition was spent waiting. Waiting for practice. Waiting for events. Waiting for your results. It was mind-numbingly exhausting.

Dana and Steph walked through the double doors into the rink and spotted me immediately. Steph was pep-stepping to get to me. We texted briefly last night, but I gave them the bare minimum.

"Spill it," she said when they sat down.

Dana handed me a Styrofoam cup of hot tea from the coaches room. "Thought you could use this about now."

"I wanted to put something in it, but she wouldn't let me." Stephanie smirked.

"You guys, I just don't get it," I started. "Why is he here?"

"And you're sure he's coaching?" Dana asked.

"He has skaters in Addie's group tonight," I confirmed. "He was in the coaches room yesterday, relaxed and chatting up everyone in there. Like he'd been here his whole life."

"None of it adds up," Dana said. "He had everything at Skateland, and he threw it away to come here? Who does that?"

"Look," Stephanie said, pointing across the rink. There, standing in the hallway leading to the locker rooms, was Jonathan with Addie's mom. "They look like they're having a heated discussion."

It was true. Addie's mom was visibly animated with her hand gestures. Jonathan's head was hanging down, hanging in shame.

"What in the world is going on?" I whispered, almost to myself.

Stephanie took her phone out and zoomed in on them, recording the entire scene. She held her hand up to stop us from talking. Suddenly, Jonathan's head snapped up, and he backed away slightly. She was threatening him with something, but what? Dana looked at me, wide-eyed, and I shook my head slowly, dumbfounded. My mind raced to scenarios as to why this would be happening.

Did they have an affair?

That was the only thing that came to mind, given the body language I was looking at. What I didn't understand was why Nicole was so upset with him. Dana hit my arm and pointed to the entrance of the rink down at the end. Addie and Will were walking towards us in the bleachers.

"Oh, I gotta stop them from coming down here. She can't see this," I said, getting up.

"Good call," Stephanie said, still recording the unfolding scene.

I pasted a smile on my face, but my heart raced a little as I rushed to stop them from coming any farther. I pointed towards the lobby to them, and both of them turned and retraced their steps.

"So," I said with too much enthusiasm. "How are we feeling today—you guys slept okay last night?"

They had practice-ice in a half hour, and they should be getting warmed up by now.

"The stupid hotel gave us a king bed instead of two beds," Addie complained. "I had to sleep in the same bed as my mom and she tossed and turned all night. Kept sighing. Drove me crazy."

Will shrugged. "I slept like a baby."

I glanced at my watch. "You guys should be starting a warm-up now, so you're ready for practice. I think they have a ballet studio upstairs they're letting the skaters use."

"They do," Will confirmed. "We just wanted to come find you and let you know we were here. How have the skaters done so far?"

"Mallory got third—skated great but missed her second double toe. Ingrid nailed her program, took first."

"Nice," Addie said. "She is so fun to watch."

"Go." I pointed to the stairs. "Get your butts in gear."

Both saluted and jogged towards the stairs just as Dana and Stephanie shuffled into the lobby.

"I don't know what happened between them, but Jonathan spotted you walking out with the skaters and he bolted," Stephanie said. "I don't know if he knew we saw them, but he also wasn't waiting around to see, either."

"That was the most bizarre thing I've ever seen." Dana scanned the rink area, looking for Jonathan, but Nicole was the one who walked through the doors.

And directly towards us.

"Oh shit, oh shit, oh shit," Dana whispered, turning

away from her. "What do we *do*?"

"Well, we don't do *that*," Stephanie said, circling her hand around Dana's face. "Pull it together."

Instead of panic, Dana's face morphed into the Joker from Batman. Very, very smiley.

"Hi, Nicole," I greeted her first, mostly to avoid her noticing Dana. "I just sent Addie and Will to warm up in the ballet room." I pointed in the general direction, although I'm sure she knew where it was. This was not her first rodeo.

"Sounds good," she said. Her voice was strained, but her face appeared normal. "I'm going to pop out and get some real coffee—can I get you something?" She glanced at me, and then Stephanie and Dana, extending the offer to them.

"I'm good," I said, holding up my now-cold tea. "But thank you." I didn't want to appear obvious, but curiosity was getting the better of me. "I haven't seen Jonathan today, but if I do, I want to make sure he's not going to get in Addie's head."

She seemed to hesitate, and an undercurrent of anxiety washed over her face. She blinked, and it was gone. "I haven't seen him yet, but I'll make sure he knows to keep his distance. I'll be back," she said and walked away.

"'*I haven't seen him yet?*' Who is she kidding, and why is she lying about it now?" Stephanie was incredulous at the blatant lie.

"Save that video," I told Steph.

I didn't know yet what I was going to do with it, if anything, but I felt like I needed the proof that it really did happen.

"I'm going up to wait for them—try to gauge their moods when they get out," I said. "I'll catch up with you two later?"

Dana nodded. "I have practice-ice in the other rink at the same time as you, and I'm staying to watch Will and Addie."

My stomach turned at the thought, nerves rolling over me in waves. Competitions always made me jittery, and the higher the level, the higher the stakes. I couldn't get rid of the feeling that something else was going on here as well, and as much as I wanted to get to the bottom of it, I also wanted to protect Addie and Will from anything damaging.

Steph rested her hand on my shoulder and looked me in the eye. "Stop the idiot voice in your head, right now. You got this."

I nodded, unsure if I really did or if I was just playing the part. A part that was now beginning to feel like a coverup from something other than Jonathan's wife getting a promotion. Walking upstairs, I scanned the lobby from a bird's eye view, looking for Jonathan. When I reached the top, he was standing at the railing waiting for me.

"Hello, Natalie," he said. His tone mocked me. "Ready for tonight?"

Mind Games

I was leaning against a cement wall in the hallway between both rinks. Addie was pacing back and forth, earbuds tucked in her ears. Every now and again, she would look to me for reassurance, and somehow I had mustered up that reassuring nod all adults give to kids, even though I felt less than confident in anything right now.

Will's program went as expected—clean, although the energy seemed a little flat to me.

"I always hold back in the first few competitions, Nat," he said, a twinkle in his eye. "Can't give them the goods all at once."

Addie and I watched him from the side right before her warm-up. The look on her face was a mixture of pride and envy. If I could give her an ounce of Will's confidence in this moment, I would.

Steph and Dana were in the stands. Steph—now with an iPad—was going to record Addie and also anyone Jonathan was coaching. I also noticed Nicole sitting next to Dana and wished I knew what they were talking about. Nicole had a habit of being super critical of anyone on the ice—even her own daughter.

Sometimes it was funny, and we would seek her out at competition just to hear her commentary.

'Does she really think that color looks good on her skin color?'

'Poor dear... probably moved up to test out.'

'I don't know what all the fuss is about that skater. Bor-ring.'

It was as if she turned into another person when sitting in the bleachers, and she had no clue or control over what came out of her own mouth. A part of me wished I was still on that side of the rink and could take this pressure off myself. And I'd give anything to hear what she had to say about Jonathan's students.

Addie's group warmed up next, and she was skating dead last in the order. Good placement, but not the easiest to withstand with all the waiting. Her practice-ice was tense earlier. She definitely looked uneasy with Jonathan coaching on the other side. He greeted her professionally, but she looked like a deer in the headlights.

The thing I remember about Addie's competition history was that no matter what, she would always pull it out in the end. Even if she was having the worst week leading up to the event, she would rise up and give the judges what they wanted.

That is, until this past January.

A flash of memory from watching her on TV and seeing how mechanical she was being reminded me of the same look on her face now. I had to try and turn her thoughts around.

Jonathan's skater was just finishing her program. There was a smattering of applause—lots of Cleveland skaters cheering loudly—and then the quiet while the live scores were announced.

From what I saw in practice, she was a solid skater. I didn't want Addie to focus on her at all, but I knew she noticed her too. How could she not begin to compare herself to the new student? I felt like we were both being compared, even if it was self-imposed.

The last group took the ice, Addie leading the pack around the ice. That felt reassuring to me, knowing she wasn't holding back from the beginning. She immediately went into her edge work, then the planned warm-up we'd practiced all week. Her goal was to find her comfort zone during this time, and not get too wrapped up in rushing through everything. She had plenty of time, and I needed to keep her calm. She still had a blank look on her face, and her jumps looked tentative. She followed through, but they were small with questionable landings.

Her double axel, while the easiest jump in the program, had given her so many issues this summer. It was one of those jumps that couldn't be done if you were uptight or holding back. We agreed she would warm up this jump once she felt comfortable with the other elements. By my estimate, she had two minutes left, and she wasn't sticking to our schedule, so I waved her over. I set her water and a pack of Kleenex on the boards for her. Her breathing was shallow, and her eyes darting around.

"Hey," I said, forcing eye contact. "Keep your eyes on mine, and just listen."

She regained some focus and nodded.

"You're scattered, and we need to clear that head of anything but what we're here to do. Clean jumps. Level four spins. Step sequence with clarity." She nodded again, entranced by my words. "Show me a walk-through for a double axel."

She pushed away and stepped forward onto her left foot, right foot behind her. She kicked through and pulled into a loop position over her right leg, arms tight to her chest.

"Good. Remember, nice knees, tight abs."

My nerves kicked up a notch when she circled twice without following through. The announcer called one minute remaining, and she tightened her shoulders through the steps leading into the double axel. First attempt at it and she popped—opened up mid-rotation—and singled the jump. I circled my hand to have her try one more before they were called off. She skated the same steps and flung herself into the air. She landed, but not without touching down with her right hand. It wasn't good enough, and she knew it, but the skaters were called off the ice before she could try again.

I stood back, waiting for her to get her guards on, and Jonathan came up behind me.

"Still hates that double axel, I see," he said. "I don't miss that."

I whirled around to face him. "Don't you *dare* talk to me about Addie," I whispered. My blood was racing. "You lost that right when you walked away."

I turned and met Addie's eye, nodding for her to follow me to the hallway again.

Jonathan's student was in second, and all I wanted was to beat her score. I knew it was petty, but all I wanted was to wipe that smirk off his face now. If Addie skated clean, it might be possible—but that was a big if. I handed her phone and earbuds back to her, so she could refocus with her music. We'd practiced every skating order in the group, and the hardest one for her, by far, was last. She began pacing like a caged animal in the small, cramped hallway.

This was the most difficult part of coaching: The utter lack of control over anything. I could tell her everything until I was blue, but unless she decided to let go of the anxiety and skate, none of it would matter. I took a deep, measured breath, trying to ease my own tension.

The skater before her took the ice, and I led her out by the ice. I had her close her eyes and see herself doing perfect double axels. The steps leading into it through to the long, landing edge. She opened her eyes and nodded at me. She peeled off her coat and gave the phone and earbuds back to me.

I pasted a warm smile on my face. *You got this*, it

mimicked, but my heart rate betrayed me. Addie spotted Jonathan and looked away, her mouth pressed into a firm line.

It was her time.

She blinked back tears, the same ones that haunted her in January. I rubbed her back, squeezed her shoulder—anything that would remind her that this was just the first competition. Her double axel was flawless. High, with a beautiful landing. Unfortunately, that was the only jump she landed. Spins and step sequence were great, but without the triple flip and combination, she was toast. Standing here, waiting for the live score, was adding insult to injury.

Jonathan stood near the entrance of the hallway—Addie hadn't noticed him—and he watched it unravel. This poor girl, who he all but raised in the last five years, was left to crumble under whatever he was hiding. He looked at her with a mixture of guilt and regret, then turned and walked through the doors to the hallway. I was grateful Addie didn't have to see him on top of everything else she was feeling.

"Let's get back to the locker room," I whispered.

She nodded and complied, her emotions flattened out into a daze. The locker room had already cleared out, and the light clicked on as soon as we entered. She took her warm-up jacket and gloves she was holding and flung them across the room.

"Why?" She yelled. "What is wrong with me?" Tears rolled down her cheeks.

Her outburst startled me so much, I was speechless.

She stared at me with an intensity I had never seen from her before. Pure anger rolled off of her, and I took in a deep breath, trying to figure out how to handle this. What would Marcy do?

I sat down on one of the benches and restrained myself from picking up her things on the floor, although my mind reeled to how many germs were crawling where they lay.

"Addie," I said, not even sure she was listening to me. "The only thing we can do is learn from this. We have to think of this short program as a puzzle, and how we can fit all the pieces in when it counts."

I knew she wasn't listening to anything I was saying. 'The sky is purple' would've been met with the same reaction I just got. She couldn't hear anything but the sound of her own voice in her head telling her she wasn't good enough. This was the one thing we did have in common. The ugly voice in our heads.

In that moment, I understood what I was battling: In order to help Addie through whatever this was, I'd have to fix myself too. I'd have to walk the walk and take my own advice that I doled out so easily to her.

Hell, I didn't even know if I *could* fix myself—it was so much easier to walk through life waiting for the next bad thing to happen than to hope for something better and never get it. It was easier to hide out than to step out. I had been saying yes to everything and going through the motions, but here I was feeling like a failure over someone else's mistakes. I didn't blame Addie, but the lack of control I had over the situation felt even more helpless now.

What did it matter saying yes to anything if I wasn't changing how I felt on the inside? It was just an external change, and in this instant I knew it wasn't good enough. In order to help Addie, I had to help myself. One of my own puzzle pieces slid into place. It wasn't complete, but it was one step closer.

"Look at me," I said to her quietly. She lifted her head out of her hands and met my eyes. "We are going to get through this and figure out what is going on with you, but I need to know you're on board with that. I can't do this for you—you have to want a different outcome."

She flinched. "You think I wanted this?"

"No," I said. "I don't think you wanted it at all, but I think you're stuck, and in order to fix that, you'll have to know what it is that you do want."

Even as I said the words, a lightbulb went off in my head.

Clarity.

She pondered what I had said and stopped crying.

"I don't know what I want," she whispered. "One second, I want to quit, and then next I want to fight back."

"Okay," I said. "That's good. That's a place to start."

"I'm so tired of feeling like this."

"I know you are, and you have to remember this is a process. Nothing is fixed overnight, and if you want this, that part of you that wants to fight back will have to show up in a big way."

There was a knock at the door, and Will popped his head in. He asked if he could come in with just a raise of his eyebrows, and she nodded. Their unspoken connection was so strong. He walked over and sat down beside her, and she gave him a teary, lopsided smile.

"That double axel, though," he said, smiling.

She breathed out a smile and looked down at her hands. "Spins were good."

He nodded and looked at her, waiting for her to look up.

"Well," he said. "What's next?"

INTERVIEW PART 4

TL: All hell broke loose… Are you referring to the rumors about your coach? There were several flying around that weekend.

[Addie closes her eyes and takes a deep breath.]

AG: There are some things I can't really get into, and that's one of them. I'll just say I was seriously let down by the people closest to me. I felt completely betrayed and didn't think I'd ever want to skate again.

TL: And now? Do you still carry that burden and betrayal around with you?

[A smile appears out of nowhere on her face. Eyes downcast again, but a softness grows from within.]

AG: Honestly, I spent a huge part of last year stuck in my head and felt so lost. When you believe the thoughts in your head that continually tell you you're not good enough, every day feels like an uphill battle. However, I'm happy to say that, with the help of my current coach, and Will Tran, I'm in a much better place. I wouldn't be here if it weren't for them. So many times in this last year I almost threw in the towel, but they wouldn't let me. They reminded me why I'm here—on the ice—every day.

TL: And what about next year? I know this year took a toll on you mentally and physically… Do you have it in you to stick around for an Olympic year?

[For the first time, Addie looks directly into the camera, determined and clear.]

Spirit Week

It was August in Michigan, which meant the world was melting outside. It wasn't the ninety-two-degree temps that would get you—it was the humidity that felt like you're wearing a wool sweater in an oven. Fortunately, it was always a cool fifty inside the rinks, when coaching time almost doubled in the summertime. Given the off-season status, ice was given more freely, and the figure skaters—without the time constraints of school—increased their training for the upcoming competitive year. The days were filled with freestyle sessions, moves sessions, off-ice classes, power classes, and exhibitions on Fridays.

In June, when the ice times changed to this schedule, everyone was excited and motivated—inspired by the luxury of all-day training.

By the time August rolled around, everyone's motivation became a little depleted. The figure skaters—after weeks of this grueling schedule—responded with the attention span of a squirrel. Exhaustion kicked in for the coaches, who never wanted to teach squirrels a double axel. I remembered complaining to Jonathan last year about one of my skaters who had clearly lost her mind, and he responded with a knowing smile.

"It's August, Natalie," he had said. "August is everyone's breaking point. The rock bottom. Give it a week, and things will turn around. Until then, try to have some fun with your skaters. Give them different challenges… change up your lesson time."

And it worked. Almost instantly, the skaters responded with my change of perspective. Similar to Friday Funday, they were eager to practice something different than just the program and choreography we had been trying to perfect all summer. This year, I wanted to build that break into our skating program with a Spirit Week.

All of the coaches—with the exception of Lydia—met the idea with enthusiasm. Dana planned the theme days, while Stephanie and Ronnie took over the power classes with Rewop, the complete opposite of power. For the parents who didn't intend for their skater to have a fun week, it was the perfect time for them to take a family vacation.

Spirit Week had the same effect on the skaters that show week did. They learned all over again what they love about this sport and each other, and the coaches embraced a lighter approach to what Stephanie called GSD: getting shit done. For Friday's exhibition, the skaters had to learn someone else's program and perform it. Lydia scoffed at the idea from the beginning and refused to partake in any of the group classes. She had the mentality that her skaters were serious athletes and tried to shield them from having any fun. They looked longingly at the others as they tried to focus on Lydia's commands. Call me silly, but I was proud of the fact that Addie could do a triple-triple in pajamas or a headband with antlers. I loved that she could be a kid again, even for just a week.

Roger and Mack noticed the difference in attitude around the rink and grilled me about it during the weekly staff meeting.

"I have to admit I didn't think this was going to work," Roger admitted. "On paper, it just looked ridiculous."

Mack nodded, looking at his notebook. "I may have wondered what you were thinking more than once." Then his eyes met mine. "But it's clear, this week has been what the skaters needed."

My heart skipped a beat, and my face flushed. "I know you both thought I lost my marbles, but I had to take a chance on trying something different. Normally, August is zero fun for the coaches and skaters, but I think we accomplished what we needed this week. That we could still work hard while having fun."

"I'm wanting to try something next week with the hockey players I've been training all summer," Mack said. "And I'm wondering if you would help me with it."

I leaned forward in my seat. "You want to have pajama day for the players, don't you?"

He barked out a laugh. "No, probably not going that far, but I'd like to try adding a power class, similar to your Breakfast Club, and have you run it."

I looked from him to Roger, then to Janie, who only shrugged. "I think it's time those players learned how to skate," she said, smirking.

"Tell me more," I said. "What is your intention for this class?"

"Honestly, I'm seeing the same burnout from them that you were with your skaters. They're tired of the same drills, and they're half-assing it most of the time. There's no drive to push themselves."

"She would definitely bring a different energy out there," Janie said. She was excited about this idea.

"But hockey players usually look down on figure skaters," I started. I was doubtful they would listen to me, let alone try any of what I had in mind.

"I think, with me and a couple other coaches out there to assist, they would know we were serious," Mack said. "And you and I could go over what drills you'd want to do with them this weekend."

"Yes," I said.

Mack smirked. "Are you saying that because you have to?"

"Nope, I'm in. This will be fun, and if I can change the mind of even one hockey player, it'll be worth it."

"We can pay you your hourly rate," Roger said. "You wouldn't have to clock out for this coaching time."

"I don't get it," I said. "What is the sudden interest in having me work with them?"

Roger cleared his throat. "Janie might have had something to do with the idea," he said.

"Might have?" she inquired. "Natalie, I learned the most about skating from figure skating coaches. I've been bugging these knuckleheads to work with you for a while."

I looked from her to Mack, and he shrugged. "We're a stubborn lot," he admitted. "But after watching your power classes with the skaters, I knew this was something we needed to work into our own program, and summer is the perfect time to try it out, since ice time isn't as stretched."

"It'll be fun," I said. "And who knows, we all might learn something new."

⌣

"You do see what's happening, don't you?" Marcy asked as I waited in line for an iced caramel macchiato.

"No, but I'm betting you're going to tell me."

The drive-through line at Starbucks was normally long, but it always moved along fairly fast. Today, it seemed to be moving backward.

"What's happening is you're saying yes to opportunities instead of shooting them down," she said. "And because of that, more opportunities are being created for you. It's like an opportunity snowball."

"A snowball of any kind sounds good about now."

"It's so hot," she agreed. "We are literally melting in the school this week."

Marcy decided she wanted some upgrades to her office this summer and started painting it this week. The school gave her a budget of three hundred dollars, and she was going to make the most of it, even if she had to do it herself. We went to IKEA this past weekend and spent half of it on office organization items that she would have to spend hours putting together, but I've never seen her so excited. She had finished her life coaching training and was going to start working virtually with clients. The school agreed that she could use her school office for those meetings as long as she worked after hours.

"But imagine how amazing it's going to be when you're done," I countered. "It'll be the perfect workspace for you."

"I know, I'm pretty excited," she said. I could hear her smile through the phone. "But I want to hear more about this Mack character. What is his deal?"

Instinctively, I smiled. "Oh, don't start in again with him," I said. "We're just friends, and he would never want someone with so much baggage."

"I think you're wrong."

"It doesn't matter—he's a hockey player, and they can't be trusted. They lure you in with charm, then break your heart."

"And you know this how? You've never dated a

hockey player," she said. "You're prejudiced against a whole group you know nothing about."

"They're loud. They're aggressive, and don't even get me started on the smell."

She laughed. "Is Mack loud, aggressive, and smelly?"

This stopped me. "Well, no, but still."

Mack was the opposite of loud, aggressive, and smelly. In fact, he smelled pretty amazing most of the time.

"You're saying no to this guy, and that is not allowed this year," she said.

"I haven't said no to anything! In fact, I've said yes all the time."

"But in your head, you've ruled him out—haven't even given him a chance. That's a no in my book."

"You and your book are wrong," I said. "There isn't anything to say yes to. He hasn't pursued me in any way other than the occasional beer after work once in a blue moon. Trust me when I say, he isn't interested. Besides, there's literally no way he doesn't have a girlfriend...guys like him are never available."

"And if he were?"

Why did she have to push this?

"If he were, I guess I'd have to figure out what I wanted," I said.

"What is it that you want? What does that look like for you?"

"Oh, don't you life-coach me right now. I've been

waiting in this line since we started talking and I need caffeine before I figure out what I want."

But in my head, the question lingered. *What do I want?* And why have I never asked myself this question?

"Okay, you get back to your line, and I'm going to get back to painting," she said. "I'll see you tomorrow."

"I just really want my caramel macchiato right now," I pouted.

"I know," she said. "Think about it, though. What you want is important."

"I suppose," I said. "See you tomorrow."

We disconnected, and I leaned back on the headrest. *What you want is important*, rattled my brain. If it was so important, why didn't anyone ever tell me this before? Why was I learning this at thirty, and not at twelve? And why was it so much easier to know what I don't want than to claim what I do want?

I flashed back to picking out my wedding dress and how the saleswoman was exasperated with me. I gave her a list of what I didn't want in a dress and nothing else.

No mermaid cut.

No sleeveless dresses.

No ivory or off-white dresses.

No poofy skirts.

It seemed that every time she brought a dress to the fitting room, I'd find another no to add to my list. I remember her and my mom exchanging a look that said *Bridezilla*, even though I felt like the perfect dress was out there. Eventually, we whittled down to a simple, straight cut with a cap sleeve. It was stunning, and the second I stepped into it, both my mom and the salesclerk smiled. That was the dress.

I shook my head and we moved up slowly, car by car. Ordering Starbucks was easy. I always knew what I wanted there, and I was the perfect customer at a restaurant. I ordered right off the menu, and never tried to make special requests. If a burger came with onions, I'd simply pick them off. No need to make a fuss about stuff like that. I heard Marcy in my head telling me this is exactly what she's talking about. Ask for what you want—don't just take what you're given.

But what if I wanted Mack—and I'm not saying I am. But *what if*?

What if I enjoyed working with hockey players and wanted to continue it after next week?

What if I told Jonathan exactly what I thought was going on when we captured that video?

What if I finally admitted that I loved being the skating director? Sure, it was a ton of work, and no one knew half of what I did, but I knew, and that was enough for me.

What if changing your life was really as easy as saying yes?

Again

The music was blaring, and all three hockey coaches stood in front of me, panting and sweating profusely.

"What I don't understand," Mack said, "is how your skaters do this on a daily basis. Have you ever killed anyone?"

I looked at my watch. "Break time is over—let's get moving in the other direction this time," I said. "And make sure you're doing actual crossovers on the ends, and not that shuffle thing."

The other two coaches that will be helping next week joined Mack on the ice to go over what we'll be doing. Given they were going to be assisting, I suggested they actually participate today to see what the class would be like. No one has puked yet, but Louie wasn't looking so hot. Johan—who didn't speak a ton of English—kept eyeing Mack, his eyes pleading to make me stop.

"C'mon, boys," I said. "This is just the warm-up. After this next round, we'll get started on the edge work, and that's when the fun begins."

I set my watch for ninety seconds, and got them moving, covering the length of the rink, and around the ends.

First thirty seconds was a medium pace.

Second thirty seconds at a slower pace, but still some effort.

Last thirty seconds at their sprinting and fastest pace.

I had yet to warn them they'd have to do ladders after the edge work. Best to keep that to myself for now.

Yesterday, I went over most of the edge work I planned on introducing to the hockey players with Mack. I also told him that I preferred it if the players didn't have their sticks during the class with me. He pushed back a little, but agreed (finally) that if they could do these skills without a stick, they would only be better with it. They had to be able to skate without their stick being a balance point.

All three coaches picked up on the edge work fairly easy while skating forwards. Doing the same edge work backward was another story, though. Figure skaters are taught from the very beginning that everything done forwards is also done backward. Same with skills on the right and left foot. The only thing skaters don't change is the direction of their rotation for spins and jumps. Once that is figured out, that will always remain the same.

Hockey players are given minimal actual skating practice. As soon as they can stand up, they're given a stick, and they're chasing pucks. They practice shooting. They practice checking. But they're rarely taught how to skate. This opportunity could change a lot of minds around here, if done correctly.

As good as Mack was, he struggled with most of the edge work backward. He would break it down to try and figure out where to balance, and how to lean to work with the edge. He wasn't just going through the actions, he really wanted to learn something. Johan and Louie looked too tired to learn anything at this point. They attempted it but didn't have an interest in getting it right. Moving to the one-footed skills sent them over the edge... pun intended. Meanwhile, Mack played the perfect student, trying so hard to figure everything out.

I didn't have the heart to make them do ladders, so I rewarded them with an early dismissal, which was met with relief.

"So, we're all on board with everything?" Mack asked of Louie and Johan. "I know a lot of players will be like these two yahoos and try to take the easy way out. I can't imagine how much this will help them in the long run if this was something we could add to our normal season."

The two coaches nodded. "I'll be curious to see if anyone can do the edge stuff backward," Louie said. "That was the hardest part. I couldn't get my feet to do what she was saying."

"Hopefully you were listening, so you can help on Monday," I said. "With a large group, I'll need a little help out there."

"I can't wait to see their faces when you tell them to put their sticks away," Mack said. "Should be an interesting week."

I wasn't sure if by "interesting" he meant good or bad, but no matter what else, I said yes to this and was following through. The idea of being on the ice with a bunch of teenage hockey players terrified me. I didn't know how I'd sleep this week, but I knew in my heart that this was going to be a great class for them.

Whether *they* knew it was a completely different story.

⌣

Me: They hate me. Like legit HATE me.

Marcy: That's the spirit!

Me: I'm not kidding. The glares I got today were intense.

Marcy: Did you expect teenage boys to like endurance training? Of course they're going to hate you.

Me: It's not all endurance... half of it's edge work.

Marcy: Which they've never done before.

My phone rang with Marcy's picture flashing on the screen.

"But still," I said, continuing our conversation. "They were mean. And they spit, right on the ice."

"Ew," she said. "That's gross, but boys spit. It

wasn't in your direction, was it?"

"No." I laughed. "Mack would've knocked them out if they tried that. I'm just not used to spitting on the ice."

"I'm sure there will be many differences you find this week in working with them, but you're gonna have to be able to hang with them if you want to get through to them. They won't listen to a figure skater, but they will respect a coach."

"What do you mean? I *am* a figure skater."

"Nooo," she said. "You're a coach. You have skills they don't, and it's your job to coach them as hockey players. You have to treat them how they're used to being treated or they'll eat you alive."

"Ha, they did today. Mack had to put a few of them in line," I said. "I hated that."

"Tomorrow, you're going to put your big-girl panties on and show them who's boss—and that's not Mack. When you're on the ice, you command their attention and gain their respect. You can do this, but you have to make it something they want to do, too. Can't just be all grind all day."

"I know," I whined. "I just thought making it extra tough would appeal to their caveman instincts. By the end, even Mack looked defeated. I never should've watched Miracle last night. I thought the 'do it again' scene was what he wanted."

"Oof." She giggled. "You probably scared the bejesus out of him."

It felt good to laugh. "All right, I think I know what I have to do," I said. "I'll rework my lesson plan for tomorrow's class, but I have to figure out a new approach first."

"That's my girl," she said, sounding a lot like my mom. "They're going to have their guard up at first, but go with your gut and you'll figure it out."

My heart clenched a little, longing for more motherly wisdom. Her anniversary was last week, and I was still carrying the sadness around.

"Thanks, Marce," I said, blowing out a breath. "Are we still good for Winesday?"

"Does the pope wear a funny hat?"

I giggled again. "I'll text you an update tomorrow."

We disconnected, and I wiped a tear from the corner of my eye. Would the thought of her always make me cry? I flipped on the TV, found an episode of *Seinfeld*, and grabbed my planner. When I first started teaching, I had to plan my lessons, like a schoolteacher—to make sure I was giving them the skills they needed to succeed. By watching other coaches, I figured out how to manage the lesson time efficiently, and eventually I was able to just go with the flow more. It doesn't happen overnight—coaching is one of those jobs that takes years to gain confidence, and even then you have days where you're just trying not to screw them up. Days where nothing you say works, and they push back with the resistance of a rhinoceros.

The nerves I felt stepping on the ice with the hockey

players was comparable to competition nerves. I felt clammy and sick to my stomach. Tomorrow would be different, but first I had to figure out where I went wrong today.

My phone chimed.

Mack: Checking in with you. You seemed a little stressed today.

I smiled. "Stressed" was a polite way of putting it.

Me: Working on a lesson plan for tomorrow. I'll be ready.

Mack: I can't believe you're willing to go back out there. They were brutal with you.

Me: Not what I'm used to, but I'll approach them differently tomorrow. It'll be good.

Mack: Just teach them like you did with us on Saturday. You don't have to prove anything to them.

That's it—I taught the class like I was trying to prove myself to a group of teenage boys.

Me: Gotcha. That helps me. See you tomorrow!!

Mack: Give me a shout if you need help.

I drew a circle in the middle of the page and divided it into thirds. Next, I labeled each slice of the pie with edges, endurance, and agility. I'd have twenty minutes with each group of skills and brainstormed a list of drills for each segment. Excitement grew with each drill. Dividing the time and keeping it organized in my head would help me feel more comfortable too. I'd start with edges to warm them up, then endurance, and end with agility, which would be a welcome relief after pushing them to the limit.

This would work, but I'd have to keep my nerves calm and be more confident and clear with them. I shook my head at the thought of today—it was the longest hour of my coaching life, and I never wanted to experience that again.

I grabbed an index card and listed out a group of skills for tomorrow. If worse came to worst, I'd have this in my pocket to remind me of any drills I forgot. My shoulders started to relax, and exhaustion crept into my bones. It was only nine thirty—still light outside—but I shut the lights out and crawled into bed.

As I lay there, I thought about my mom and what she'd say to me right now. Would she be proud of me for everything I took on this year, or would she shake her head in disappointment? In my head, I saw a flash of her smiling at me. It was brief, but it was there, and I rolled over, hugging a pillow to my chest. I would never get over missing her, but I knew in my heart she'd be proud. No question.

And I also knew tomorrow would be a better day. It had to be.

Teamwork Makes the Dream Work

On my desk was a tiny gold trophy with "Mini-Mite MVP" on the gold plate glued to the base.

"What's this?" I asked Janie, who tried to appear busy and watch me at the same time.

"Oh, just something Mack thought you deserved for this week," she said. "I think you even impressed Roger." She motioned to his office door, which was closed with him and Mack inside.

"What are they meeting about?" I asked. Roger rarely closed his door.

She merely shrugged and walked back into her office. "They've been in there a while, but I haven't heard anything interesting. Roger's been weird all week though. I guess we'll find out in the staff meeting."

I looked at my watch. "Crap, I forgot about that. I've lost all track of my days this week."

"Understandable," she said. "You've had a busy week and summer. Spirit Week was such a good idea... I never actually told you that. I think the kids loved it."

"Okay, what gives?" I said, sitting down. "First, a trophy, and now a random compliment—something is going on that I don't know about."

A look of guilt crossed over her face, and she did that paper shuffling thing again to look busy. "I have several emails to get to before our meeting."

I spent the next half hour tracking program numbers and comparing them to the last two years. My heart started to race a little as I configured the estimates of how much we were down. Only five percent, but still, down just the same. The pit in my stomach told me I knew what they were meeting about now, and why Janie was full of compliments. I was getting ice time taken away for the fall schedule. Roger and Mack were plotting my demise. Any good feeling I had coming in here was immediately washed away. Of course this week was too good to be true. Of course it came down to money and numbers, and not about happy skaters, players, and coaches.

It didn't matter if I said yes to everything that came my way—life had it out for me, and nothing else would matter.

Roger's door suddenly opened, and Mack walked out, smiling. "Hey there," he said, standing in the cubicle opening. "How's your morning so far?"

I turned to face him, and his eyebrows raised up.

"You okay?" he asked. "You look upset."

"I'm fine," I said, and Roger chuckled.

"Mack," Roger said. "When a woman says she's

fine, it usually means she's anything but. Best to back away slowly."

"I said I was fine, and I meant it," I said, sharpening my tone.

Mack backed away slowly, and Roger kept his comments to himself. An awkward silence fell over the office, and the country music station playing overhead seemed to be blaring Randy Travis now. He was singing something about "rock bottom," and I thought it was only fitting given my circumstances. I didn't even make it a full year before they took my ice away, and I wasn't sure how I was going to tell the coaches. What was I going to do? Anger began to burn in my stomach.

From his office, Roger cleared his throat. "Um, Natalie? Can I see you for a sec?"

He eyed Mack briefly before I entered. Here it was—the moment of truth. It felt ominous as he motioned for me to shut the door behind me.

"Two closed-door meetings in a half hour—that's gotta be a record for you," I said, sitting down. "Should I be worried?" Anger made me say things that I almost always regretted.

He chuckled again, and I realized it was nervous laughter.

"I know what you're doing," I said, stopping him mid-laugh.

"What I'm *doing*?" He played dumb. "What would that be?"

"I've added up the final summer numbers for learn-to-skate and freestyle. I know you're going to take fall ice time away from me. You and Mack had your little powwow to decide what to do with it, and it's not fair. You are punishing the program because I was the person to take over."

He tipped his head. "So, you have it all figured out then, huh?" he said. "I didn't even need to call you in here. Hell, I don't even need to be here if you're going to make all my decisions for me."

"That's not what you two were talking about just a minute ago?" I could feel the crease in between my eyebrows tighten up.

He shook his head slowly. "Not even a little bit," he said. "We were talking about you, but more of a plan to restructure the learn-to-skate to include a beginning hockey class—one to include the skills you introduced this week. Mack seems to think this is the beginning of something big, and he wants to start a Breakfast Club for hockey players now. He's all wound up."

I was listening to the words, but they weren't sinking in. "Then I'm not losing ice time?"

"Like I said, you're not going to lose any freestyle time, but we'd like to look at your learn-to-skate times and see where we can fit in a couple classes strictly for hockey players. Any numbers or revenue will go towards your overall numbers, but it will cut into the number of figure skaters on the ice at times. Mack is a little nervous about cutting into those times, but after what we both saw this week, we agree that you need to be included in any discussion for hockey development."

"This is not at all how I imagined the conversation would go," I said, shaking my head.

"Clearly," he replied. "You had a chip on your shoulder coming in here. Are you okay with all of this? I mean, it won't be a major change, but will take some extra planning on your part to see how we run the learn-to-skate ice."

A part of me was still dazed, thinking how wrong I was when I came in here. How I was so quick to believe the worst was happening without once thinking something good would win out.

"You guys really liked the class this week that much?"

"Not just us—we've had so many hockey parents calling, trying to get in and wondering when the next one is running. They would pay anything for this kind of instruction. It's incredible!"

"I'll admit that Monday was rough, but once I had the plan clear in my head, everything fell into place. I didn't get to half of the drills I wanted to do this week. Next summer, we could run this every week if you wanted."

His eyes lit up. Finding lucrative ways to fill the summer ice was always an issue—especially for the hockey program. Only the dedicated were motivated to skate year-round.

"Is that all, then? I want to start playing with the ice

time before our staff meeting. If we're going to start this next month, it has to be done quickly."

"That is all," he said. "Happy to hear you want to work with us. Should be good for both programs—a win-win, as corporate likes to say."

I refrained from rolling my eyes. Corporate didn't care about a win for either of our programs. Its only goal was the bottom line. The financial outcome of the win-win.

It didn't matter to me. I wanted to grow something different and better than what we'd done. If it made our programs better, then that would just be the cherry on top. It was the skaters that mattered, plain and simple.

Regionals

The only saving grace we had was the fact it was Regionals, and not the Midwestern Championships. The talent was thin in our region—especially at the senior level for some reason. If Addie were skating at the junior level, we'd be ending our season this weekend. She threw out another disastrous short program yesterday, but she was starting to feel more confident after her practice-ice this morning.

Jonathan was here, lurking in the background of everywhere we went like *Where's Waldo?* His skater, Janelle, wasn't necessarily better than Addie, but she had managed to perfect a clean short program in the last two competitions. I know I shouldn't blame her for any of Jonathan's mistakes, but it was hard not to hold it against her. The competitive part in me wanted to use black magic on her to encourage some falls.

Unfortunately, I had left my voodoo doll at home.

Dana, Steph, and I sat at a table in the café area in the lobby, splitting an order of mozzarella sticks. Coaches lived on coffee and bad food for comfort in between events.

"I still can't believe Kari bombed as badly as she

did," Dana said.

"It's apparent her dieting is affecting her mentality" Steph said. "I imagine she'll have to do a cleanse to get rid of the season's bad juju when she gets home."

"Nat—I think I'd like to bring you in to see if you can help with her eating," she said. "Or at least introduce some common sense to Jeannette."

"Absolutely. I was hoping you'd ask at some point. Wait—aren't you done now? I'd get on the road if I were you," I said.

We were in downtown Indianapolis—one of my favorite places to go for competitions. Great hotels and restaurants always made the trip memorable.

"I'm staying the night," Dana said. "We both are—thought you could use the support with Addie and Will later."

"Or at least a stiff drink after," Stephanie said.

I looked from one to the other. "Seriously, you're staying?" Relief flooded through me. "You guys are the best."

"It's not like there's any ice tomorrow, and we'll just get on the road early."

"Yeah," Stephanie confirmed. "Plus, I wanted to check out the junior ladies… they were rockin' practice-ice earlier. That little one from DuPage is unbelievable."

"I swear she comes up to my boobs with her skates on. Can't be four-foot-ten," I said.

Dana sighed. "I wonder if I'll ever get to teach

someone talented like that."

"Ha, it's not all it's cracked out to be. The stress alone is eating me alive," I said. "But yeah, Will is pretty fun to work with. Plus, he is just so driven. I think he could do all of this without me."

"Oh, you had to get on him during Hell Week," Stephanie said. "He'd be a slacker if no one was there to keep an eye on him."

"Ladies," a familiar voice said behind me. Dana and Steph froze in mid-smile.

"Oh—Jonathan," Stephanie said, with forced kindness. "How... nice to see you."

He had the audacity to pull up a chair to our table and grab the last cheese stick. I hoped he choked on it.

"Dana—unfortunate skate for Kari earlier," he said. "She looks light as a feather, though."

She rolled her eyes and stood up. "I'm going to get some fresh air," she said. "I'll catch up with you later."

"Something I said?" he said after she left.

"What's your angle, Jonathan?" Stephanie asked. "Exactly what are you trying to prove?"

"I don't know what you're talking about," he said, holding his hands up defensively. "I just thought it would be nice to catch up with my old friends. I miss you guys."

"Tell me," Steph said, pulling out her phone. "Have you had any conversations with Addie's mom lately? That last one looked like a doozie." She didn't show him her phone, but she narrowed her eyes at him.

His smile faltered. "I don't have any idea what you're talking about—she and I have always had a difficult relationship. Hopefully, she isn't as hard on you as she was with me," he directed at me.

"We get along just fine, but forgive me for wondering what you're talking about," I said. "You two were thick as thieves in the last few years you were at Skateland. Makes me wonder if something other than a professional relationship was taking place."

"And I'll sue you for slander if those words ever get repeated to anyone," he said. His stony expression stared at me. He stood abruptly, the metal chair sticking to the rubber flooring and almost tipped over. "I guess I'll see you later—best of luck to Addie."

My cheeks flamed red as I held back a bitter comment.

"That escalated quickly," Steph said. "What the hell?"

"He's obviously hiding something about Nicole," I said. "And I'm not sure I ever want to open that can of worms. I just wish I didn't have to deal with him at all."

"You don't. Your only job is to get your skaters ready for their long programs—they should be getting here soon, so put your happy face back on," she said. "They're gonna take one look at you and know something is off."

She was right. I had to get my act together for them. Will was so far ahead after the short program, he could probably skate blindfolded. But I knew him—he would be skating lights out tonight. I still couldn't believe he had to go through Regionals and Mids, but not skating at Nationals last year eliminated any International competitions.

"I can't wait to see him skate tonight. His *Godfather* program literally gives me chills."

The moment I heard the music—the beginning with just the horn playing that iconic melody—his program came to life in my head. I knew Fredrik would choreograph a program worthy of Will's style and technique. Nothing compared to how proud I was of Addie's long program. I can still see her eyes light up the second she heard the music I loved for her from the beginning. Her short was different, not quite the same enthusiasm, but the long program she felt in her bones. I didn't know how to work that magic into her short program, but we'd have to before Mids.

"I have a good feeling about both of them," I said, more of an affirmation than a statement. "Addie just has to skate solid enough to stay in fourth."

I hated that I doubted her even just a bit. She didn't deserve that, but I wanted her to keep going. I wanted her to have her chance at Nationals again, and to prove to herself that she could compete at that level.

Another important detail you need to know about figure skating competitions is that ultimately, it's a numbers game. A math puzzle for the insanely talented. Whoever ends with the most points, wins.

As a coach, it was my job to make sure the program is choreographed to utilize the most points possible to the best of their ability. You have to know your skater's strengths, and—especially—their weaknesses. You have to understand what jumps they love (open with that one), and what ones they hate (hide it before the halfway mark). What jumps they can do in their sleep (second half), and what combinations are their strongest. It's not unlike building a house from the ground up.

The foundation is the music and theme.

The structure consists of the jumps, spins, and step sequences.

The style is the choreography and in between steps.

And the decorations—well, that's probably the hardest part to get right. The skater has to feel the music to the point you think they recorded it themselves. It has to match the music and overall theme. Every note, every beat, every nuance needs to be brought to the judges' attention, preferably in a good way.

Technical elements placed in the second half get 'extra-credit' and can boost the score even more, making it extra important a skater can get through the program easily. Every skater hates the double run-through until they're competing. Then, they're grateful for them.

Currently, Addie wasn't skating her worst or her

best. Middle of the road at best, and I paced back and forth along the side of the boards saying silent Hail Marys to myself. The voice in my head was definitely talking non-stop and wouldn't let me calm down. Will was standing behind me about ten feet back, not wanting to distract her, but also wanting desperately to cheer her on. She still had two triples and a combination left in the second half. If she could nail them, she would be through for sure, but that was a big if. She started strong. Confident. Then a fall on her first triple lutz let some air out of her sails.

I tried to slow my breathing down—only breathing through the nose—but also felt like the other coaches were watching me.

Next up, triple lutz triple toe combination.

And she nailed it. The triple loop was next after her step sequence. My heart raced, and I glanced at Will. I nodded for him to come up with me.

Triple loop off of the rolling back three-turns.

Yes!

Okay, ohmygod, ohmygod, ohmygod, the combination and layback were the only thing left. She seemed to slow down on purpose going into the toe, but why? Ohmygod. I blew out the breath I was holding as she popped open, and the triple turned into a double. She ended with her gorgeous layback and pulled up into a Biellmann. When she finished, she covered her face with her hands.

I felt as if I had skated the program myself while

Will cheered wildly beside me. I pasted a brave smile on my face. We would go over any issues next week. Right now, she just needed support, and I prayed it was enough to stay in fourth.

I glanced behind me as Addie skated off and noticed Jonathan. His mouth set in a straight line and he simply nodded. It felt like a gut-punch that he doubted her. Doubted us.

She skated off and fell into my open arms.

"I'm so sorry," she whispered in between gasps. "I can't believe I just popped at the end."

"Shhh," I tried to soothe her. "It's over, and I think it's enough to stay in fourth. It's up to everyone else now."

She gave Will a quick hug before we moved to the kiss and cry area. Her legs started to shake as soon as we sat down, her adrenaline working overtime. Nerves affected every skater differently, and some didn't feel anything till after it was over. Me? I felt them before, during, and after.

Bruno Mars played overhead while the next skater—Jonathan's—skated laps to warm up her body again. Jonathan kept his back to us, but it was hard to ignore him standing there.

The score was read, and Addie blew out a sigh of relief. She was in first with three other skaters to go. No matter what, she would be moving on to Mids, so she could relax for now. I led her down the stairs, where she was attacked by Will.

"You did it! You're going to Mids," he whispered loudly.

We headed away from Jonathan, not wanting to give him the satisfaction of being interested. I just wanted to call Marcy, but I knew there wouldn't be enough time, so I quickly shot her a text.

> Me: SHE DID IT. More skaters to go, but she qualified for Mids!

> Marcy: YES, you BOTH did it. She couldn't do it without you.

> Me: xoxo, I'll call you tomorrow on my drive home. Will is up next.

> Marcy: Good luck!

Will went to get his skates on, and I found the bathroom. Washing my hands, I glanced at myself. Drawn and pale, I looked like something the cat dragged in. My hair was flat and somehow frizzy at the same time. A feat one can master only by being in an ice rink all day long. I blended dots of concealer under my eyes and brushed on some light lip gloss to appear more alive.

Will would be an easy win, but we still had to go through the process as professionally as possible. I had a few minutes, so I rushed to the bleacher side to get Steph and Dana's take on how she looked.

As I walked up towards them, Nicole smiled at me and mouthed 'thank you.' I winked and nodded back to her.

"I thought that was fair, and I'm so happy she will get to go to Mids now," I said. "We have several things I want to work on and figure out, but I'm not saying a word until Monday. She needs to celebrate tonight—this is a win for her."

Her mom winced. "I doubt she'll see it as a win, especially since she didn't even have to compete at Regionals or Mids last year. But I'll take her to dinner tonight and make the most of it. She'll want to stay for Will, obviously."

"I was going to let her stay over with us, if she wanted," I said. "He was so supportive during her group."

"That would be good for her," she agreed. She started to say something, then hesitated. "I hope you know how much I appreciate what you've done for her this year. It's been so hard on her, and I know you've had your hands full too."

I sat there, stunned. She was so unlike anything I expected. "I genuinely care about Addie and want what's best for her. I'm still not sure what is going on with Jonathan, but I will get to the bottom of it," I said.

She bristled. "Just let him go. He clearly isn't the person we thought he was. Try not to let him get to you."

This, coming from the woman we have on video irate with him. Nodding, I let her believe he wouldn't bug me anymore, but there was no way I'd let it go. I needed to know why he had to leave town so quickly.

"Well, I'm heading back over," I said, standing. "Wish us luck!"

I winked at Steph and Dana, who were listening to everything we were talking about. Jonathan's skater had taken the ice, and I stood in the corner of the rink to watch. She was in second after short, and if she skated clean, she'd most likely win. It frustrated me to no end that he could treat us the way he did and still come out on top. My phone buzzed.

Stephanie: When Addie decides to skate clean, she's gonna kick her ass.

I snorted out a laugh and covered my mouth.

Stephanie: I heard that!

I looked up in the stands to Dana and Steph smiling at me. I blew them a kiss and waited until the program was over. I didn't watch her, because my only focus had to be on Addie—I had no control over what Jonathan or Janelle did, so it didn't matter if she skated clean or fell on every jump. When the music ended, I continued the walk around the rink back to the check-in area. I double-checked the order in Will's group (he skated last) and felt Jonathan's eyes on me while Janelle's live scores were being read. I ignored his presence and looked back towards the locker rooms, where Addie was helping Will warm up.

It felt good to rise above the drama Jonathan was trying to create—or hide—and as I walked towards my skaters, I felt for the first time that they were better off without him.

I don't think I could've said that a few months ago, but I knew they were better off with me now. I'd make sure Jonathan knew that too.

Queen for the Win

It was Saturday morning in October, which meant Michigan had turned into a brightly colored palette of rust, reds, and yellows. The air was crisp, and everyone was wearing either green or blue, supporting their favorite college football team. Saturday morning ice was a melting pot of skaters, from the elite to the recreational. The sessions were packed and difficult to get anything done with the higher levels, so Marcy and I had devised a plan to use this time to work more on the mental side of figure skating.

Last Wednesday, I spilled my guts about my insecurities and doubts in dealing with elite skaters. Will was fine, but I didn't have a clue how to give Addie the help she needed. The Midwestern championship would be here in six weeks, and Addie would have to perform a hundred percent better than she has so far this year.

"She needs some mental training, if you ask me," Marcy had said. "I know you can handle the technical side of what she is doing on the ice, but she has to learn to control her thoughts in order to succeed."

The idea of "thought control" made me feel uneasy,

and I let her know that.

"Close your eyes," she said.

I tipped my head as if to say *not a chance*, but in the end, I complied.

"Now, imagine you are standing on a white sand beach. The sand is hot beneath your feet, and there is a light breeze blowing your hair out of your face. You can hear the seagulls in the distance, and the waves and washing over your toes. There are no thoughts in your head other than how comforting the sun feels on your skin. The water is so cool, and the sun is so warm against your skin. Do you go in farther or stay where you are on the warm sand?

As she was talking, every muscle in my body seemed to melt into the sofa. I felt the ocean on my toes. I heard the seagulls in the distance. I smelled sunscreen. I wanted to stay here forever and not open my eyes. I sighed, and I heard her giggle.

My eyes fluttered open.

"You might have gotten a sunburn if you stayed there much longer," she said.

Every muscle in my body felt relaxed in this moment. "What is that? How did you just make me feel like I was at the beach?"

"It's just guided visualization, but it's so powerful," she said. "And if you can get in the habit of doing it regularly—with images of what you want—your life will begin to change. Your brain doesn't know any different from really being at the beach or going through the visualization. And the more senses you can incorporate, the more real it feels."

"And you want to do this with Addie and Will?"

"What have you got to lose?"

"Only everything," I said. "What if it backfires, and both of them start to freak out?"

"Let's just try it once," she said. "And take it week by week to see how they respond. I have several techniques to help them regain their focus."

"I'd have to run it by their parents first," I said. "Give me a couple business cards, and I'll see if we can schedule something."

"I know I'm just starting out in this life coaching business, but I'd venture to say that skating is ninety percent mental when it comes to competition. Every skater is trained physically, but it's the mental part that will make or break them when the pressure is on. Hell, I'd say that about any sport."

"You're not wrong," I agreed. "The entire competition process is one big mental game. The strongest mind wins."

"So, let's try something new. Let's say yes to trying something new."

"Ummm, some of us have been choking on the word since January," I said. "Everything I've done this year is new."

"And how do you feel about that?"

"Exhausted." It was true. I was exhausted from constantly being outside my comfort zone. There were days I missed my mom so much and just wanted someone to take care of me. There were also days where I looked back on the year and couldn't believe how much I had changed. Everything about me was different from a year ago. And yet, I couldn't get rid of the feeling that it could all just crumble around me at any second.

"Exhausted isn't the worst thing you could feel," she said.

"I get that. But there are days when I just don't want to get out of bed, still. Not every day, but enough to make me wonder if all of this is worth it."

She grabbed my hand. "I think you're still carrying around a healthy dose of fear about everything that happened last year—which is completely understandable. The challenge of saying yes to everything this year was more about overcoming that fear. Seeing it, feeling it, and ultimately still saying yes. It is exhausting, and I'd wonder about you if you didn't feel this way."

"Do you really think you can help them gain some control over their thoughts?"

"I'm willing to stake my brand-new business reputation on it," she said, smiling. "Will is probably fine, but Addie is the one I really want to help."

"We have roughly six weeks before Mids, and I want that last week to be tapered, so why don't you come in this Saturday. I think the parents will be fine with some positive mental training."

"Yes!" she cheered, fist-pumping the air. "Let me get the business cards…"

～✓

I stood outside Rink One, trying to warm up my toes before I went back out for the last session this morning Will had chosen "Radio Ga Ga" by Queen for the edge song, and the energy and magic on the ice could be felt in the lobby. Dana, Steph, and Ronnie chose to dance and lip-sync to warm up, and Lydia crossed her arms and stood erect on the other side, just waiting for the song—and lightness—to be over.

The skaters felt the energy too, smiling through the tricky and intricate turns, edges, and twizzles, never missing a beat. A great song could change the feeling on the ice.

Ohmygod, that's it.

My eyes snapped to Addie, smiling and energized— the complete opposite of what she had been all week. The last time I saw her skate with this kind of passion was during the show. My mind was spinning. Did I dare think we could do this? Would she even go for it? I knew I had to at least ask the question.

Not feeling cold any longer, I pulled the door open and danced my way out to the ice. Steph hit Dana, and both watched me step onto the ice and skate towards them.

"I have a plan," I whispered to them, beaming.

"Are you drinking already?" Stephanie asked,

straight-faced.

I grabbed Ronnie's hand and twirled myself under his arm. He was laughing with me.

"She's gone off the edge," he fake-whispered to them. "Someone call nine-one-one."

I let go of him and turned to watch the skaters. "This," I said as if it were apparent to anyone around me. "This is the answer to Addie's short program hang-up."

"Radio Ga Ga?" Ronnie said slowly.

"Look how happy she is—all of them, really. They are using the whole song, instead of just the first couple passes."

"Okay, they like the song," Dana said. "But what does that have to do with Addie's short program?"

"Have you ever seen her skate it—even in practice—with this kind of enthusiasm?"

They all paused to see what I was seeing, and slowly shook their heads.

"She doesn't love it," I exclaimed. "I'd go so far as to say she doesn't even like it."

The music from the play *Carousel* was classic and flowing—a dream to choreograph, but she didn't *love* it. That was so crystal clear to me now. I needed to change her music, and I wanted to use the song from the ice show this year. That program was magical.

Sure, Fredrik would probably disown me, but I believed in my gut this was right for her. The only question now was, would she think so? Changing a program this late in the season could be disastrous—it was unheard of. But sending her out with a program she doesn't love would stop her from getting to Nationals. She would have to skate a clean short program to even have a shot.

"You can't be suggesting what I think you are," Stephanie said. "Nat, you can't change it this late in the season. It won't work."

"But what if it's a program we've skated before, and we just have to tweak it for the short elements?"

Dana smiled. "The edge of glory… that's it. You want to use her show program music from this year."

I nodded, and Steph raised her eyebrows, thinking it over. "Okay, it's not the worst idea, but still, you have to see if she even wants to change it."

I spotted Addie and Will stretching across the ice. "I guess we just have to see…"

Will turned and whispered something to Addie as I approached them. She turned, a questioning look on her face.

"You look way too happy for a Saturday morning," Will said. "Are we still meeting after this session?"

"Yep," I replied. I had almost forgotten about Marcy during my epiphany. "But I need to go over something with Addie right now… I'll take you second today."

Addie wiggled her eyebrows, clearly having won a small victory of the first lesson. Will smirked and skated away to get to work.

"What's up?" she asked. "You look excited about something."

"Tell me how you felt during that warm-up," I said.

Her smile grew wide. "I love that song," she explained. "It was my favorite scene in the movie."

"But how did you *feel*?"

She looked at me like I lost my marbles. "Umm, relaxed? Happy, I guess. I'm not sure what you mean, though."

"What I mean is your whole body language changed while you were just warming up, and I noticed it from the lobby. You were skating with confidence and joy."

"Oh-kaaaay," she said. "So what? It's just a warm-up."

"How would it feel to skate a short program like that... happy and relaxed."

She shook her head, and her face dropped. "Not possible."

"Now, I'm going to suggest something, and I want you to give it some serious thought."

She leaned on her elbow at the boards. I felt her resistance immediately.

"Do you remember your program from the ice show?"

Her eyes lit up and flashed to mine. "I do." She hesitated. "I loved that program."

"I know you did. Everyone knew you did," I said. "How would you feel about changing your show program to your short program? Obviously, we'd have to re-choreograph parts to add in all elements, but we could crank that out in a day."

Her eyes started dancing around the rink, spotting different skaters, while she thought it through.

"Do you really think we can?" A slice of hope broke into her voice.

I smiled and nodded. "Not only do I think we can, I think we have to," I said. "I think we have to try something different to get a different result, and clearly, this program isn't working for you."

She bit her lip, and I couldn't tell if she was on board or not.

"I can cut the music tonight to make sure it's the correct length, and we can work out the steps Monday. I'd like to keep a lot of the choreography because it was magic," I said. "But in order for this to work, you have to want this. I don't want to change anything for the sake of changing. We have to have a reason, and you have to want it."

She nodded vigorously, and tears sprang to her eyes. "Yes," she whispered. "Yes, I want to." She looked to Will and gave him a huge smile.

I prayed I was doing the right thing, but following your gut had to count for something. I knew Marcy would be proud of me.

"Okay, so we are doing this?" I asked one final time.

"Absolutely," she said. "One thousand percent."

I glanced to the lobby and noticed Marcy watching us. I gave her a thumbs-up, looked around the rink.

This was all I needed right now, and for the first time, things felt like they were falling into place.

How long this would last, I had no clue.

I'm an Excellent Driver

Because of Mack's persistence in having me help with his own Breakfast Club, I had several teams reach out to me to work with them during their practices. Once one team had me out there, the other teams caught wind and wanted to try it out. I coached on Monday and Tuesday evenings after our regular ice time and learn-to-skate. We also created the first hour of learn-to-skate on Tuesdays, specifically for young hockey players.

Lydia mentioned several times that I was crossing to the dark side, and we would lose more and more ice if I continued down this path. Dana, Steph, and Ronnie wanted to know how they could get in with more teams. The money the teams were paying was well above what we were making even in our private lessons.

Mack and I leaned into an easy coaching system on the ice. He and his helpers gradually picked up on the edge work and could demonstrate more each week. It was exciting to see how quickly they improved, and they even grew to enjoy the skills and wanted to increase the difficulty. They also became increasingly competitive with the ladders to see who could complete it the fastest. At the end of every learn-to-skate class, we'd pull the kids to the side, and I'd time the coaches to see who was the fastest. The kids loved seeing the speed up close and cheered for their favorites. It fed completely into the parents, who all wanted their players to skate that fast someday. The fact that a figure skater was helping them get that fast made me feel like I was making a difference, and I knew that this was something Jonathan never would have agreed to help with. I took some pride in that.

Hockey players weren't the enemy, and they didn't want all our ice time. The main goal was, and has always been, the highest rate per hour. It was a math problem for me to solve. Either increase skaters, session prices, or risk the chance the hockey players would. I could see that now and had to work with the system instead of complaining about it.

Mack and I sat at Pauley's, sharing a plate of breadsticks. We had grown more comfortable going out after the hockey classes we coached together. Tonight was learn-to-skate, and his cheeks were still flushed from the final ladder.

"You know, you could let one of your helpers win a ladder from time to time," I said between bites.

He made a face. "Never gonna happen," he said, chugging a large glass of water. "They need to remember their place."

"Oh, my, someone is full of himself tonight," I said.

"Not at all," he said, switching and taking a pull from his beer. "Don't get me wrong—they're good— but neither of them will make it in juniors. They'll get lost in the shuffle in the first month."

"Why? How can you predict that a year away?" I wasn't questioning him, per se, but wondering what he saw in them that made him say that.

"One, neither of them has leadership skills. If you can't stand out, you fade away. The coaches keep their eyes on the ones making plays and willing to go the extra mile on the ice."

"That's fair," I said. "And the other reason?"

"And two, have you noticed how long it's taken them to lean into the edge work? They resisted it for so long, and just now get the hang of it."

"Actually, I was sort of impressed how they've done with all of it—so much of it was completely new to them."

"True, but their head was the biggest roadblock, and that tells me they are not as coachable as they should be."

I thought he was being a little tough on them, but if anyone knew how challenging playing Juniors was, it would be Mack.

"Do you miss it?"

He made that face again and took a bite before answering. "I will always miss playing hockey. It's not something you get over, especially when an injury took you out of it to begin with," he said. "But I've been out for so long now, and I've obviously found other ways to be a part of the sport. My only real regret is not being able to play college hockey. Having to go to those games, knowing I could've been out there too, was a bit rough."

"Where were you supposed to play?"

"Michigan," he said, his shoulders drooping.

"Oh, man, I didn't know that. You must be a smarty pants," I said.

"School came very easy to me, and it helped that my grandparents were both schoolteachers in Sarnia. They watched me when my mom was working, and my grandma was a stickler for math and science."

"What did your mom do?"

"You're asking an awful lot of questions tonight," he said. "Is this an interview?"

"Yes, and it's rude to answer a question with a question."

"It's not like you're giving me a choice," he said. "To answer your last and final question, my mom owned a coffee shop, and we lived in the apartment above it. She still runs it, too." He was smiling easily at the memories. "I loved being able to go downstairs at any time and get a cookie or something. It was the best."

"That is so cool," I said. I began to ask about his dad, but he cut me off.

"That concludes the question-and-answer portion of the evening for me," he joked. "You, on the other hand, are going to answer rapid-fire questions now… are you ready?"

"Oh my God, no way," I said. "I'm not a fast thinker."

"Too bad—take a drink while you can, if you're thirsty."

I sighed and took a sip of my wine. "This is zero fun, by the way."

"I'm okay with that," he smirked. "Okay, here we go. Favorite Netflix show?

"Ummm…"

"No, there's no ummmmmm in rapid-fire answers."

"Schitt's Creek."

"Good one. Favorite ice cream?

"Rocky road."

"Worst childhood memory?"

"Having the whole class come to the rink for a field trip, and I fell. They all made fun of me because our teacher had made such a big deal about me being so good."

He winced. "Favorite summer Olympic sport?

"Diving."

He rolled his eyes. "Favorite movie?"

"*Jaws*."

"You have *got* to be kidding me." He chuckled.

"Nope, I could recite every line to you if you ever wanted to watch. It's a classic. What's your favorite?"

"Without a doubt, *Rain Man*. Now, *that's* a classic, and like you, I know every word," he admitted proudly.

"Moving along, name your favorite band."

"Backstreet Boys."

He closed his eyes and leaned his head back against the top of the booth. "Now I know you're lying."

"Shows what you know. I even went to their concert two years ago."

"Favorite NHL team?"

"Rangers."

"I feel like I don't even know who you are," he said, shaking his head. "Favorite food?"

"Pizza."

"Okay, I can actually agree with you on that one," he said. "Favorite pet growing up."

"I had a cat named Alan when I was little." I sighed. "I loved that cat."

"*Alan*?"

"My mom loved the Tigers—Alan Trammel." I shrugged one shoulder.

"I have known you for months, and there isn't one answer that I would've guessed right."

I shrugged again. "It's a gift. I like to keep people on their toes." In the back of my head, I was screaming *just stop talking*, but a part of me was enjoying this little banter. "Will that conclude the question-and-answer portion of the evening?"

"One last question—what are you doing Saturday night?"

The wine I had just sipped went sideways, causing a coughing fit to erupt. My eyes watered, and everyone turned to make sure I was okay.

Mack held up his hands. "You don't have to answer if you don't want to—I just thought we could hang out somewhere other than here," he said, looking around.

"Like a date?" I knew that came out wrong, but this was not what I expected.

"Well—yeah? I guess we could call it something else if you wanted."

Nothing was coming out right. "I guess I thought you already had a girlfriend."

"With all my free time? I'm at that rink every single day and most nights."

"True," I agreed. The rink had a way of taking over your life, especially in the fall and winter months.

"It's cool," he said, draining his beer. "I just think you're so easy to be around. Thought we could do something outside the rink, but it's probably not a good idea to just… not, I guess." His eyes darted around the restaurant—trying to find another focal point other than mine.

"Yes."

He raised his eyebrows. "Yes?"

"Yes, I'll go on a date—or whatever—on Saturday night… with you." My voice, steady and calm, surprised both of us. The right side of his mouth twitched up as his eyes landed on mine. "I still tend to resist anything new without thinking," I explained. "My comfort zone has a very small window of opportunity."

"I know," he reassured me. "No pressure, just fun."

"I could definitely use a little fun about now." My heart thudded at the knowledge of how true that statement was. In saying yes to everything, I became so wrapped up in the details of life, I always felt a little unsteady, unstable, and more than anything just needed a solid place to land. I didn't know if Mack was that solid place, but it felt right. There really wasn't fear involved in saying yes tonight, but I still didn't understand how someone like him wasn't dating anyone already. In my head, he was always taken, my imagination creating the perfect blonde-size-two-perky girlfriend.

On the drive home, I realized I had been comparing myself to this imaginary girlfriend of his for months. And no matter how good of a day I had, I'd end up feeling bad- because I never measured up. I dialed Marcy's phone.

"Am I crazy?" I asked when she answered.

"You're gonna have to elaborate on that one," she replied.

"I'm just now realizing that I've been on the losing end of comparing myself to an imaginary person— someone who literally doesn't exist. Who does this?"

"Someone who loves to create stories about why their life isn't what they want it to be," she said. "It's not crazy at all—just a protective reaction to everything you've been dealing with. Wait—what happened?"

"Mack asked me out on a date," I admitted.

"Yesssss," she said. "It's about freaking time. That boy is taking the slow boat to shore."

"It doesn't feel slow to me at all," I said. "In fact, I always assumed he had a girlfriend—a perfect, Barbie-like girl—and that's why we were just good friends."

"Ahh, the imaginary person was his girlfriend?"

"Yep, and I didn't even think I was in his league, so I ruled him out a long time ago. Why would he want to go out with someone like me?"

"Because you're smart, and beautiful, and crazy talented—why wouldn't he, is the better question. You're better than Barbie. You're real."

"I come with a lot of baggage, and Barbie has a cute carryall."

"Good lord, Nat, BARBIE DOESN'T EXIST!" she yelled into the phone. "Everyone has baggage, even Mack, and he clearly wants a woman who can hold her own."

"You think?"

She sighed loudly. "We still on for Winesday?" She sounded tired and clearly done with this conversation.

"We are," I confirmed. "I'll see you tomorrow."

We disconnected, and my mind continued to wrestle with the thought that my mind made something up for the sole purpose of protecting myself. Where else am I doing this in my life? Marcy had always talked about the voice in our head, but I didn't know how to shut it off, and suddenly I wanted to know what was real and what was just a story my head produced.

I pulled into my driveway and turned the car off. I shivered in the chill November air as I got out and looked up at the stars. I still didn't know what all of this meant, but I knew in my gut I was going to figure it out.

Until then, I might question everything I thought I knew.

INTERVIEW PART 5

[Cut to video of Addie's last remaining seconds of her program at Nationals from this year. Ending pose, and the emotional tears that stream down her face as she acknowledges the crowd and judges.]

AG: I think what I need most is to take a week off and see where I'm at mentally. An Olympic year is overwhelming and not something I can decide just yet. My only focus is to skate the next two programs as clean as I can and embrace every moment out there. There are no guarantees, and I want to make sure the decision is right for me in the long run.

TL: Fair enough, but you have to know everyone is going to be asking you this week. In a sport known for its over-the-top drama, your story reminded us to root for the underdog. To believe that hard work and perseverance pay off.

AG: I just want to go out and skate. I can't carry the weight of all those expectations and stay focused. Everyone has been so supportive and kind, but I don't want to lose sight of why I'm here.

TL: Do you mind if we bring your coach in for the last few minutes? I think the world would like to know more about the dynamic duo you two have become.

[Her face lights up, and she looks to the side.]

AG: Sure, but you'll have to get her to say yes first...

Giving Thanks

Thanksgiving was upon us, and my sister was furious with me for not making the trek to Chicago to be with her family. She didn't understand why I wanted to be alone and had a hard time believing it was all because we were getting extra ice-time that day and all weekend. Roger gave me the go-ahead to let Addie and Will skate today. He even carved out some ice for them during the hockey tournament all weekend.

In truth, I probably would've skipped even if we didn't have ice. Celebrating with her perfectness only made me see how much I was missing right now, anyway. Marcy understood and said it was my only free pass for the year, and that I had better find my party pants before Christmas. She was going to Florida for the weekend to see her parents, and while Roger invited me to be with his family today, I wasn't up for awkward social gatherings.

I was happiest at the rink and found solace in the fact we had the ice to ourselves. Will pulled out his favorite hip-hop music from the early nineties, and I surprised them both by cranking up the volume. Something caught my eye in the lobby, and I turned to find Mack watching us with wide eyes and a blank expression. The glass was thin, and I knew it was loud even in there.

I smiled and waved. He just shook his head and walked back towards the office, smiling. He knew I'd be here today, but never said he was coming in. I felt better knowing someone else was here.

Will and Addie were stretching when I skated over to them. "Who's going first?"

"Not me," Addie said.

"No way," Will said.

"Someone is," I said. "I guess we can always flip a mitten for it." I pulled off my mitten and pointed to Addie.

"Thumbs-up," she said, and Will tipped his head back. She smiled smugly.

"Thumbs-up always wins," he said. "Completely not fair."

"You got to go first last time," I reminded him.

The mitten twirled in the air like a gymnast on a floor routine and landed thumbs down. Will's eyes grew wide, and he jumped into the air.

"Yes!" he shouted. "The mitten never lies."

Addie simply rolled her eyes. "Whatever," she said.

He continued to dance around her chanting, "I won," in a sing-song rhythm. Her face broke into a smile, and she laughed as she pushed him away.

"How rude," she said. "Go away, William Tran."

He wiggled his eyebrows one last time and then

proceeded into the middle to warm-up his spins.

"You know what this means, right?"

She eyed me carefully. "Not a six-minute warm-up?" Her face cringed into a tight ball.

"Indeed," I nodded. "Let me know when you're ready…"

"Like, *never*," she retorted. "What's the skating order?"

"Ohhh, let's be the first skater today. Short program."

Her eyes bugged out. "Nat-a-leee," she whined like a five-year-old. "Honestly, it's a day of thanks—can't you cut me some slack?"

"Ummm, nope. Slack time is officially over until the season is complete," I said. "You'll thank me for this someday."

"I highly doubt that, but I guess I don't have a choice either."

"Smart girl." I held up my stopwatch hanging around my neck. "Ready, and go!"

The rink filled with "Super Bass" from Nicki Minaj—Addie's hype song for five years or longer. It had already been a thing when I started teaching, and the coaches always put up with the quirks of what motivated skaters. Even I had to admit, my blood got moving hearing this now, and Addie seemed to immediately get focused in the zone when it came on. She skated faster. Landed cleaner. Choreography was sharper with more extension. Why I didn't have this playing on a loop for the month before a competition, I didn't know. Will had our backs and found a way to play it every day.

Will didn't have a hype song—more like a hype list. Every day it changed, and it would range from Michael Jackson and the Beastie Boys to Post Malone. Of course, we'd have to make sure younger skaters weren't on the sessions or he'd have to find the clean versions. No one knew music and how to motivate athletes like Will. It was a gift.

I looked at my stopwatch and noticed she was halfway through the time. She looked relaxed and in the zone. She attacked her jumps with perfect execution and clean rotation. Even Will did a double take on her triple flip-triple toe combination and graced her with a whoop and clap. She moved on to spins next, fast and centered. I hadn't seen Addie skate like this since pre-Nationals last year. This was what she used to be like all the time, and my eyes welled up seeing her so focused and calm.

I pulled my iPad out of my tote bag. She probably wouldn't want me to video her program, but she needed to see this.

With one minute remaining, she came back over to me, slightly winded.

"That felt really good," she said, eyes bright.

"I haven't seen you skate like that in a year," I agreed. "I'm going to video your program today—you need to see yourself skating with this confidence."

She surprised me by nodding. She blew her nose and took a small sip of water. "Can I leave my gloves on?"

"I don't know—can you at Mids?"

She rolled her eyes and peeled off her mittens. "Did you see that combination? Felt so easy," she said.

"Okay," I said, showing her the six-minute mark. "It's time. Stay fluid and focused."

Will was in the box, waiting for the go-ahead. "From the Skateland Figure Skating Club, please welcome, my homie, Adeline Gray," he said into the microphone.

She giggled and presented to a fake crowd, taking her opening pose in the middle. The breath was heard in the silent rink, and she closed her eyes and smiled before beginning. We had worked so hard on making this music change before Mids, and I couldn't love the program more. Even Fredrik agreed this was a much better choice for her.

Will came and sat on the boards next to where I was standing. My only focus was keeping her on the screen, so I couldn't truly see how beautifully she was skating. He clapped louder and louder with every jump, and when she nailed her combination, he threw his arms in the air. She finished her program, and turned to look at both of us, her hands covering her mouth—eyes wide. Will jumped off the boards and went to hug her, and I kept the video rolling. No matter what else, she would be able to see this video over and over again and know she could do it.

I wiped a stray tear and shut the video off. We were two weeks out, and the last thing I wanted was for her to peak too early. Marcy would have to help us keep all of this in perspective, and I couldn't wait to show her this video.

Addie took a slow lap to catch her breath, and Will went back to his warm-up.

"I can't believe I just did that," she said, breathless. She blew her nose again and took a long drink of water. "That felt so good."

"I'm speechless," I said. "Wait till you see it—it's amazing."

"Honestly, I've been visualizing every night like Marcy said, and it felt exactly like I see it in my head. It was like floating."

"I don't think I could expect anything better than that," I agreed. "But I'm going to send this to you, and I want you to watch it over and over again. If you see something you don't like, we have plenty of time to make a minor change."

"I had forgotten how good it feels to skate like that," she said quietly. "Do you think I can do that when it counts?"

"Addie, you have it in you to skate like that every time," I said. "You just have to let your mind work *for* you and not against you. What you did today, though— this was a huge step in the right direction."

She nodded, her cheeks flushed from the cold air

and exertion. She took a final big breath and blew it out slowly, like Marcy taught her. 'Pretend you're blowing on hot soup…'

"What's next?" she asked.

"Why don't you be Will's DJ, and I'll have him do his short now."

The difference between Addie and Will was the fact that Will was part machine. Consistency was his greatest asset, and he was the definition of calm under pressure. I think he still got nervous like everyone else, but it never showed in his skating.

Post Malone filled the rink and I held up the stopwatch. Going through a warm-up wasn't much different than the choreographed program. There was a certain order the skaters like to warm up the jumps, spins, and connecting steps, and I made sure they practiced the warm-up every day, so they would fall into a groove during competition. The less they have to actually think and they can just feel, the better.

Addie came and sat on the boards to watch him. "Want me to video him?"

"Would you rather video or watch and cheer?"

"Oh—never mind," she said. "I'm cheering. I'll introduce him too."

I would have to do something nice for Roger for letting us come in here today. This was the best Thanksgiving I had in years.

"Time," I yelled to Will, who was already winding down with his final lap.

I gave Addie, who had scooted back to the box, the thumbs-up.

"From the Skateland Figure Skating Club," she bellowed into the mic. "Please give a warm welcome the king of music, Williammmm Trannnnnnn."

I lifted the iPad, but noticed Mack watching from the lobby again. I'm certain he heard Addie and wondered what the hell we were doing.

Effortless. Easy. Entertaining. The trifecta of E's was something I joked with him about at Regionals when he demolished the competition. His short program music—"Wanted Dead or Alive"—was the combination of cool and swagger that only he could pull off. He had his quad toe—triple toe combination first and flowed out of it with speed. The rest of his program filled the rink with speed and a precise technique only a few skaters would ever possess. To Will, this was no big deal. To the rest of us, it was like watching a perfectionist at work.

It was brilliant.

The Hallmark Effect

The lights in the office were off, with the exception of Mack's cubicle light glowing in the dark. I knew he wasn't going home for Thanksgiving, but I didn't know why he was here today.

"Surely, you have better things to do today than work," I said.

"I could say the same to you," he retorted, his face brightening up.

"But the thing is, I don't have anything better to do, and I know you could've gone home to visit your mom and been back by tonight."

He pushed back from his computer and crossed his arms over his chest. "You're right, I could've, but she's been seeing someone for a while, and they were eating with his kids. Not anything I'd want to be a part of no matter how much I love my mom," he said. "Plus, we're short-handed tomorrow and I'm trying to figure out how we make it work with what we have."

"It just so happens I'm free tomorrow," I said, shrugging.

"No way, you have enough going on with competition coming up."

"It's not tomorrow," I said. "Besides, I need to come here tomorrow for a morning session. You bring me a coffee, and we'll call it even."

"You'd seriously help out tomorrow?" His eyebrows raised in hope.

"If you'll commit to being Santa again this year for learn-to-skate and the ice show, then yes. I'll help."

His head tipped back. "Come on," he groaned. "Don't make me do that again."

Laughter bubbled up inside me. "I barely knew you last year, so you'll have to blame someone else," I said. "But you were so good, and I won't take no for an answer."

He looked at me with a twinkle in his eye. "You won't take no for an answer? Then, I guess you have to give me tomorrow *and* another date."

My stomach flip-flopped, but I fake-flinched. "I don't know about that. It would have to be something special."

"Are you implying the first one wasn't? I thought a haunted maze was straight out of a Hallmark movie."

A memory of me screaming into his chest as a zombie killer scared us from behind flashed in my head. "As hard as I try, I can't seem to forget that date." I shuddered. "But I don't think I've ever seen anything like that on Hallmark."

He waved me off. "Hallmark movies are overrated and all the same."

My mouth dropped open. "You take that back," I

said. "That channel helped me get through Christmas last year and not collapse from crushing depression."

His entire body seemed to soften. It was crazy how someone with so many muscles could look so comforting. "I admit the haunted maze was a bit terrifying, and I'll refrain from Hallmark-bashing if you agree to let me make it up to you."

"Nothing haunted."

"Hard to find haunted holiday events, but I'll agree to that term," he said.

"Okay, you have a deal," I said. "Let's get back to tomorrow. What do you need help with?"

"Would you want to be here in the office or out front at the check-in table?"

I made a face. "In here," I said quickly. "No way do I want to deal with crazy hockey people."

"The rink is going to be filled with crazy hockey people, so not much of a chance avoiding them."

"Why do you have a tournament on Thanksgiving weekend? That is so weird to me."

"Players don't have to miss school. Most parents have the weekend off from work. It's a no-brainer." He shrugged. "You're in here training today, and all weekend, so don't call me crazy. Being here at six a.m. on a Friday morning after Thanksgiving is bananas."

He had me there. "I don't disagree with you, but someone ate up all the ice time this weekend."

"Okay, truce. We're all a little crazy for working here, anyway," he said. "How did they look today?

Addie seemed to be a little more relaxed."

"Addie skated the best program she's done in about a year." I beamed. "She was focused and seemed to be floating over the ice. It was so fun to watch."

"I watched most of Will's program—he's pretty incredible, even for a figure skater."

"You know we rule."

"Pfffft," he blew out. "I know no such thing." Even as he said the words, I knew he was just joking. He had given me full reign over the hockey class we started in the summer, and there was a waiting list every week. Even Roger had to admit the class was gold.

"I've come to the conclusion that Will is part droid—it's just not possible to be that good all the time. Even on his bad days, he's better than most."

"That's exactly what people say about me," he smirked.

I laughed. "Is it, though? I mean, is anyone really saying that?"

"Ouch," he said. "I guess just me."

I grabbed my bag from the floor just inside my cubby and slung it over my shoulder. "I'm going to go home, order pizza, and watch Hallmark movies for the rest of the day."

"And I'm thankful that you didn't invite me," he said, laughing.

"Oh, you're more than welcome to join me once you're done here."

"I'll probably go home and try to sleep. I haven't

gotten much this week, and I know this weekend is going to kick my ass."

"If you change your mind, you know where to find me," I said, although I knew he wouldn't. Probably best for now. I wasn't ready for anything more than this casual flirting, and he seemed to understand that instinctively. Marcy met him last Saturday and told me if I didn't want him, she had dibs. I didn't know what I wanted, but I was curious to see where it was going, and he made me feel good.

After eighteen months of feeling like I was going through hell, it was nice to look forward to something again. Everything finally felt like it was falling into place, and my only fear was that somehow it would get taken away from me.

The skaters, the program, even Mack... I was still holding my breath with worry that something would go wrong and ruin it all.

Midwestern Sectional Championships

Halfway through Addie's short program, I felt my phone buzz in my pocket, and I knew it was Stephanie who was streaming it online at home. My heart was thudding against my chest, and I wanted this moment over and to last forever, simultaneously. She simply had never skated so beautifully in competition, or ever in my opinion. The fact that she was able to do this now made every horrible moment this past year worth it. As she completed her final spin and ended the program, I noticed Will in the corner of the rink jumping up and down, arms in the air.

Addie skated a clean short program, and I could see tears on her face as she curtseyed to the crowd and judges. Her hands covered her mouth as she skated towards me and fell into my arms.

"You did it," I whispered in her ear. "You just did it."

Her body began to shake in my arms, her nerves and adrenaline catching up to her. She peeled herself off of me and wiped the tears away as we found our way up to the kiss and cry. She was in the first group, so I knew the score would be good, but we would just have to wait and see how everyone else performed. It would be a waiting game, but one of the best kind, when you could relax in the fact that you did your absolute best.

Her score—68.3—was the highest she had ever scored in a short program. Ever. And I was tackle-hugged sitting next to her as she squealed with joy.

Cloud nine was the only way I could describe what she was feeling, because I felt it too. I remembered my phone and pulled it out to find twenty text messages from our group—the last one from Steph: She did it!!!!!!!!!!!

Once we got back to the locker room, I snapped a selfie with Addie and sent it to Marcy, with the caption 'best program score, ever.'

Addie was talking a mile a minute as she took one skate off, then the other, meticulously drying each blade before putting covers on them. I wanted to scream 'hurry up!' so we could get out and see the rest of the skaters, but she also needed this time to process what just happened. She pulled on joggers and her Skateland warm-up jacket.

"Are you ready?" she asked me.

"Umm, sure," I said. "Let's go find your mom and Will."

She picked the last locker room at the end of the hall for privacy—she always wanted her space at competitions. When we walked out, we saw two things at once: Will stopped in his tracks at the hall entrance, and Nicole and Jonathan breaking from an embrace when they heard us open the door. The phrase "it all happened at once" came to mind, and I felt I truly understood what it meant now.

I looked from Jonathan to Nicole, and my mouth gaped open. Addie's entire face fell into a stony glare, and she walked towards Will, who was looking at me for guidance. It was a matter of five seconds, but it felt like ten minutes.

"Addie, wait," her mom said, following behind her. "Adeline—*stop*."

Addie stopped and turned, her eyes cold. "You said it was *over*."

"It was—it is," her mom stammered. "I was just coming to see you because I was so proud of you."

None of this made sense to me, since parents aren't even allowed down here during competition. "How did you even get through?" I asked.

"Jonathan saw me and led me back," Nicole admitted. "He knew I wanted to see you."

I looked at Jonathan, still unsure of what I just saw. His eyes were downcast, his head dropped down.

"I don't even want to see you right now," Addie said. "You two said it was over—I trusted you!" She walked away and a concerned Will followed, leaving me with Nicole and Jonathan.

"Can we take this into the locker room?" I asked them, opening the door for them to follow.

"Jonathan, what the *hell* is going on? What did she

mean she thought it was over?"

He looked to Nicole, and she nodded.

"Last year, right before the short program at Nationals, Addie caught us. I had already made plans to leave, and we were going to end it, but she still saw us and knew what was going on," he explained.

"But where?" I asked. "Where did she find you?"

Nicole's head dropped to her hands.

"Are you kidding me? She caught you guys in *bed*?"

"She was supposed to be heading to warm up before her short but she had forgotten her headphones," Nicole choked out. "We knew we had about forty-five minutes before either of us needed to be at the rink."

"Oh my God," I whispered. "This was why she looked so spaced out that night," I said, remembering watching her practice-ice. "You never answered my texts that night."

"What exactly was I supposed to say? Sorry for that Nat—Addie caught me screwing her mom? Not sure that you could've helped the situation."

"Is this why you left in the first place?"

His eyes slid to Nicole's, her mouth in a tight line. She slowly closed her eyes and shook her head slightly. "You might as well get it all out there," she said. "Or I will."

He sat on the bench and leaned his head against the cement wall. He took a deep breath and began. "Nicole and I had been... seeing each other for almost a year when she figured out I had been embezzling money from the Club." He leaned on his elbows, head dropped. "She gave me the choice to leave or she would've turned me in."

My mind was spinning, and the entire time I was listening to him, all I could focus on was my phone buzzing in my pocket.

"Addie doesn't know about the money—she believes, like everyone else, that I followed my wife to Cleveland. In truth, my wife and I split shortly before Nationals. We're going through a divorce now."

My mouth dropped open.

"That's why you went off the grid completely," I whispered. It was all falling into place. "And this is why you've treated me so badly—you were afraid of me finding out the truth."

"The truth coming out wouldn't help anyone now, and only hurt Addie more than she has been."

"But don't you think I deserved to understand what I was dealing with? I've spent this entire year wondering why she couldn't skate a clean program, and here you two are, hiding behind everyone's backs." I was furious with both of them for putting me in the middle of their mess.

"I have never seen her skate like she did tonight," Nicole whispered. "It was so incredible to see."

Jonathan looked at his watch. "I know this is bad timing, but I need to find my skater and get ready for the next group." He stood and looked at Nicole. "I'm so sorry this happened again."

"Are you, though?" I snapped. "Or is this just your way of getting into Addie's head again?"

His face dropped. "No matter what you think of me, I would never do that to her."

I wasn't convinced. Clearly I knew nothing about this man standing in front of me who I used to idolize. I blew out a breath and shook my head.

"Go, get out of here, and don't you ever talk to me or Addie again. If you do, I'll go public with all of it."

He nodded and walked out of the locker room without another word.

I pulled out my phone and noticed a text from Will.

Will: We're outside rn. Can you meet us?

Me: I'll be right there.

I slid my phone back in my pocket and grabbed my bag. "I don't really know what to say. I imagine you've lived with this guilt for a year, but I will need some time to process this," I said. "What I don't understand is how you knew what he was doing—you went so far as to threaten him to leave—and *still* chose to sleep with him one last time. That makes no sense to me."

Her chin quivered as she stared at her hands. "You're right about one thing... I have lived with this mistake for almost a year and wake up every day wondering why I did that." She met my eyes and shrugged. "I knew what was best for everyone else, but I couldn't help myself. I loved him... a part of me *still* does. "

I nodded, knowing I could question her all night, and I'd never understand. "My only concern is for Addie and getting her through the next program and Nationals. If you're not on board with that, I need to know that now." I stood and looked down at this shell of a woman.

She nodded, her face drained of any emotion. "We never meant to hurt her."

"And yet you did. Twice, now."

I didn't wait for a response. Will skated in two hours, and we would have to make sure he was mentally ready for this. If ever there was a time that I wished Marcy was here with me. I thought we could all use some of her magic right about now.

What Would Marcy Do?

I pushed through the double doors at the front of the rink into the bright sunshine. Shielding my eyes, I scanned the sidewalk for Addie and Will. Will's SUV was parked in the front row with the trunk door open, and Addie sat cross-legged in the back. Her eyes were red, and Will's face was drawn. Drawing in a deep breath, I sat on the edge of the car next to Addie and rubbed her knee.

"This was not in the coaches' instruction manual," I said with a sympathetic smile. "I have no idea what to even say, but is there anything you need right now?"

Her eyes continued to stare at a stone on the ground and a smile appeared on her face, but only out of obligation. "I really thought this would all go away if I didn't think about it," she said, her voice cracking. "Even after I found out he was coaching in Cleveland, I thought as long as I don't see them together, I'd be able to forget."

My mind flashed back to the video I still had of them fighting in the hallway. It all began to make sense in light of the last twenty minutes.

"Will—do you want to go in and start getting

warmed up? You still have a job to do tonight."

He nodded and handed Addie his keys. I stood so he could get his bag out. "We will see you in there shortly."

Her eyes followed him towards the front entrance.

"What can I do?" I asked. "I already told Jonathan he can't speak to you, but I don't know how to help you through this."

"I just want to go home." She sighed. "I don't want to do this anymore." Her eyes met mine, pools of tears in the corners. "Do I have to skate tomorrow?"

"You are the boss right now," I said. "If you want to bag it, I totally get it, but that's when you let him win. You just had the skate of your life tonight—we don't even know the results yet, and I would hate for you to regret throwing that away."

She closed her eyes and slowly shook her head no. "I'm sorry, Nat, but I just don't care right now. None of it matters to me."

My heart thudded in my chest, knowing I needed to help her and couldn't. "I wish you had come to me last year when this all went down. I could've helped more, and we wouldn't be here now."

"I didn't even tell Will, and my mom pretended nothing happened," she said. "What a joke."

In my head, my mantra became 'what would Marcy do,' but my heart was sinking back into the disaster comfort zone it knew so well. It didn't matter how much progress I had made this year, life would always reflect my biggest fears, and like Addie, I didn't know how much more I could take.

What *would* Marcy do?

"Tell me about your short program," I said. She needed to remember why she was here.

She blinked twice and looked at me. "What place did I get?" It was as if she had forgotten altogether why she was here.

I shrugged and smiled. "I have no idea," I said. "It might still be going on."

I looked at my watch and noticed I had a bajillion message alerts. My phone showed the coach group was responsible for one hundred and eight of them. A single text from Marcy showed a heart, prayer hands, and a fist bump. One from Mack telling me to call later tonight. The last one made me smile.

"Tell me how you felt after your program. Give me three words to describe how you felt in your ending position."

She closed her eyes and tipped her head back against the seat behind her. "Elated. Relieved. And proud."

"Highlight of my coaching career," I said. "I don't think I've ever been so excited watching a program."

My phone buzzed with a text from Will. "She's in first!!!!!"

I held it up to Addie, and a slow smile spread across her face.

"*You* did that," I said. "And I know you don't have

a clue what you want to do yet, but just remember when you go to bed tonight… you fought for this and made this happen. And now it's Will's turn. I'm going to head in and get him ready—you can join, or you can stay out here."

"Do you mind if I hang out with you guys right now?"

"This whole energy drain will have to change if you do," I said, circling my hand in front of her body. "Good vibes only."

She nodded. "I can muster up some good vibes from somewhere. I'm going to tell my mom to go back to the hotel, and I'll ride back with either you or Will… is that okay?"

"My job is to take care of you—if that makes you feel better, then go for it. I do think the three of us will have to have a conversation next week, though."

She rolled her eyes as only a teenager could.

"And I warned Jonathan not to ever speak to you again," I continued. "He is not the person I thought he was, and we are not putting up with his BS anymore."

We walked through the front doors, and the results were posted on the right wall in the lobby. Addie walked over to confirm what she already knew. We took the steps down to the lower level where the warm-up area and locker rooms were. I scanned the area to make sure Jonathan wasn't down there, and spotted Will jumping rope in the corner. He saw us and smiled, but never broke his quick rhythm. He could jump rope for days, if needed.

Addie took a moment to text her mom about her plan to stay with Will, and then spent the next half hour warming up with Will. Didn't matter to either one of them that she already did this once today, competed, and had her life blow up again. This was a warm-up for Will and therapy for Addie. They giggled and tried to outdo the other one, Will easily winning any contest Addie attempted. At one point, I snapped a picture of them, both lost in the moment. Will looking at Addie, a twinkle in his eye. She was looking down, but her smile was confident again. I didn't know if they would ever turn into anything romantic—in fact, I hoped they didn't—but Will was her person. That much was clear to me. He was the one person who made everything better, and I knew he would have to help if she were going to continue. She would have to continue to work on herself, but he would also be a part of the process somehow.

"Why don't the two of you stretch it out before he has to get his skates on," I said. "He's in the first group, and I'm going to go make a couple calls upstairs."

"Aye, aye, Cap'n." Will saluted. "If you don't come back, Adds can take me through."

"Huh, nice to know I'm so dispensable," I said, miffed.

His eyes grew wide, and I winked. Addie slugged him. "Like she'd not come back."

Walking upstairs, I dialed Marcy. I needed some

reassurance that I handled everything okay today. I prayed she had something enlightening to say right now, because this rollercoaster I had been on today was starting to make me queasy.

"Yo," she answered. "Tell me there's good news."

I smiled, knowing this was exactly what I needed. The back of the lobby was empty and had some benches along the wall. If someone were to take a picture of me right now, it would be the same look that Addie had on her face downstairs. Eyes downcast, but the smile coming from the inside out. Marcy's calm reassurance was everything I needed, and gratitude welled up in my chest. I told her about my mantra, and she made me promise to keep saying it—that it worked like a charm.

After we disconnected, I walked back downstairs, determined to make sure Will got the preparation and focus he needed. The scandal we survived didn't have any space with us tonight and needed to be left alone.

This job was never done.

LESSON 3

*Our greatest glory is not in never falling,
but in rising every time we fall.*

~Confucius

What's Your Why?

Saturday mornings were always a little crazy at the rink. You had the figure skaters early in the morning, and then the hockey players took over the rest of the weekend. Scrimmages, games, tournaments, high school hockey—all of it was one giant mess of smelly, loud boys. Addie, Will, Marcy, and I were locked inside our ballet studio, just off the lobby, and while we could hear all the sounds of the hockey world, we were in our own bubble. The ballet studio was my favorite room in the entire building. It was calm. Soothing colors of cream and pale blue made you want to take a deep breath as soon as you entered.

I was sitting on the floor, back against the wall next to the space heater. This morning was exceptionally cold in the rink, and I had stopped feeling my toes about an hour ago. We were doing our weekly recap before she went into the visualization part, and I was observing, listening, and trying to process what I could do to help them. My job was only to take the information in—never to give my opinion or thoughts.

"Will—what was your win for the week?" Marcy was the perfect combination of confidant and Yoda.

Wisdom exuded from her when she was in her zone.

He glanced at Addie before answering. "I think last weekend was… tricky for all of us," he said, regarding Mids. "I always knew I could separate my problems better than most when I stepped on the ice. It's like the second I'm on the ice, nothing else matters, but that night was the first time I was ever really aware of how much that helps me."

"It's a gift to compartmentalize like you do," Marcy said. "A lot of people can't do it, and their minds end up taking over."

"It's more of a zone for me," he said. "Sometimes, I don't even notice the audience until I finish."

"I would kill to have that ability," Addie said. "Instead, I have this head that gives me the play-by-play of everything I've ever done wrong."

"From what I hear, you were pretty incredible last weekend, though," Marcy said and winked.

Addie's face melted into a smile filled with pride. "I can't remember ever feeling so free as I did on my short program. It was the highest of highs." Immediately, her face dropped.

"Until it wasn't," Marcy finished. "Talk to me about your long program." I was relieved Marcy didn't push a conversation about Jonathan.

"My long is the only thing that has saved me this year," she said. "I was first going into the long, and I didn't want to blow it. Even with all the other crap going on, I had to constantly remember why I still wanted to go to Nationals."

"Knowing our 'why' is the key that unlocks everything," Marcy said. "What *is* your why?"

"I don't think I have ever been like Will—I always have something I'm worried about or wanting to fix. I remember the first year I came here, I was so worried that if I skated badly my mom would make me switch rinks again. And all I wanted was to stay here and make it home. Every competition was a disaster that year. Now, I just want to prove to myself that I can do it—I'm done skating for other people."

"I love that. You're a classic overthinker," Marcy confirmed. "One thing you don't know is more people are like you than Will. Most people have a running dialog in our heads that is working against us. The goal is to get that voice working for you—then you can harness all that power towards your why. Will—what is your why? What makes you come here every day and push yourself so hard?"

"Olympics," he said. "Ever since I was little, I have only wanted to get to the Olympics."

"Impressive." Marcy nodded. "Let's make that happen."

Marcy chatted a bit more, then moved into the visualization part with them, and I closed my eyes as well, half listening and half pondering what my why was. I knew I had to say yes to all of this back in January, but now it was my life and there was no way was I giving it up. I hadn't ever seen myself as a coach for elite skaters or the skating director, but now that I'd done it all year, there was no turning back. But *why*?

I turned my focus to what Marcy was saying and tried to let go of the nagging thought that wasn't letting go of my attention. *Why*, it whispered to me. Did I even have a why? My breathing slowed down to match the rhythm she was setting for them. She wanted them to visualize something else today—something that had been giving them problems on or off the ice, and my mind focused on Jonathan. I smiled slightly and tried to shake the thought from my head. The last thing I wanted to think about was that lying scumbag. He was smiling at me, the crinkles in the corners of his eyes tightening in that charming way they did when he was joking about something.

We were so close, and yet I'm not sure I ever really knew him. He was having an affair with a parent, embezzling money from the club, and got divorced without me suspecting anything. I didn't know if that meant he was devious or that I was blinded by what I wanted to see. And then it hit me... he was the illusion. I only saw what he wanted me to see, and he played me so well. My mind jumped to watching Addie on practice-ice at Nationals last year—how drawn and distant she looked. She had just found out two of the people she trusted most in this world had lied to her about everything.

My eyes snapped open. Marcy noticed my shift in energy and raised her eyebrows at me.

Addie was my why. I'm not sure how I didn't see it before, but it was crystal clear to me now. She was so much like me—the doomsday attitude, the struggle to get everything just right, and the need to rise above the constant anxiety that seemed to seep into her everyday life. She spent half the year trying to push me away, probably because she could sense I was as lost as she was, or she was afraid I'd figure out how to help her. Either way, I knew that moment from Nationals last year was why I was busting my butt every day. I wanted to fix her, even though I knew Marcy would argue that we can only fix ourselves—no one else. If the best I could do was give her tools to help get out of this hole she was in, then my job would be complete. I didn't care what place she came in—only that she was happy with how she skated. At the end of the day, that's all that really mattered. Students would come and go. The glitter and glory would fade away. But helping her figure this out was what truly mattered to me.

Come to think of it, what Marcy was doing was something I'd like to start introducing to other skaters. Giving skaters the tools to help themselves under stressful situations was giving them life skills they'd never get anywhere else. My mind exploded with ideas of off-ice classes, and competition training that didn't look like anything we had ever done before.

I smiled and closed my eyes, trying to harness the racing thoughts pinging through my brain. Matching my breath again, I focused solely on the sound of Marcy's voice, calm and steady, but found my energy wanting to run down to the office and take notes. Opening my eyes, I found all three of them staring at me.

"What the heck?" Marcy said. "You're killing our calm vibe over here."

My laughter echoed throughout the small room. "I just had a couple revelations—I'm so sorry."

"Care to share?"

"Honestly, yes!" I exclaimed. "This—what you're doing is exactly something I want to start incorporating with *all* of the skaters. Start them early and get them learning how to stay calm and visualize the perfect program, and understand why they're even on the ice at all."

All three continued to stare politely at me.

"Wow, Nat," Will said after a beat. "You visualize way better than I do."

Addie giggled. "No doubt—I was just trying to get through my step sequence without looking tired."

I stood and started pacing. "If you don't mind, I'm going down to the office to take a couple notes while it's fresh in my mind."

She shook her head and smiled. "Go ahead. It's great to see you so excited about something for a change."

I gave her a stink eye and bolted from the room, hearing the lock behind me as I walked away. I knew she was going to have them try one more time without me in there. Mack sat at a check-in table in the center of the lobby by the entrance doors. He noticed me walking in that direction and smiled. My stomach flip-flopped, and I didn't know when I'd ever stop feeling like I was twelve around him. A part of me hoped never—this was not a feeling I ever wanted to go away. This feeling was a weak-kneed yes, and I was ready for it.

But first, I had to take notes on how I wanted to change the model of the skating program. It wasn't just adding Marcy to our training—my mind started racing to so much more. Once I became clear, I'd see what Steph and Dana thought, but this gut feeling was too big to ignore.

It felt right.

It felt like yes…

Santa and the Mrs.

"You have *got* to be kidding me," I said, looking at a Mrs. Claus costume. "No way, no how, am I going to wear that thing."

"But Janie thought it would be great for the kids," Roger said. Even as he said it, he was holding back a smile.

"Then Janie can wear it," I said. "So, Santa and Mrs. Claus are hockey players... only fitting for this rink." It was a dig, and Roger's expression dropped.

"You know that's not true," he said. "I have done everything possible to keep you with as much ice as possible."

He wasn't wrong. Roger had been more than fair with ice time, and I finally involved the coaches in understanding the system and how the ice was distributed. Once they understood the numbers, their goal was also their responsibility, and I didn't feel like the battle was mine to win or lose. Hell, it wasn't even a battle anymore.

Mack walked into the office, looking like the cat who just ate the canary.

"Oh, look, there's Santa now." Janie giggled from

her office.

"Ho ho ho," Mack boomed.

"Seriously," I said. "You all need to find a Mrs. Claus."

"You won't be my Mrs.?" he asked. "I thought the rule was you had to say yes this year."

My eyes grew wide. "You can't use that against me."

"Oh, but I just did," he said, taking the hat from the package and placing it on my head. Janie snorted as he took the wire-rimmed glasses from the package and slid them onto my nose. Next, he held up the dress, and his eyes grew wide.

"Uhhh, where is the rest of that costume?" I barked. "I can't go on the ice wearing *that*. The parents will have a fit!"

Janie fell to the floor in a puddle of laughter. "Oh. My. Gawd," she said. "I ordered the wrong one."

Even Roger was doubled over, holding his stomach. "I have to agree with Natalie on this one," he said, wiping his eyes. "We cannot let you wear that—I'll be sued... for *something*."

Mack wiggled his eyebrows but set the costume on my desk. "Well, we still have the wig, hat, and glasses. Surely, you have a red sweater or something."

"I seem to recall that we did just fine last year with just Santa," I resisted.

"You wouldn't want Santa to be sad and lonely without his wife, would you?"

"Yes. Yes, I do," I said, sitting in my chair.

I fired up my computer and opened my email. Mack hadn't moved from beside my chair, and I felt his presence next to me. I'd know he was there if I were blindfolded.

He tapped my shoulder, and his look said '*Well…?*'

"Fine," I said, loud enough for everyone to hear. "I'll be Mrs. Claus, but I'm picking the costume."

Janie cheered. Roger chuckled. Mack took the naughty Mrs. Claus costume. "My job is done for the day," he said, walking around to his cubicle.

"Ha ha," I retorted. "Janie, where did you even find that costume?"

"Where do I get everything? Amazon," she said. "Although, I had two picked out, and must have chosen the wrong one."

"Huh, weird how that happened." I didn't believe her for a second. She was a professional Amazon shopper and knew exactly what she was doing. She kept her eyes on her screen but bit her lip and shrugged.

"How about this," I said for everyone to hear. "How about I do Mrs. Santa for learn-to-skate, and we have just Santa during the show and mini-mite hockey players?"

"Negative," Mack yelled back. "You're in for the long haul. When I get dressed, you get dressed."

I started to stammer, trying to talk my way out of it.

"You can't say no, remember?"

My head dropped to my arms on my desk. "I

remember," I mumbled. I'd have to kick Marcy's ass for this one.

"You two should make up a number for the show," Janie said. Roger's eyes grew as wide as his smile.

"Am I being punk'd? Is that what's going on here?"

"I take offense to that," Mack yelled.

"No offense to you, but I feel like you're all having fun at my expense," I said.

"I wholeheartedly admit to having fun at your expense," Janie said. "What can I say? Christmas spirit and all that." She waved her hand around her overly decorated office.

"You and your Christmas spirit need to pick on someone else. I need to get on the ice," I said, noticing the time. I grabbed my coat off the hook and headed towards the door.

"Think about what you want to skate to, Mrs. Claus," Roger yelled.

Stephanie was walking in when I exited the office. "Mrs. Claus?"

"Don't ask," I sighed. "They're trying to torture me."

"If Mack is Santa, then hell yes, you're going to be Mrs. Claus," she said. "Wait—why doesn't she have a name? Why does she have to be Mrs.?"

"Deep thoughts," I said. "I'll have to ponder that one."

"Maybe he'll kiss you under the mistletoe," she teased. "Please tell me there's mistletoe hanging somewhere in the office."

"Oh, for God's sake," I snapped. "Enough about Mrs. Freaking Claus!"

She bit back laughter, and then both of us busted up.

"You gotta get a grip," she said once we calmed down. She unlocked the coaches room, and we walked in to find Lydia already in there.

"Oh, good, Natalie," she said. "I've been meaning to ask you about Jonathan. I heard he's coaching at Cleveland, and I wondered why you didn't tell anyone."

My eyes darted to Stephanie, who had been sworn to silence. "Uh, gee, Lydia," I stalled. "I don't know—guess I just forgot. We really didn't have much to say."

"That's not what I heard," she said.

My head snapped up. "What do you mean? What have you heard?"

"I heard you had words with him because he talked to Addie and Will without your *permission*." She said permission like it was vinegar.

"I did no such thing," I said. "And honestly, it's none of your business if I do or don't talk with Jonathan."

"I guess, I would just hate to see another coach leave Skateland and go teach down there."

Stephanie looked at her incredulously. "What are you even talking about? Natalie isn't going anywhere, especially not to coach with Jonathan."

"She always seemed to be in his back pocket before,

and he did leave you the best students…"

"Because she's a great coach," Steph said.

Lydia rolled her eyes. "I sure hope that Zamboni driver is on time today. Always such a problem."

She walked out, and I looked at Steph bug-eyed. "What the hell was that about?"

"And why would she think you were leaving?"

I stood to make sure the door was closed and locked. "All I can think of is someone told her I had been talking with Jonathan and Nicole in the locker room. If you didn't know why, then it might have looked suspicious otherwise."

"I still can't believe that was happening last year," she said.

Dana didn't know, and I only told Steph about the affair—not about the embezzling funds part.

"I can't believe poor Addie caught them," I said. "No wonder she hadn't trusted anyone this year."

"Until you." She smiled. "You've saved her, and whatever Marcy is doing with her, it's working. I haven't seen her skate this well in a long time—well, since a year ago."

The clock on the wall told us the session had started. As soon as we walked out we could hear the bass from the speakers in rink one. There were only five skaters in this session, but they did their edge work as a group, as Katy Perry serenaded them. Will gave me the double guns as he finessed his way by us.

Steph laughed. "That kid is too much," she said.

"It's not fair for one skater to have all the charm in the rink."

"Ingrid is a close second behind him," I said. "That girl says the funniest things in the morning. She's full of useless information that will win her millions on Jeopardy someday."

"Oh my God, yes."

We stepped onto the ice to begin our lessons, the skaters lined up and stretching at the boards. Lydia's words and accusations were gnawing a hole in my brain.

Too many secrets. Too many people were aware something was going on. I didn't like the anxiety building in my chest over Jonathan. I would have to push it down to move forward. My responsibility was to myself and doing what I could to help those around me.

And all it took was a "What's up, Nats?" from Will to regain my focus.

I nodded in my head towards the center of the rink. "Go."

Santa Baby

I had been running late all morning: getting to the rink, with lessons, and now with final tasks for the holiday show. This show was less stressful as the skaters were in charge of their own costumes and programs. As coaches, we would oversee and help them if they need it, but for most of them, it was a time for them to create and choreograph their own programs.

Plus, they got to choose their own groups or skate solo if they wanted. It resulted in show death at times, but for the most part, the joy of skating was what surfaced. It was fun, playful, and the music definitely put you in the Christmas spirit.

Unless it was your job to direct it.

Then, it was skating order, programs, collecting music, and fitting it all in on a busy Saturday afternoon in the middle of hockey season. Chaos, in other words. Running behind, even in my own mind, made everything feel the opposite of holiday spirit.

Three different skaters texted this morning, needing the order changed because of prior commitments. This meant all the programs I printed yesterday had to be reprinted with the new order. Luckily, Amanda scheduled extra front desk staff today and they were always more than willing to help with some of the creative stuff.

I hadn't seen Mack most of the day, but knew he was here. Roger was out of town, and he was the manager today. Hockey games were going on in rink two, and I was starting to watch the clock, waiting for him. As Santa, he needed to get dressed and be ready for the opening of the show. The two of us would skate out, do a little dance, pose, and exit. Simple, quick, and the skaters were way too excited that I was Mrs. Claus. I found red leggings at Old Navy, and Dana had a red, puffy coat. Paired with a white scarf and the costume hat and glasses, it was perfect.

But I needed Santa. We were on the ice in twenty minutes. I looked at the Santa outfit hanging on Roger's door and picked up the walkie-talkie.

"Yo—Santa," I said. "You have to get dressed."

"Is this my nagging wife?" he replied.

The front desk girls giggled.

"Fifteen minutes," I said. "We're on the ice in fifteen minutes."

He walked through the door, smirking. "Too much coffee this morning?"

"It's no secret I like everything to be on time," I said. "A little consideration would be nice."

He leaned on the doorway of my cubicle. "Is this what marriage does to you?"

More giggles.

"Will you stop that? You need to get dressed." I pointed to his costume.

"I'm going to need help once I get my skates on," he said, sliding his coat off. "Last year was a little awkward with Jonathan helping. Roger even took pictures."

Tension released in my shoulders as I giggled at the visual. "I brought two pillows, but we'll see if we can make it work with one."

"Two? How much are you feeding me throughout the year?"

Giggles.

"Can we just get on with this? Go!"

He saluted and went into Roger's office with the costume, shutting the door behind him. I took the last of the programs to the front table, decorated with lights and tinsel, then ran to the coaches room to grab my skates. Several parents greeted me, hugged me, and wanted to talk with me. It felt rude to rush away, but the clock in my head was ticking.

I noticed Mack poking his head out of Roger's office as soon as I walked back into the office. "What are you doing?" I whisper-shouted.

He flashed a smile. "I need some help with my pants."

My stomach dropped. Suddenly, I felt like the twelve-year-old again. "Okay, do I have time to get my skates on first?"

"Nope, not if you want me to be on time."

I took a deep breath and blew it out slowly, like Marcy taught me. '*When you do it like this, no one will notice your stress.*'

Grabbing the pillows, I let myself into Roger's office. "Why are the lights off?"

"Do you want everyone in the office to see me in my underwear? I believe there are Safe Sport rules about that." He smirked.

"But it's okay for me to see?" I joked. Hell, I'd probably pay to see him in his underwear.

"I trust we are both adults here. Plus, you need to stuff my shirt with those stupid pillows."

"Okay, let's do this so I can get my skates on."

He was a good six inches taller with his skates on and towered over me. My heart started racing as I grabbed one of the pillows. He lifted his white T-shirt, and his breath caught when my cold hands touched his torso, trying to hold the pillow in place. He cleared his throat, and I became very aware of the sound of his breath.

He let go of his shirt and lifted my chin, and my heart thudded in my chest.

"You okay with this?" he whispered.

I nodded into his hand as he pulled me closer. He paused an inch from my lips, his breath warming me from the inside out.

"Yes," I whispered.

He smiled before closing the gap and softly brushing my lips with his. He pulled me tighter with one arm around my waist as he melted me with every touch of his lips on mine. My mind exploded with fireworks—it was all true what they said. And even though I had felt this before, it had been over a year of living in a void of any human contact. I leaned into him, and a small groan escaped from me, causing him to pull me in tighter.

A sharp knock on the door jerked both of us to reality. I looked at my watch.

"Dammit!" I shouted. "We have to go!"

I tried to fix my hair and pulled down my coat, but I knew we had just been busted.

"Wow," was all he said.

"No, not wow," I snapped. "Put your belt on and finish up. You have two minutes."

I pulled the door open, and Dana and Steph stood there, smiling.

"Ummm, the Zamboni is almost off the ice," she said. "Go figure, he's on time today."

"I'm coming," I said. "Can you make sure Santa is dressed?"

"Isn't that what you were supposed to be doing?" Steph said. Dana snorted.

"Guys, c'mon, I have to get my skates on."

"You get a pass now, because of the time, but there will be details later."

I heard Mack chuckle behind the door. My cheeks flamed bright red to match my outfit. "Here—I'll get you fixed up while you tie your skates," Dana said, going through my makeup bag in my purse. She found a bright lip gloss and swiped it on my lips, then dusted a little powder on my chin and forehead. "Not sure I can get the red out of your face right now."

"I feel like I'm completely overheated," I complained.

"I bet you do," she snickered.

She slid my hat on and placed the glasses on the bridge of my nose.

She stood up, and Mack followed Steph out of the office. "Santa is in the house," she said.

"Ho-ho-hoooo," he bellowed in a deep voice. "Mrs. Claus is looking hot."

I shot him a look and covered my face. "I wish I could disappear," I mumbled.

"You can later," Steph said, looking at the clock. "Right now, you two need to get your asses on the ice."

Mack grabbed my hand, and we ran through the lobby to get into rink one. My mind raced to the last time I felt this alive in anything. He squeezed my hand as we made our way to the ice.

"I hope you remember what we're doing, because I totally forgot," he whispered as he waved to the crowd.

"We'll just figure it out as we go," I said, leading him around the perimeter of the rink.

He glanced at me and his eyes softened when they met mine.

"Yes, we will," he said.

Birthday Dinner

The "death by chocolate" dessert we ordered came with a candle and a group of waiters singing happy birthday off-key to me. Marcy's eyes lit up by the festivities she had planned all along.

"Happy birthday toooooo youuuuu," she sang the final note like Pavarotti while I hung my head in embarrassment.

"Make a wish!" she exclaimed. "Before the candle melts the cake."

I closed my eyes and sent my wish up to the universe to be heard and answered. Then, I blew out the candle.

"You're not gonna tell me what that was, are you?" she asked, digging into the decadent dessert.

"Not a chance," I said, following her lead. The cake was warm and gooey with a white chocolate sauce drizzled over the top.

"Oh. My. God. This might be the best thing I've eaten in a year."

"Might I remind you that we had takeout and Double Stuf Oreos last year," I said.

"Oh, I remember last year. In fact, I remember

everything about this past year."

I had made it through my year of embracing yes, and while I couldn't argue with how much better my life was than a year ago, I was secretly happy that I wasn't required to say yes any longer. I had the choice now.

"Any regrets?" she asked.

"Hmm, great question," I said, sipping wine. "I don't think so, though. While it was the most challenging year, it was also the most rewarding."

"It was pretty amazing to watch it all unfold," she said, a dreamy look in her eye.

"Have you heard from any agents yet?"

Marcy had sent her book proposal to about thirty literary agents to try and get signed. I was beginning to feel like this part of her process was harder than writing.

"A couple rejections, but the majority are still out there," she said, scrunching up her face. "If it happens, it happens. I'm not holding my breath, and still moving forward on starting a side business for coaching virtually."

"I love that you're doing that—you truly have a gift," I said. "I'm glad we got you when we did, otherwise you might not have time for us."

"You will always have first priority," she said. "Besides, working with athletes is so rewarding. I can see why you love coaching them."

"I'll be curious to see how the competitive side rates this year, now that we're incorporating the mental training along with their regular activities."

"More than anything else, I want to help create well-balanced people—not just athletes," she said.

"Roger and Mack were asking about what you were doing with the skaters the other day," I said. "Seemed interested in maybe having you work with teams, if you're up for it."

"Are you kidding? That would be amazing."

"That's what I told them already." I laughed. "They weren't for sure, but definitely interested. Mack might want to sit in on one of your sessions with the skaters."

"Sounds good," she said. She reached down and pulled out two beautifully wrapped gifts in light pink paper with black ribbon. "It appears to be that time of the evening where we celebrate you."

"Oh no," I said, moving the cake aside. "Please tell me there are no challenges this year."

"Nope," she said. "You passed that test with flying colors, but you need to keep growing. Open the small one first."

The ribbon slid off easily, and I peeled back the tape on each end. I hated ripping paper if I didn't have to, wanting to savor this moment.

A tiny card lay inside the box with Marcy's handwriting written in blue ink.

"We have this hope as an anchor for the soul, firm and secure. Hebrews 6:19"

I lifted the card to find a beautiful silver bracelet with an anchor charm attached. It wasn't like anything

I had ever seen, and a smile spread across my face.

"Oh, my," I said. "Marce, it's gorgeous." I slid it on and admired it on my wrist.

"Okay, now you know what's coming next, but hopefully it's still a surprise."

I knew what was coming—another self-help book from the latest guru she was following, but the package was a little bigger than the usual book size.

Peeling back the paper, I found a softcover three ring binder. I shot her a look as I lifted the cover and squealed.

"*Living with Intention* by Marcy Johnston" was on the inside cover. I covered my hand over my mouth, and tears welled up in my eyes.

"Don't cry, for Pete's sake," she said. "Other than an editor I hired on the side, you're the only one to have a full copy."

"I can't believe how real this is," I stammered. "You really wrote a book."

She nodded and a smile covered her face. "I guess I did, didn't I? I still can't believe how much we've both done this past year."

"Yeah, but I was forced," I said. "You just did this because you wanted to—I mean, who just writes a book because they always wanted to? Most people just talk about things they want to do."

"That is the primary reason for the book—it is about moving from that dream phase into reality. I watched you do it all year."

"I'm speechless," I said. "And I have never been more proud of you."

"Well, when I have a talk show, you can be my fly girl."

I choked on my water. "Ummm, hard pass," I said. "But I'll be your DJ like Twitch is for Ellen."

"Actually, from what I've heard, I think Will might be in for that position."

"Good call, he's brilliant with music," I agreed. "Okay, then your assistant. Or the one you send out to give away millions."

She was laughing now. "Whatever you want works for me. Producer might be the best position for you though. You have a way of making things happen."

"Here's hoping," I said. Nationals were in two weeks—we would leave a week from Wednesday—and the pressure was building in the rink. Addie and Will were the only ones going, and excitement and nerves were high.

"Addie and Will are both on track," she reassured me. "I'm more worried about you."

"Honestly, it hasn't hit me yet," I said. "Mids is the highest competition I've been to, so I'm not sure what to expect with the pressure as high as it will be."

"Your only job is to stay focused on yourself and skaters. Nothing else. Outside forces will be strong, but you just need to put blinders on."

"And keep you on speed dial."

"That too," she agreed. "Truthfully, that's not a

horrible idea. I'll make sure Will and Addie program my number in so they can reach out when they want."

"I've been thinking about Hell Week and maybe changing it up a bit for them."

She shoved the final bite of cake in her mouth and closed her eyes. "Give me a moment to savor that," she said. She chewed slowly and wiped her mouth with her napkin. "Worth every calorie. Okay—Hell Week. What do you have in mind?"

"I'm not sure yet… just a feeling that I want to go for a different vibe other than 'let's see if we can reach your breaking point before competition.'"

She laughed easily. "Why did he ever start Hell Week? I mean, I get the final push before you taper, but mentally it's tough to keep it together when perfection is the expectation. There are so many other ways to get them to work hard without breaking them down mentally."

"I do want to push them, but more physically, and work on the mental in positive ways," I said, taking my final sip of wine. "Thoughts?"

"Let me think about it, and we can discuss it with them on Saturday. I have a couple ideas, but I would love to see what they think too."

The waitress set the bill in the middle of the table, and Marcy swiped it from me. "My treat, birthday girl."

"You've already done so much," I said. "You don't have to do that."

"Oh, but I want to. Besides, after the hell you went through last year, I owe you one."

"Every yes—no matter how painful—brought me to a much better place."

"Hell yes, it did."

My head snapped up, and my eyes brightened. "Hell yes," I repeated. "Marcy, you're a genius."

She eyed my wine glass then me again. "Did you have extra wine? What did I do?"

"Next week," I said, holding my hands out for emphasis. "Hell-*Yes* Week. We can find things that will challenge them to say yes."

"That is brilliant," she said, breaking into a smile. The waitress brought the receipt for her to sign, along with her credit card. "I'll get working on it... maybe make a binder for them with hell-yes activities."

The more she talked, the bigger I was nodding. "It's fitting and puts a positive spin on the week. Plus, it'll give them control and confidence."

We both slid out of the booth and pulled our coats on. For January, we didn't have much snow, but the temps were in the teens today, and dropping more tonight. I started my car from inside the restaurant.

"When I'm shopping for a new car, remind me of that little gadget."

"Deal," I said as we walked outside. Cold air blasted us in the face.

"This is booger-freezing cold," she said through her scarf.

I pulled her into a hug. "Thank you for everything. You make everything better," I said.

"No, no, girlfriend. We make everything better, together." She pulled away and pointed to the two of us. "This here is a partnership."

"I'll call you tomorrow," she said, walking towards her car.

"Sounds good. I'll be on the ice most of the day but I'll catch up after."

I got in my car and turned the heat on higher. Nothing could get the chill out this fast. I pulled out her manuscript and ran my hand across the title again. She really did it, and I knew this was the beginning of something big. It felt like both of us were standing at the bottom of a mountain and looking up.

I couldn't wait to see what was coming next...

Shattering the Illusion

A mite tournament this weekend meant that hundreds of extra players, parents, and coaches filled the lobby. I had told Mack I could help check players in after my off-ice with Marcy, and a wave of relief covered his face.

"You'd do that for me?"

"Well, I am getting paid, but yes, I'll happily stay today."

He gave me the side-eye. "What do you want in return?"

I wiggled my eyebrows. "I'll think of something— maybe dinner?"

"Deal," he said. "I was gonna do that anyways, so win-win for me."

"Don't worry, I'll cash in come show time," I countered.

His head dropped back. "Never mind. I don't need help that bad."

I slugged him. "Sure you do, and just start saying *I love the show* over and over again, till you actually believe it."

His blank expression and raised eyebrows said he

wasn't buying it.

"Don't worry, I'll make it worth it." He winked as I walked out the door.

We'd had dinner a few times since the holiday show, and he had kissed me goodnight each time, but nothing more than that. I was beginning to wonder if he'd regretted it, but every now and again, I'd catch him looking at me, and he'd blush. I didn't know what I wanted anymore, but I no longer assumed the worst about hockey players. He had been nothing but a gentleman and seemed to worry about moving too fast.

In all honesty, I appreciated it. With Nationals coming up, my mind was elsewhere, and I didn't have the capacity to juggle that many life changes at once. Plus, with both of us working so closely at our job, we couldn't afford to rush into something and then regret it. These jobs were our lives right now, and it would be horrible if we didn't get along. I had no problem taking things slow, even though Steph and Dana thought I was crazy.

"Jump him," Stephanie said after last week's dinner. "How can you possibly let him go with just a kiss? That's like having a snack after fasting for three days."

"He *is* a snack," Dana joked. "Yummy."

"Remind me to never tell you guys anything again," I said, laughing.

I shook the thought out of my head and tried to focus on the task at hand as I headed into the ballet room. Marcy was already in there with Will and Addie.

She was going over the binders we had put together last night.

"What did I miss?" I said, locking the door behind me.

"Not much," she said. "Just going over the binders, but I hadn't gotten into the theme for next week yet."

Will put his head in his hand. "You made a theme for Hell Week? What, like *torture* or *demolish*?"

Marcy smiled at me. "You want to do the honors?"

"How about I give them a little back story first?" I asked.

She nodded. "For sure. They need the context of what's coming."

"You guys are cruel," Addie chimed in, laying down on the floor.

"How about a little trust?" I said, sitting down cross-legged in front of them. "This little story starts exactly one year ago, with my birthday and a book that Marcy gave me."

"What was the book?"

"It was called *The Beautiful Yes*," I said. "And she challenged me to say yes to everything for an entire year."

"A *year*? You couldn't say no to anything for a year?"

"How do you think I ended up with the skating director position? Coaching you guys? All of it—I said yes."

"So you didn't really want to coach us?"

"I wouldn't say I didn't want to, but I was definitely

intimidated by coaching skaters at your level—I didn't feel like I would be able to give you what you needed."

"But you did it, and look at us now. We're both skating better than ever," Will said.

"I don't take credit for that, but I believe I was the best coach for you now, even though it wasn't always easy. The point is, even when it was difficult, and I sometimes didn't want to, I had to say yes. I had to try things I didn't feel comfortable with and forced myself to get comfortable with being uncomfortable."

"Uh-oh. I don't like where this is going," Addie joked.

"I can't believe you accepted that challenge," Will said. "You're either crazy or didn't realize you could say no." Marcy laughed with him.

"The thing is, once I started saying yes, more and more things popped up to make me realize how little I was living. Now, I know that part doesn't apply to you, but I want you to know that we all have these limits we carry with us of what we think we can or can't do. And after this year, I know that there isn't anything I can't do, but I had to say yes first, then figure it out. You're both going into Nationals as underdogs because we didn't get any Internationals this year. Make that work for you—be okay with their focus being elsewhere and just keep your thoughts self-centered."

"Agree with her one hundred percent," Marcy chimed in. "The worst thing you could do is go into next week thinking about what others are doing, or

God forbid, comparing yourself to anyone. The spotlight is going to be bright, but you have to block everything out except your vision of how you want to skate and feel when you're done."

"What do you mean by that?" Addie asked.

"Let's try something," Marcy answered. "Let's close your eyes. If you want to lay down, that's fine, just make sure you're comfortable."

I scooted myself so my back was against the wall facing them. Will continued to sit up, and Addie rolled to her stomach and rested her head on her arms. I closed my eyes and waited for Marcy to continue.

"Good. We're going to imagine the best possible program ever. Clean landings, centered, fast spins, all of it. I'm going to start a timer for two minutes, and even though I know your programs are longer, I want you to go through your short with perfection. Feel the jumps. See yourself in your beginning pose, staring down the judges. For two minutes, give it everything you have."

I followed along with Marcy's instructions, focusing on Addie's short program. In my head, I was standing at the end of the rink, watching her program unfold like we had planned it. Every step, every jump, and every spin done at a level four with positive grade of executions.

It was better than at Mids, and I could feel my body start to react to what I saw in my head. My breathing sped up, and I started to feel tears well up in my eyes from joy. The crowd erupted in applause, and Addie covered her face with her hands in disbelief. I could feel my chest rise and fall as a smile spread across my face.

As a coach, we're used to holding back. Don't get too close. Don't expect too much. Don't get your hopes up. The vision never matches the outcome. Day after day, we work with these gifted athletes, trying to give them every morsel of knowledge we have to get them through. We spend hours looking for the perfect music. We wake up in the middle of the night wondering why the combination isn't working. We put up with mood swings, PMS, bad days, and moments when they just want to be normal kids. On most days, all of that is overlooked—our job is to be there, steady, truthful, and ready for whatever is flung our way. And I wouldn't ever give it up for anything. My mom was wrong to want me to leave this, because even with all of that, my heart would always be grateful with just a chance to see a program like I envisioned.

I was one of the lucky ones because I'd seen her skate like that already, and I'd do anything to see her do that again in front of an even bigger crowd. More than that, I wanted her to know her worth even before she went out to skate. The clean program would be the cherry on top of an internal knowing that she was just as good as anyone else on and off the ice. We all had to perform our role at competition, show our best faces, in order to appear as though we were perfect.

The illusion.

What did it all mean? The competitive side of me would say the mentally tough were the ones who survived. If anything weakened that toughness, it would appear in your skating. The other side of me felt like there was a lesson to be learned in every experience, good or bad. It didn't matter if you had an off day—chalk it up to a learning experience.

Deep down, I didn't want to train them to be robots—void of emotion or strength. I wanted to teach them how to be in this world as they were—flaws and all. If they knew at the end of their career that they were a better person for having skated, then my job would be complete. They needed to know they mattered, no matter what.

Marcy looked at me and winked. Both skaters had grins on their faces, and Will even motioned a bow while sitting there.

"Okay," Marcy said quietly. "Keeping your eyes closed, I want you to come up with a word describing how that felt. Or a couple words—whatever feels right to you."

My eyes voluntarily shut again. What was I feeling—what was this? *Clarity*. My goal became clear to me in that I wanted a whole package in a skater. Not just a perfect skater on the ice—I had no interest in the illusion. What we needed was to create a skating program that encouraged mental toughness while giving them the techniques for the best performances.

It didn't have to be just Addie and Will going to Nationals every year. All of them should have the chance and be told it wasn't unattainable.

Will broke my concentration. "Relief," he said. "All I ever feel at the end of a program is relief."

"Does that feel good to be done?"

"Yeah, especially if it was clean." He chuckled.

"I felt elated and proud," Addie said, her eyes still closed. "The world would be a different place if everyone could feel like this."

"Amen to that," Marcy said and looked at me. "Will, anything other than relief?"

"Honestly, I think relief is the only emotion he has when he gets off the ice," I confirmed. "It's very business-like for him. A job well done." He nodded in agreement.

"Interesting," she said. "Tell me, was your mom born in China?"

"He wasn't, but my grandparents were. Very traditional. And strict."

"So, skating a clean program *is* like doing your job, then?" she asked.

"Absolutely," he said. "Truthfully, it's expected."

I saw Marcy make a face, but Will's eyes were still closed.

"Okay, that's good to know." She sat on the floor with us. "You can open your eyes now."

Will had one more year of high school still, then I knew he would be expected to attend Harvard or Yale for pre-med. Both his parents were doctors, and while I saw very little of them, his mom texted me often and always full of praise. He also spoke of them with nothing but love and respect. He had two younger brothers, and both were soccer players.

"What would it mean to you to skate a program like that you just envisioned at Nationals?"

"It would mean all this practice meant something," Will shrugged. "That it would be worth it."

"Is it bad that I want to show Jonathan we don't need him anymore?" Addie asked.

"There are no wrong answers here," Marcy said. "But tell me about that answer."

"Every time I competed this year, I knew he's there watching... judging me. Thinking that I'm broken because of everything he did. I want him to know that I'm not. Broken."

"Nope, you're sure not," she agreed. "In fact, just the opposite. I think you're stronger than you were before."

She sat up a little straighter.

"How about you, Coach? What would it mean for you to see them skate the programs of their lives?"

I took a deep breath to stall. "It would mean that we created something special for them to be able to succeed. And while I'd love to stick it to Jonathan as well, I really just want both of you to experience the freedom of knowing you worked as hard as possible and gave it one hundred percent. Anything less than that will feel like a failure to either of you, no matter the placement."

"Good point," Marcy said. "You have to be okay with any placement as long as you go out and do your best."

"Now, let's get those binders out and see what we have planned for your new, improved Hell Week."

"Ugh, come on," Addie argued. "We were doing so good."

"Just open them—we worked hard on these this week. I think you'll be surprised."

They opened the cover to a quote from Paulo Coelho: *"The secret of life, though, is to fall seven times and to get up eight times."*

"That's uplifting." He smirked. "No offense, but if I fall down seven times, I'm getting off the ice."

Addie giggled and shoved him. "It means to never stop trying," she said. "Probably meant for me."

"It's about life," I said. "No matter what happens this week or the next, there is always going to be something standing in your way. Your job is to keep your eyes focused on what is important to you—no one else. If you get knocked down, just get back up."

"It'll be difficult, somedays, but getting up is the only option," Marcy agreed.

We went through the rest of the binder and planned out what would become the standard in our rink, the "yes week" before competition. Yes to all of it. Nerves. Emotions. Brilliance. And getting up.

So much getting up.

Falling Down

The week had flown by, and Thursday learn-to-skate couldn't be done fast enough. My brain was fried, and while the skaters had embraced every moment of Yes Week, I think they were antsy to get there already.

Nationals were in Boston this year, and I couldn't wait to go, even though they currently had more snow than we did. I had been to Boston once—two nights at a skating conference—but what I saw of the city, I loved. It would be cold, but a much-needed getaway from my regular routine.

One of my junior hockey coaches bailed on me tonight, so Mack was helping me with the smallest group of players. More than anything, he was the player-picker-upper. Every five seconds, one of them—if not several—would fall down, sometimes causing a domino effect.

Things had been going so well between us, and I loved being around him, whether on or off the ice. It didn't matter, and Roger didn't seem to care that we were hanging out more than usual. Mack still kept me at arm's length, and I couldn't tell if that was because he just didn't want to get close or was trying to get out of it.

"I think that parent wants you," he whispered in my ear. I hoped the parent didn't notice how I jumped when Mack got close to me.

When I turned, my stomach lurched. Kevin stood in the doorway, looking handsome and sad at the same time.

"You okay?" Mack asked. "Who is that?"

I took a deep breath. "That's my ex," I whispered. "Can you take over till I get rid of him?"

"Can *I* just get rid of him?"

"I wish," I mumbled as I skated away. There were only ten minutes left in class, so Mack would be fine.

Kevin backed out of the doorway and stepped out of the hockey box, and I followed him out to the lobby. I gestured to the tables in the café area, and we walked in silence to sit down.

"Good to see you," he said. "You look good."

"What are you doing here?" I genuinely tried to soften my voice, but it still came out harsh.

His eyes darted around the lobby, trying to find something to land on.

"Um, I have some news, and I just wanted to tell you face-to-face." His eyes finally locked on mine.

"Let me guess, you're getting married," I said.

"Yeah, um, yes, we married in the fall," he stammered. "But that's not what I'm here to tell you."

"What's wrong? Are you ill or something?"

"No, it's not that. Nothing is wrong, really," he stalled. "Listen, Kaitlyn is pregnant, and I knew that this would be difficult for you…"

"Wait—what did you say?" I whispered. My blood boiled, and it all became clear why he was here. "She's *pregnant*? Are you kidding me?"

For the two years that we were married, Kevin claimed he wasn't ready for kids—that he might never be. 'Let's wait till next year,' was his famous line, and all I wanted was to start a family. I wanted it all: the family, the mess, the chaos, the sleepless nights and midnight feedings. I haven't thought about kids since the day he left me. I had figured that he just would never want them.

He just didn't want them with *me*.

He flinched at my anger. "This was a mistake—nothing would've made this easier."

"Because you denied me a family for two years," I snapped. We sat in silence for a minute. His eyes focused on the TV hanging in the corner with SportsCenter playing. "So, when is your baby due?"

He bit his lip and shook off a thought. "It's twins," he said, eyes downcast. "A boy and a girl, due in June."

A sharp pain pierced my heart, and jolts of pain shot through my ribcage. "Okay," I said, standing. "I have to get going. Good luck with… everything."

I didn't look back, only moved forward to the coaches room, where I took my skates off as quickly as possible. Learn-to-skate was just wrapping up, and I raced to the office to shut down my computer and grab my purse. The last thing I wanted was to talk to anyone, so I rushed out without saying a word. The front desk girl eyed me carefully but didn't say anything.

The second I walked outside, the tears started to roll down my face, and I wiped them away angrily. He didn't deserve my tears, and I was so mad for reacting this way. By the time I got to my car, my eyes were watering from the cold and tears. My nose was running, and I felt like everything was closing in on me. I punched the radio off and tried to focus on getting out of the parking lot without hitting anyone.

Why, was my only thought. Why with her and not with me? What was so wrong with me that he couldn't stay and work it out? It was as if the last year hadn't made a difference at all, and this was the moment I had been dreading the whole time.

My third in my list of threes.

And it all made sense and clicked into place at once. Nothing had changed at all with me. In one three-minute conversation, I was right back where I started a year ago. What was it all for—saying yes to everything—only to arrive back here? Feeling alone and worthless.

I didn't remember anything about the drive home. My phone rang from the depths of my purse, but talking to anyone was the last thing I needed. As soon as I got home, I curled up on my couch with the blanket from my bed and turned on *Grey's Anatomy*. Anything to shut out the voice in my head. The old hag was back, and she meant business.

Getting Up

There was a pounding on my door, distant at first, then louder.

"Open up, or I'm breaking a window," I heard Marcy yell. The clock on the wall in the kitchen read six fifteen. "You have to the count of three."

Sitting up, I realized I still had everything on from last night. It all came flooding back to me in a flash.

"One!"

All I wanted was to sleep.

"Two!"

Damn her for being so stubborn.

"Three—I'm coming in!" she yelled as I opened the door.

She stood there, holding two cups and bakery bags from Starbucks.

"Do you know how worried everyone is? Couldn't you answer the damn phone?" She walked through the entryway into the kitchen. "You're lucky I love your sorry ass."

"Lucky isn't what I'm feeling right now."

"You stood me up for shopping. And do you know that Mack didn't sleep last night? He stalked me on

Facebook and messaged me this morning."

I grabbed the coffee and bag, saying a silent prayer it was a scone. "I'm sorry," I said. "Truly—I didn't mean to worry anyone."

"What happened? What is going on, and where is your phone?"

"My phone is in my bag, and I'll text Mack as soon as you leave."

"No—text him now, so he can stop worrying." She dug through my bag and pulled out my phone.

The first sip of coffee hit my system and felt like a jolt. She wasn't kidding about worrying Mack. He called twelve times and texted just as many. I opened the last text and replied.

Me: I'm so sorry. Everything is okay. I'll call soon.

Bubbles immediately popped up, like he had been waiting for me.

Mack: You left so fast. Are you okay?

Me: Yes. I'll call you in a bit.

Marcy took the lid off her coffee and blew on it. "Wanna talk?"

"And if I said no?"

"I'd keep asking until you said yes."

She was relentless. "I'm done saying yes. I did for a year, and I'm right back where I started."

"Talk to me—what the hell happened? Mack said Kevin showed up at the rink, and you left before he got off the ice."

"They're married," I said, taking a sip of coffee.

"Woof," she said. "But we knew they were going to do that, right?"

"And they're having twins… in June."

"Oh," she said with finality. "Now I get it. And he came to your work to tell you? Of all the insensitive and asinine things to do."

"I came home, got under covers, and slept," I said. "I'd still be sleeping if you didn't come here to threaten me."

"Threaten, schmeaten." She waved me off. "I brought you caffeine and sugar. You will thank me as soon as you bite into that scone."

"I felt so helpless—so worthless all over again."

"Stop," she interrupted. "We did not go through this entire last year, make all this progress, to have you be taken down from one conversation. Screw him and his life. You are so much better off without that sack of poo."

I choked on my scone. "A sack of poo?" I said, laughing. "I was not prepared for that."

"I got written up last week for cursing in front of the kids," she shrugged. "I'm trying really hard not to swear around them, but *goddamn*, it's hard."

"I promise not to ever write you up, unless you keep saying sack of poo. Use your big girl words."

"This is so not the point," she said, sighing. "Do you remember our conversation with the kids last weekend?"

"I do." I crossed my arms over my chest. I knew where she was going with this, and I felt angry she was pushing me.

"And remind me again, the quote we discussed the most?"

My entire body slumped back into the sofa. "Fall down seven times, get up eight," I droned.

"Tell me about that quote… do you really believe in it, or was that talk last weekend just for the skaters?"

"No, it's not just for the skaters, but this is different. This is my life. And he keeps messing with my head."

"How exactly is he doing that? You asked him to stay away, and he did," she said. She moved to the sliding door and looked out at the lake. "I had forgotten how pretty this was in the winter. It's gorgeous out there."

The sun was rising, and the snow and ice on the trees glittered.

"Why are you taking his side in this?"

"Natalie—you need to understand there are no sides to take," she said, turning to me. She came and sat next to me, tucking her feet underneath her. "He is living his life. You're living yours. What he does with his life has no effect on yours, just like yours doesn't affect his. You moved your focus onto him instead of where it should be. You."

"But all I wanted when we were married was a baby—literally, that's *all* I wanted when we were married."

"And thank God you didn't have one with him. Babies don't save marriages, and he clearly wasn't in the same frame of mind that you were."

"His life is perfect—perfect wife, perfect babies on the way—she has everything I wanted."

"*Wanted* being the operative word there," she said. "Do you still want that kind of perfect? Or do you want to go to Boston with two of the top skaters in the nation?"

"I want it all," I admitted, pouting. I heard what she was saying, but I still felt left behind like the trash.

"Preach," she said. "And that's okay, as long as you understand you just aren't going to have it with him. Let him go."

"I'm not holding onto him in any way. I hadn't thought about him in a month," I argued.

"Then let go of the person you were when you were *with* him. She doesn't exist anymore, and that hag in the attic needs to understand that you can't be bullied anymore."

A single tear snaked down my cheek, and she wiped it away. "I'm scared," I admitted.

"I know you are. This is not a little thing you're dealing with. It's years of self-blame and doubts you're trying to let go of, and you're not sure who you are without it."

"So, what do I do now?"

"You get up."

"You were waiting to say that, weren't you?" I rolled my eyes.

"You teed it up quite nicely."

"You're relentless," I sighed.

"And you love me for it. Besides, who else would come all the way out here at six on a Friday morning to save your butt?"

"No one," I said, and a sob escaped my chest. "I'm alone except for you."

"Oh my God," she snapped. "That is the furthest thing from the truth, and now you're getting up, taking a shower, and preparing for next week. Put your focus where you want it."

She was right, and I knew it. What was I clinging to? Why did I feel almost comfortable with this sadness and angst? It has been so long, and yet they felt like a well-worn pair of shoes.

She looked at her watch. "Look, I have to get going, but I'll check in on you later. Please call Mack and put him out of his worry."

I stood to follow her out, my body feeling like a thousand pounds. She pulled me into a hug and held me there. "You got this," she whispered. "And until then, I got you."

When I closed the door behind her, I leaned against it, wondering if I really could just get up from this fall. Was it that easy?

I found my phone and dialed Mack's number.

"Are you okay?" he answered.

"I am," I said. "Sort of—I have some baggage to sort through today, but I will be fine."

"You scared me," he said quietly. "No one knew what happened or where you went last night."

"I'm sorry about that. I didn't want to break down at the rink and just came home. Couldn't talk to anyone."

"I'm guessing Marcy kicked your butt for that this morning," he said. I could hear the smile warming up his voice. "She's a good friend."

"She is," I agreed. "And yes, my butt is officially kicked."

"Anything I can do to help?"

"Honestly, no, just something I have to work through on my own."

"You know where to find me if you do," he said. "Will you be in today?"

"It's the Friday before Nationals." I finally smiled. "Nothing would keep me away."

"There she is," he chuckled. "Knew your competitive spirit would come through eventually."

"You think I'm competitive?"

He laughed openly. "You're kidding, right? I've never met anyone like you. You could've played hockey."

In all of my years at the rink, not one person had ever called me competitive. I always felt like I even lacked the competitive drive needed for coaching.

"I usually think of myself as more go-with-the-flow."

"As long as the flow is going your way." He smirked. "I think Roger is afraid of you."

"Okay, stop. Now you're just pulling my leg."

"No way… I'm telling you how it is. That's why we kinda freaked out last night when you just went missing."

"I wasn't missing—I just came home."

"And didn't answer any calls or texts from anyone. I was probably more worried than anyone."

"I fell asleep on the couch and didn't wake up until Marcy was banging on my door this morning. I really didn't mean to worry you."

"It's all good now, as long as you're okay."

"I'll see you later," I said. "Maybe we can do pizza tonight?"

"High school hockey."

"Ah, okay. Then I'll just see you at the rink."

"Later," he said and disconnected.

I sat there, feeling slightly deflated. So many emotions had gone through my system in the last twelve hours, and Marcy was right: I needed to put my focus on what counted, and that was Nationals. The pull of Kevin and his wife didn't have any bearing on my life, and I wanted nothing more than to be free from that relationship.

If only I knew how to let that go.

Good Luck Wishes

On Monday, I busted out of the rink early once I double checked learn-to-skate was covered for the week. Most of my figure skaters were taking a couple days off, so I only had to find lesson time with Stephanie and Dana for two of them.

It was snowing again, and the view out my bedroom window was magical. My suitcase laid open on the bed, and a pile of clothes sat beside it. Packing was up there on my list of things I hated to do, and I started to panic that I didn't have anything nice enough to take with me to Nationals.

This was a big deal, and the coaches were usually dressed to impress, but I literally didn't have anything that would impress anyone. I did have some basic neutrals that went with everything and could be dressed up or down. Plus, I did have a wool coat my mom got me for Christmas a few years ago. With my cashmere scarf, that would work.

A knock at my front door broke my mental dressing... probably just my Amazon package being delivered. I peeked out the front window in the hallway and noticed a blue SUV parked in my driveway.

Mack.

I quickly checked the hall mirror to make sure I wasn't a mess and ran downstairs. His face looked somber when I opened the door.

What's going on? Is everything okay at the rink?"

He took one step in the door, gently reached for my face, and pulled me into a long, slow kiss. My heart thumped in my chest, and I reached inside his coat to pull him tighter. He pushed me against the entryway wall and leaned into me. Every cell in my body was screaming for him.

He broke the kiss, leaning his forehead on mine, and I felt his chest rise and fall with mine.

"Hey," he said, chuckling. "You forgot to say goodbye to me."

"Remind me to do that again," I said, giving him another small kiss.

We had kissed several times since the Santa dressing incident, but nothing like this. This felt real.

He pulled away and looked around. "I really like your home," he said.

I grabbed his hand and led him into the open kitchen/family room and sat him on the couch.

"Do you want anything to drink?" I looked at the clock and it was only four thirty. "Wait—what are you doing here?"

"I told you," he said. "You didn't say goodbye, and I wanted to properly wish you luck."

A slow smile spread across my face. "How did you

know where I lived?"

He slid his coat off and set it beside him. I came and sat cross-legged next to him, my knees touching his.

"Truthfully?" He scrunched his face like he held a closely guarded secret.

"Uh-oh, you're not a stalker, are you?"

"No, but last week when you took off from the rink, I might have looked up your address in Roger's employee file," he admitted. "And, I might have driven by to make sure you made it home okay."

I grabbed his hand. "You did that for me? It's such a horrible drive, and I'm surprised you didn't give me crap last week."

He tipped his head back, laughing. "*Right*? I thought I contained myself quite well. And you're not kidding. Why do you do this every day?"

I pointed to the sliding door, and he stood to look out. "Oh. I get it, now." His eyes danced around the trees and lake. "This is where you paddle?"

I nodded. "I can't wait to get back out there."

"It's beautiful. Doesn't anyone play hockey back there?"

"Sometimes, but this year has been quiet." He came and sat back down next to me and grabbed my hand. "Why do I get the impression something else is going on with you being here."

"I was just wondering if, maybe when you get back, you might want to see where this goes…" He trailed off and looked at his hands. "Asking for a friend."

I laughed, and my stomach did a flip-flop. "Does your friend know what he's getting into? I'm a bit of a hot mess."

"I told him that, but he thinks you're a beautiful mess," he said, still looking down and smiling.

I swallowed hard. Did I want this? "Technically, my year of saying yes is over," I stalled.

His shoulders dropped a bit.

"But I suppose I could extend it just this one time," I said. His eyes locked on mine. "And I'm terrified of these feelings right now."

He pulled me into a hug. "I know you are," he said. "That's why I haven't rushed anything so far, but knowing you're gone for the rest of the week was making me crazy. I wanted you to know how I felt and wish you luck. I'll be right here, waiting, when you get back."

I smiled into his shoulder.

"I'm taking that as a yes," he said.

I pulled away and found his lips with mine, heat building in my belly. His breathing quickened as he leaned into me, his hand reaching into my hair and pulling me even tighter.

"Whoa," he whispered, pulling away. "When are you coming back?"

I laughed. "My flight is on Sunday at five forty-five. And I can't wait to come back home now."

His phone rang, and his head tipped back when he realized it was Roger.

"Roger," he answered.

His eyes locked on mine while he listened to the other end, his thumb rubbing lazy circles in the palm of my hand.

"Gotcha, I'll be right back." He sighed. "Give me twenty."

He closed his eyes and shook his head slowly.

"We can continue this on Monday?" I said, trying to make light of it.

"Monday night is Italian night," he said, imitating *Rain Man*.

"Here's to swimmin' with bow-legged women," I countered with *Jaws*.

He checked out my legs and raised an eyebrow. "They don't appear to be bow-legged, but I'll go swimming with you any time."

He pulled me into a tight hug, and I snuggled into his neck. He smelled like soap and aftershave.

"I hope you have a great week," he whispered.

"Me too." I giggled. "But I'll be back before you know it."

He gave me one final squeeze and grabbed my hand, walking towards the front door. "Text me, anytime, day or night," he said. "Preferably at night."

I reached up and kissed him on the cheek. "Thank you for coming over."

"Kick some ass in Boston," he said, squeezing my hand. "I told Steph she had to keep us informed in the office."

My stomach rolled with nerves at the thought of Nationals. "I'm excited, but I'll also be so relieved when this is all over."

He bent down to meet my eyes. "You'll be great," he whispered. "I know it." He gave me one more kiss, then pushed through the front door.

As I watched him pull away, I realized I had been holding my breath. That, or he took my breath away. Either way, I knew I was in trouble. This feeling meant trouble for my heart.

Johnny Drama

My flight to Boston was uneventful, with the exception of the turbulence coming in for our landing. An hour later, I still felt queasy. The only thing we had today was the draw party in the hotel banquet room later tonight, so I curled up in bed and fell into the deepest sleep I'd had in weeks. I woke to my phone alarm. I'd had no intention of sleeping this long and made a mad dash to get ready for the event downstairs. It was all about the skaters, but I knew the networking scene would be strong.

Truthfully, I dreaded it, and if I could order room service and stay in bed all night, I'd be a happy camper.

The first person I saw when I finally entered the room was Nicole. I knew Will's parents wouldn't attend the reception, but he said they would be at both programs this week. Nicole was always dressed as if she had just stepped out of a high-fashion magazine. Hair, makeup, shoes—she was a total package, even if she was dressed for a workout. I found it intimidating at first, but once I got to know her, I understood it was just one of the things she could control.

We all have our something that makes us feel better.

Hers was appearance.

"I'm glad I found you," she whispered to me. "I had a strange phone call from the skating director in Cleveland earlier, and I lied about all of it."

I pasted a smile on my face in case anyone was watching. "What are you talking about? What specifically did they ask you about?"

She raised her eyebrows, as if that specified every rotten thing Jonathan did.

"You two?"

She nodded.

"Money?"

She nodded again.

"Oh my God," I said. "How did they find out?"

She shrugged again.

"Do you think he's doing the same thing there?"

"That was the impression I got. And she said she wanted to talk with you too," she added.

"What? You lied, and what am I supposed to do?"

"Think about what this would do to Addie if it became public knowledge," Nicole said. "It would crush her—and she doesn't even know about the embezzling."

"I still don't understand why you protected him."

She sighed heavily. "I needed him gone, and this was the only way to make him go quietly. He promised that if anyone ever found out about the money, he'd confess to the affair too. I can't hurt my husband like that."

This woman was a lunatic, and I didn't understand how she raised such an incredible kid.

"So in protecting him, you're saving yourself too."

"I didn't have a choice," she snapped.

A couple parents looked our way, but quickly went back to their own gossip. These events were definitely powered by who knew what.

"I don't understand how I got to be in the middle of all this," I said. "My only focus this week is the skaters, and I can't worry about saving you or him... or *whatever*."

My stomach still felt queasy, and the wine I sipped threatened to come back up. I found the buffet table with light snacks—pretzels, snack mix, and veggie and cheese trays—and loaded up a small plate. I needed something solid in my system to combat the stress coursing through my veins. I found a spot on the side, where most people were already talking to someone else. No one even noticed me standing there. The skaters were all gathered in the middle, mingling and relaxing before the stress of the week hit them tomorrow. Going through the process of each skater drawing their skating order for the short program took about forty minutes. Addie drew sixth, and Will drew eighteenth.

The skating gods were always with Will.

Luckily for Addie, several of the top skaters were skating in the first group, so that would help her a bit— at least to know what the score was to beat. Now is when the game began… the mental game of sizing each other up and seeing who would crack.

Coaches—while friendlier—weren't much different. As I looked around the room, it dawned on me that everyone's main goal is to get on the podium, and they didn't care how that happened. I spotted Jonathan across the room, and as if he sensed me, he locked eyes with mine. He took a sip of his drink and nodded to me, tight-lipped. He pointed to the entrance to the banquet room and excused himself from the coach he'd been talking to.

This was the last thing I wanted to do, but I found my way towards the entrance as well. Nicole was nowhere to be seen, but Will and Addie tracked me down before I could make it to the hallway.

"You're not going to talk to Jonathan, are you?" Addie said.

"I just want to lay down some ground rules for the week with him," I lied. Protecting Addie at all cost had become my new goal for the week.

"But he can't be trusted," Will said. "I think he's proven that already. He's not going to get to us this week."

"And why is that?" I asked, smiling.

"Because we are focused on ourselves," they droned back to me, like robots.

"Oh, don't make it sound so appealing," I joked.

"You can't control Jonathan, so just let him be," Addie countered.

"I promise this will just be a quick conversation that doesn't involve you two."

With that, I walked away, sensing they were watching me head out to the hallway. Jonathan was down the hall to the right, near the kitchen entrance. Only staff would be down here, and he waved me over.

"Not conspicuous at all," I said, looking back where we came from. Anyone walking out of the party would be able to see us.

"I couldn't care less if anyone sees us," he said. "My concern is what you're going to say to Roberta when she finds you."

Roberta—Bobbi to everyone in the skating world—had been the skating director at Cleveland for almost twenty years. She was a legend, a class act, with impeccable standards. And I was certain she would toss Jonathan out in a heartbeat if she knew the truth.

"Honestly, I don't know yet," I said. "Nicole just gave me the rundown, and lying just isn't my thing."

"Think of Addie and what it would do to her," he pleaded.

"Did you think of Addie when you were sleeping with her mom? Or stealing from the Club?"

He rolled his eyes and tipped his head back. "Yes, I've made some mistakes, but I am trying to rebuild a life in Cleveland. If word gets out about this, no one will let me coach anywhere."

"I don't know why this is my problem," I said.

"Because you have the power to take everything

away from me if you want to be vindictive," he said.

"You're right about one thing," I said. "I do have the power, but you're wrong about me being vindictive. I don't use people to get ahead, unlike you."

"Please, Natalie," he said, shoulders dropped. "All I ask is that you say you don't know anything, and I promise to never meddle in your life or the skaters. You have my word. This is my *life* we're talking about."

"If anyone ever finds out about this, it won't be from me," I said. "But I have to warn you that Lydia was asking weird questions after Mids, and it wouldn't surprise me if this gets out another way."

I walked away from him and felt a release of pressure I had been holding for a long time. It wasn't my battle to fight. It wasn't my place to air his dirty laundry. Doing that would only hurt Addie and our club. Plus, I had a feeling that his life would blow up of his own doing, not mine. Bobbi wouldn't be asking questions if she wasn't suspicious for some reason.

We keep the focus on ourselves. I repeated the mantra in my head.

As if on cue, my phone buzzed in my pocket.

Marcy: Success consists of getting up just one more time than you fall.

Me: You're like Yoda in a pocket.

Marcy: LOL. I figured I'd just send little quotes randomly for you and the skaters.

Me: It's perfect. They will love it too.

Marcy: How is it going? Can you talk?

I hit the phone icon.

"I guess you can talk," she answered.

"You won't believe the conversation I just had with Jonathan," I said. No one was in the hallway with me, but I kept my voice as low as possible.

"What's Johnny Drama up to these days?"

"And we have a new name for him." I laughed. "Walls are closing in on him, and his skating director is asking around for dirt."

"Oh, sugar," she said.

"Still on the cursing ban, I hear."

"In my defense, I'm in Target," she said. "What are you going to do?"

"I can't be the one to out him—I need to keep my attention where it matters this week," I said.

"Such a good student you are," she said. "But you're willing to lie for him?"

"Until I saw Nicole and Jonathan at Mids I was completely in the dark," I said. "I never knew anything while he was at the rink, or the circumstances of why he left. I figured that is all I have to say."

I bypassed the party, which was still going strong, and found my way to the elevators. Room service and a quiet room were calling my name. "Look, I'm heading into an elevator and gonna let you go. Buy something fun," I said.

"Already have," she said. "I'll text you in the morning. Have a good night."

The door opened as we disconnected, and I was grateful no one else got in with me. I pushed the button for the eighth floor and leaned back against the back wall and closed my eyes. I saw Addie stepping on the podium, but the door dinged before I could see what spot she took. Smiling, I pulled my key out and unlocked the door.

Once inside, I texted Addie and Will to make sure they ate healthy tonight and to get some sleep. Our group text was filled with quotes, emojis, and hearts. We had grown a lot in the last year, and I considered myself lucky to be a part of their lives.

Everything was going to work out… I would make sure of that.

Nationals

We sat in the kiss and cry box, Addie still crying, the crowd cheering on her emotions.

The two things fans loved most at Nationals was a clean skate and genuine emotion at the end of a program. When the score was called, they booed. Granted, it was still her personal best for the year, but the component score was lower than it should've been. It was early in the group, and they had to make sure to leave some points on the table for some of the other big names skating later. I understood the game, and Addie was so happy to have had that moment on the ice that it didn't matter to her.

We were ushered through the curtain to the back hallway that led to the open area for skaters to warm up. Skaters were everywhere, walking through their program, jumping rope, and stretching on yoga mats. U.S. Figure Skating had even brought in spin bikes for skaters to warm up on before they skated. It was an underground gym just for skaters, and the energy was electric. All the nerves bouncing around created an atmosphere of excitement.

Coaches stood near their skaters, bored and

scrolling their phones. A TV in the corner was playing the short programs, but no one appeared to be watching.

I spotted Will running toward us, but Addie wasn't paying attention, still in her post-skate high. When she did, she opened her arms wide to let him lift her up in a hug. "You did it," he whispered. "That was so good."

He set her down, and she covered her face with her hands again.

"I want to go back out there and do it again," she said.

"Get your skates off, and we'll watch the rest of the group upstairs," Will said.

My phone buzzed as I watched them walk towards the locker room.

Stephanie: OMGOMGOMG

Dana: Holy shitballs that was good.

Ronnie sent the red dress dancing emoji eight times.

Me: I can't even right now. I am so proud of her.

Stephanie: If this is Marcy's work in action, I want in on that.

Dana: Samesies

Me: She's been so helpful.

Stephanie: We recorded it so we could watch it over again during the first break. Her score was crap.

Me: It's a game. Always has been. But I'm hoping

she is at least in the top five so she has a chance.

Dana: How has Janelle been skating?

Me: Clean on the practices. She looks good. There's about six that could potentially get on the podium.

Stephanie: Woof.

Ronnie: Addie did her job—it's out of her hands. Yours too.

Me: She's just going to relax and have fun watching tonight. I might go puke.

Addie came out of the locker room, and Will had jumped on one of the bikes that was waiting for her. He had his lanyard on, so no one questioned him. As soon as he spotted her, he jumped off, and they took off upstairs.

I sent a text to Marcy and followed them up. I knew she was meeting with a potential client tonight and would call me later. As I walked up the stairs, I noticed a feeling of emptiness inside me, like something was missing. It wasn't until I reached the top of the platform and looked at the crowd watching the event that I realized what it was.

Loneliness. I was utterly alone in this crowd and wished I had someone to be here with me. I didn't know enough coaches at this level. Things with Mack were too new to feel a connection. Hell, even Marcy was busy.

I walked the steep stairway to the upper level of seating, which was empty for the most part. *Focus on what matters*, I heard in my head as I took a seat. The Zamboni was on the ice clearing for the next group of skaters. My phone buzzed, and Mack's name pulled up.

"Hey there," I answered.

"You do know this is the first time I have ever watched figure skating on TV, right?"

"I'm honored, especially since you had to pay to stream the live events."

"Roger put it on the rink expense so we could all watch it." He chuckled. "Janie, Roger, and I have been texting the whole time. It's kind of exciting when we have skin in the game."

"No way, you all watched? That is so cool."

"Yep, you were on TV and everything. I don't know how you stand there watching without going crazy with nerves. I was nervous just watching here from the comfort of my couch."

"Yeah, I don't eat much on the day of events—my stomach is too wonky, but I'll get something when the event is over. Room service."

"She looked amazing—better than the video I saw from Mids."

"It was her personal best, so I can't complain. I'm so proud of her," I said.

"I don't know, I kinda think her coach had something to do with her skating so well."

My entire face heated up. I didn't know where we were going, but I loved this feeling I got with him.

"We still have free skate programs, but maybe we can celebrate when I get back."

"You bet your ass we will."

My phone rang with a FaceTime call coming in. I pulled it down to look at it, and Mack had switched it, mid-call. I tapped the button.

"There you are," he said. My stomach flip-flopped like it always did with him.

"It's good to see you," I said. "Wish I was sitting there next to you."

"Me too," he sighed. "What's the deal with these announcers on TV? They're a little out there."

I laughed. He had to be talking about Trish and Thomas, both former Olympic competitors, now TV analysts. You loved them or hated them. Very little gray area where TnT were concerned.

"You'll get used to them eventually," I said.

"Doubtful," he mumbled. "I'm fairly certain he has a bird on his head."

"It is the ladies' event, so that sounds about right."

"What time is Will tomorrow?"

"His event starts at six, but he's in the last group—his slotted time is seven eighteen."

He furrowed his brow and studied me. "That's oddly specific," he said.

I laughed. "All the music is turned in ahead of time, so they allow for judging times and can specify how long it'll take for each skater."

"I'm an excellent driver," he quipped.

I covered my mouth to stifle the laughter. "Well played, and you're right. It is oddly specific. Next time, I'll give you an estimate."

The announcer called the next group of skaters onto the ice and began to introduce them one by one.

"I'll let you go," he said. His eyes were saying he wanted to stay on the phone.

"We can catch up tomorrow in between practices. Lots of downtime."

He nodded. "I hope all of them fall tonight."

I shushed him. "Thank you for calling. It made my night."

He winked and disconnected.

We may not have been together, but I most certainly wasn't alone anymore.

The Free Skate

Midway through Friday, I began to notice that other coaches were casting glances my way. They were watching Addie and Will during practice-ice as well, and all of it made me feel like a bug under a magnifying glass. Sitting in the sun.

Intense.

Addie had come in fifth after the short program, but there were only three points separating the first five skaters. Anyone in that group could take the lead with a great skate. Will had a small bobble on his triple axel landing and was in second, but less than a point behind.

He took the placement in stride and seemed to enjoy not being in first.

"It's cool," he said. "Everyone loves the underdog."

It was long program day, and my stomach was threatening to ruin everything. Nerves kicked in around three a.m. and I'd been dozing in between panic attacks. "Exhausted" didn't even begin to describe how I felt right now. It wasn't a big enough word. All I wanted to do was hide under the covers and let someone else take over.

My phone buzzed. My eyes started to water at the

sight of Marcy's name.

Marcy: Rise and grind, girlfriend.

Me: I can't. Calling in sick today.

Marcy: LOL, good one. Seriously, get out of bed, and go get some breakfast.

Me: It's adorable you think I could eat today.

Marcy: By breakfast, I meant coffee. Silly girl.

Marcy: I saw you post the Starbucks in your lobby. #Winning

She had me there. Just seeing the name made me stir inside. Flinging the covers back, I blew out a breath I had been holding.

Me: I'll call you when I get back in my room.

Marcy: word.

The hotel at this early hour was hushed and peaceful—thank God because my messy bun and leggings wouldn't impress the Nationals networking scene.

Starbucks was located to the right of the elevators when you exited, and I smiled at the bored-looking barista. She scanned my phone for payment, then went to work on my latte and scone. My phone buzzed again.

Marcy: You could be on an episode of What Not to Wear.

My head snapped up, and across the lobby, she held up her own Starbucks cup.

I didn't know if it was the loneliness, the nerves, or the lack of sleep, but I broke down right there, covering my face with my hands.

"Ma'am, are you okay?" the barista asked, eyes widened.

"She just really wants her coffee," Marcy reassured her as she pulled me into a hug. "Shhhh, it was supposed to be a good surprise."

"It is," I slobbered into her shoulder. "I think I'm just a little nervous."

"You're hiding it so well, though," she said, laughing. "Thank God I got here when I did."

She pulled me away, handed me my coffee and scone, and pointed to the elevator. "Go."

"Did you know that's the shortest sentence in the English language?"

"I'm sure it is," she said. "We need to regroup for the big day."

"I have so many questions," I said. "How did you even know what hotel I was at?"

"The event website had all the host hotel information listed on the main page. I had planned this all along, but knew you'd try to stop me if I told you."

"I'm so glad you're here. Wait till the kids see you."

"I got in last night and watched Will's program in my room," she said as I slid the key card into my door. "Is he really okay with being in second?"

"He seemed to be."

I slid my shoes off and sat cross-legged in bed, pulling the covers up over my lap. She pulled the lounge chair closer to the bed and sat down, propping her feet up.

"I still can't believe you came for us," I said.

"It'll reflect in your bill. Tell me what your focus is today."

The latte felt like a giant sigh, and my shoulders began to release. I closed my eyes and tried to figure out what I needed right now.

The word flashed in my head, one letter at a time, like it was being typed out... c o m f o r t.

"I think, what I need, and what I want to give the skaters is—comfort. Does that make sense?" I cringed because I felt like the answer should've been more fierce.

"Given your anxiety level, that makes perfect sense," she agreed with me. "And more than anything else, it's probably exactly what the skaters need. Remember, they are the ones with the job to finish—their stress will be magnified today."

I offered her my scone. "I ordered this out of habit, but there's no way I can eat right now."

She wiggled her eyebrows. "I was hoping you'd say that."

"So how can I possibly bring comfort to anyone today? It's a pretty big day."

"What is the one thing you *can* control?"

I tipped my head back to the headboard. "Myself."

"Good." She broke off the corner of the scone and popped it into her mouth. "So the question is, how can you bring comfort to your sweet self?"

I held up my coffee.

"Good. What else?"

"Showering. Taking my time getting ready. Wearing the cashmere scarf and anchor bracelet you got me."

"Things are looking up already. I'm honored you brought those things."

"We should text the skaters and see if they want to meet with you this morning after their practices."

"I would love that," she said.

I unlocked my phone and smiled as I opened our group text.

Me: Knock-Knock.

Will: Who's there??

Addie: Who?

Marcy: Me!

Addie: ???

Marcy jumped on my bed and took a selfie with me, bedhead and all. Then she sent it to them.

Will: Is this because I got second? :)

Marcy: lol, hardly. I wanted to see some good skating today.

Addie: You're really here?!!

Me: she heckled me in the lobby when I got my coffee. She's really here.

Will: hahaha yesssss :))

Marcy: Hoping for a team meeting after the morning practices, if you're good with that.

Addie: In!!

Will: In

Me: Okay, see you guys at the rink in a bit. Don't be late. Full warm-up before you get on.

Thumbs up emojis from both.

"Okay, I'm going to skedaddle and let you get ready. Take your time—deep breaths all day long. You got this."

I leaned in to hug her again. "Love isn't a big enough word right now. Thank you for being here."

"I got you," she whispered. "I'm going to my room to get some work done—just text me when you're ready, and I'll go to the rink with you."

After she left, I curled up into a ball on my bed, tucking the covers under my chin. I closed my eyes and saw Addie stepping onto the podium again. If figuring out how to stay calm today was the price that I had to pay for that vision to come true, then I could do that. My emotions wouldn't override what was needed from me today.

Comfort. Calm. Present. Clarity.
Those were my words today.

⌒〜⌒

Addie's practice was atrocious, and Will's wasn't going much better. The pressure was closing in on them, but I didn't know if this was something we were prepared for. Marcy texted me and said she was in the stands with Addie. She reminded me of my word. I was grateful I could get her in for practice, but she knew a ticket to the event wouldn't happen. It had been sold out for weeks.

I pulled Will over to the boards and made him stand there for a moment.

"Close your eyes."

He rolled them instead.

"No, no, I said to *close* them."

He sighed heavily but complied, the right side of his mouth twitching up.

"See your first combination. Speed going in and flowing out of the landing. Strong core. And smile."

His entire face relaxed into a broad smile. "Can I do my triple axel?"

"You can do your whole program if it makes you smile like that."

He closed his eyes again, then blew out a breath of air. "Okay," he nodded. "I'm ready."

"Show me the section with that first combo and then the triple axel."

Will was back. Addie and Marcy clapped from the audience along with other spectators watching. The best-kept secret in figure skating was the practice-ice sessions were more entertaining than the actual event. Seasoned fans knew this.

He finished his session way better than he started it, and I only wish I could've gotten Addie to do the same. Her head was definitely more resistant. I trusted Marcy was working with her already.

We had roughly three hours of free time before we needed to be back at the arena for Addie's final practice before her event started. Will's group was later tonight, but he would be at the rink during her event for support. The four of us found a tiny area in the lobby of the hotel where it was quiet and empty.

"Tell me about your practices," Marcy said. I was a bystander in this meeting, and happy someone else was here to help me.

"It sucked," Addie said.

"I was able to turn mine around with the visualizing," Will said.

"Addie—did you visualize anything in particular?"

"I tried, but I just kept starting over. I couldn't see what I wanted. It was like someone changed the channel right before it got good."

"That is a great description," Marcy said. "The energy on that ice was crazy, and you were probably just not zoning out enough to see the visual through to the end. You were easily distracted because your attention was on everything outside of you."

"I think I was doing the same thing until Natalie pulled me aside," Will said. "My wheels were just spinning."

"Exactly," she agreed with him.

She led them both through another visualizing exercise right here in the lobby. Even though our area was empty, you could still hear people talking and the sound of hissing coffee machines. It would be tough to zone out here, and that was exactly what Marcy wanted.

As I watched her lead them through various exercises, it dawned on me: Their placement really didn't matter at all—at least not to me. I wanted them to feel the joy of giving one hundred percent in front of the biggest crowd either of them had ever seen. It wasn't about the skating at all. It was about facing fear and doing it anyway. Saying yes to all of it, good, bad, and the ugly cry. We are given this one life, and some embrace that from the beginning, but some of us have to learn how to live in the yes lane. Marcy was living her dream—that much was clear by how much she lit up when helping people.

I didn't want to be afraid of living anymore. I didn't want to expect the worst thing was going to happen anymore. I didn't want to be alone in this world, afraid of getting hurt by love.

We're meant to love hard, and I finally felt like I could let all the baggage go. This is what life is about…

these moments that fill in the gaps of the big stuff. If you're only worried about the big stuff, you completely miss the beauty of what is in front of you right now.

There was beauty in succeeding, and there was beauty in failure. It was all in your perspective and what you chose to carry with you or let go. It was all part of life.

It was always my choice... I saw that now. Choosing the fear over the love. And more than anything else, I wanted to choose love now.

Life wouldn't instantly be easy knowing this. There would still be ups and downs, but by embracing it all, the experience was guaranteed to be a full one.

I couldn't make the skaters choose that, but hopefully they had learned as much as I had. And no matter what, I could lead by example. I could show them it was enough to live fully.

Would it be enough for them?

Yes... the only answer was a resounding yes.

INTERVIEW PART 6

[Cameras continue to record as Natalie gets mic'd up and seated. Addie has a smirk on her face—an inside joke with her coach.]

TL: Natalie, take me back to Nationals a year ago... were you there?

[Natalie glances at Addie before answering.]

NB: No, I was at home watching the whole thing unfold on TV.

TL: What was your relationship with Addie like before you took her on as a coach?

NB: Everyone at our rink loves Addie, and I was no different. She's hardworking, kind, and always seemed happiest on the ice.

TL: Was it a difficult decision to take her and Will on when Jonathan left the rink?

NB: I wouldn't say difficult, but definitely overwhelming. I hadn't coached anyone at that level before, and I wanted to make sure they were getting what they needed.

TL: I'm sure you're aware of all the rumors swirling

around her prior coach, and your former skating director—care to shed any light on that story?

NB: That is not my story to tell. You would have to go directly to the source on that subject.

TL: *(laughing)* Fair enough. I think the answer everyone wants to hear about is how did you do it? How did you lead these two skaters to have the performances of their lives under the most stressful situation any of you had ever been in?

NB: *(also laughing)* I can't give away all my secrets. [She ponders the question for a moment.] I think ultimately all three of us learned what we needed to focus on, and we worked very hard on and off the ice. We have an off-ice coach who has made it her mission to help keep them focused on the right things.

TL: Are you supportive of their Olympic dreams? Are you ready to take on that challenge?

NB: I would say a hearty yes to any dream they had. If they want to take on that challenge, I'll be by their side. And if they don't, then that would be okay too. This sport isn't about me and what I want.

TL: You might be the first coach ever to utter those words. Any last words of wisdom you want to share with us?

NB: Only that I'm grateful to be on this ride with them.

It's been enlightening for all of us, and I can't wait to see what life has in store for them.

TL: Well, I can't thank you and Addie enough for being here with us today. Good luck tonight with the short. We can't wait to see what you have in store for us.

～～

They both removed their mics, and Trish stood to shake Natalie's hand. "I shouldn't say this," she whispered, "but I hope Addie kicks Janelle's ass tonight."

I chuckled. True to form and catty as ever. The skating world had finally gotten wind of what Jonathan had done—with no help from me—and he was banned from coaching until his legal issues were settled.

It wasn't wrapped in a red bow like a Hallmark movie, but maybe there was such a thing as a happy ending.

World Figure Skating Championships

Montreal, Quebec
One hour before...

Ronnie: I legit have nervous diarrhea today.

    Stephanie: UGH! TMI RONNIE

    Dana: Agree…UGH! But also samesies :)

    Me: Still here, and this isn't helping. Brian Boitano just walked by me! #legend

    Ronnie: Doesn't count unless there is a picture.

    Dana: You know the rules.

    Stephanie: Pretty sure you created that one…

    Me: Seriously, I love you guys, but you're making me more nervous.

    Ronnie: Make sure you know where all the bathrooms are.

After silencing the notifications, I leaned my head against the wall behind me. The lower level of the Bell

Centre in Montreal was abuzz with figure skaters from all over the world warming up. The first group of skaters would go out shortly, but Addie was in fifth and would be skating in the final group. Her short was clean—beautiful, even—but the Russian skaters were unbeatable point-wise if they skated clean, and they were expected to sweep the championships.

And who was I kidding? *If* they skated clean? They skated like it was their job.

Because it was.

Addie and a Canadian skater would be the only non-Russian skaters in the last group. That alone should've gotten her a medal.

Janelle was in seventh, with nothing to lose. GG in tenth. Both of them skated in the group ahead of Addie, and while they were still the competition, they also grew closer on this trip. Being only one of thirteen American skaters, Addie quickly warmed up to the new group of teammates.

I slid my earbuds in and relaxed into the sound of ocean waves with the Calm app. Marcy insisted I try, and I'll be damned if she wasn't right again. Addie was on the mat to the left and walking through her long program. Her movements were clean and crisp, matching the music playing in her ears. While her short program was fluid and flowing, her long was sharper and forced her to exude more confidence.

When she skated it with determination, it was perfection. I took my phone out and recorded a small portion and sent it to the yahoos. They loved backstage stuff.

Glancing around, I tried to take it all in. The skaters, the world-level coaches, and the electric energy. It was something I had only heard of before, and I still had to pinch myself for being here. A wave of emotion rolled through me, forcing me to take this in and be present.

To be here, now.

To remember that this wasn't about skating or medals or the podium. It was about letting go of our own limitations and taking on the challenges life threw at you.

Giving up was never the option.

~~⌣~~

One minute before...

Josephine Brodeur exited the ice in a puddle of tears.

Not the good ones.

Addie stepped on, slipping off her other guard before handing them to me. Her eyes darted around like a cat watching a toy before it pounced.

"Take a lap. Feel the ice underneath you," I ordered.

She nodded and took off towards the end. We had at least one minute while we waited for Josie's scores to be read. My heart thudded in my chest, but I pasted a look of calm compassion on my face for Addie. Lady Gaga played overhead, and she matched her edgework to the beat of the music.

That was the moment I knew everything would be okay.

She came back, face relaxed, eyes calm.

"That felt good—like we are home and Will is playing music."

"That's exactly what it looked like, too," I said, smiling.

She took a sip of water, finding Will in the stands. A momentary flash of excitement lit her eyes up as he held up an American flag, and then she nodded, back to business.

"In case I forget later," she said. "Thank you for helping me get here."

My eyes met hers, and she pulled me into a hug.

Josie's score was read—not what she had hoped for, but this was figure skating. I grabbed her hands.

"Close your eyes," I said. She did. "How do you want to feel in four minutes?"

A slow smile spread across her face. "Free."

"Representing the United States of America," the announcer boomed. "Adeline Gray."

She gave me a final nod and took off for her presentation that we had practiced so often.

She took her beginning pose, eyes focused on the ice. There are usually three seconds from when the skater takes their position to when the music begins, and I saw her chest rise and fall. I took a slow breath with her.

Three… two… one.

And like a lion waking from a long nap, Addie's eyes snapped to the judges as the first note echoed throughout the stadium.

the end

Acknowledgments

It's been six years since I left the skating world, and there isn't a day that goes by that I don't think of something about that other part of my life. The memories—while faded, slightly—came flooding back to me when I began writing this. My heart would race and tears would form in my eyes... all the feels. As with most of my books, there's quite a bit of me in this fiction—either how I remembered it, or how I'd like it to be now.

The heart of this book is about the kind of friendship that holds us up in life, and I can write about it so easily because I have been blessed to be surrounded with the most amazing women, even if it is through a text most days. For so many years, the running joke has been, "Will that make it in the book?" It wasn't a matter of *if* I'd write a skating book—just a matter of *when*. There is also something about a friendship grounded in a sport—especially figure skating—it endures time like none other. The bonds I share with my skating family run deep and stand the test of time.

To my first readers: Amy, Chris, Lara, Linda, and Pam - I don't know how you can keep reading the first drafts and seeing what it's supposed to be. I'm forever grateful that you do, and love and appreciate the comments and encouragement you send my way! Thank you isn't enough!

To my editor, Susie: Do you know how often I wish I wrote faster, just so I have something to share with you? Your constant support and love truly means the world to me. Plus, your comments make editing fun… well, sort of. Thank you for agreeing to be a part of everything I write!

To my SI team: This last year of learning how to make it all work remotely has been the craziest kind of roller coaster. Spoiler alert: we did it! From Schitty Tuesdays to Pirate Fridays, there isn't another group of people I'd rather spend forty hours a week with. Thank you for letting this financial rookie be a part of the team.

To my family: Of all the things I learned in 2020, gratitude for my family was at the top of the list. Words just aren't big enough to express my love for Toby, Evan, and Blake… and now Darby too, our fur-baby. Living with a writer isn't easy, but they always support me every step of the way.

Are you still reading? I hope so… I saved the best for last.

To my readers—the ones who love the characters, and want to know when the next book is coming out, and bring me joy every day. I can't say it enough—I do all of this for you. You're the ones who make this dream so damn fun for me, and I will forever be grateful for each of you. Special shout out to Jen from

In Literary Love for all the book love and keeping our TBR piles forever high.

Happy Reading!

XO, Mo

Mo lives in Michigan with her husband, Toby, and together they've raised two boys—Evan and Blake. She works full time at Smalley Investments and also writes for her website, mjparisian.com. When she isn't working, she can be found reading, working on a new writing project, or bingeing on Netflix shows.

She is passionate about all things figure skating and hockey, and will never give up the search for the best chocolate chip cookie recipe.

Made in the USA
Middletown, DE
28 June 2021